To Bob -

I hope you enjoy the book.

Have a great holiday season.

-Colin Patrick Garvey

THE DISAPPEARANCE

THE
FALLEN RACE
TRILOGY

BOOK ONE: THE DISAPPEARANCE
by COLIN PATRICK GARVEY

www.thefallenrace.com

PaddyPiper Books, LLC

ISBN: 978-0-9847675-0-2

Book Cover/Website Design by Jacob Matthew
Book Design by GKS Creative
Original Cover Photograph by Colin Patrick Garvey

Printed in the United States of America

To My Wife Kate, who never doubted,
To My Wee Loves, Declan and Shea-bird,
And to Mom and Pops, who always encouraged.

ONE

Tamawaca Beach, Michigan

It is Fourth of July evening and Tamawaca Beach is covered with blankets, towels, coolers and cabanas. The fireworks show is set to begin as little kids scamper across the sand holding sparklers while the bigger kids launch bottle rockets down by the water. Scattered pockets of teenagers huddle together for the sole purpose of consuming as much alcohol as possible before their parents have a chance to notice. Despite their caution, the adults fail to pay them much mind anyway or even think to monitor their brood, as the majority of the former appear occupied themselves, drinking and talking with one another. The silver and gray-haired sit quietly on the benches lining the sidewalk, patiently waiting for the show to start. Most of them do not attempt to brave the unsteady terrain of the beach for fear they may break a hip or sprain a wrist.

The sidewalk runs practically the length of the beach, ending in a plethora of massive dunes that stretch for several miles to the north. As the dunes move west toward the lake, they diminish in stature before completely leveling off. Once they do, the sidewalk resumes, leading to a large pier that protrudes nearly three hundred feet into the waters of Lake Michigan. A rail inhabits each side of the pier to prevent people from trying their luck on the large, slippery rocks that encircle it. Standing watch at the head of the pier is an enormous, cherry-red lighthouse known as "Big Red." The old sentry has seen much in its day, but continues to remain in pristine condition courtesy of an annual scrubbing and polish during Memorial Day weekend.

Directly over the dunes to the east sits the much smaller Lake Tamawaca, where most recreational skiers and wakeboarders can be found on calm days. The current is more manageable and the water less choppy than what one typically encounters on Lake Michigan. Lake Tamawaca eventually empties into the Great Lake, but the channel connecting the two bodies of water is nearly five miles north of Tamawaca Beach.

On the east side of the sidewalk are a dozen cottages fortunate enough to be located directly on the beach. Behind these beachfront properties reside approximately twenty cottages and this, simply put, is the town of Tamawaca. To the south is a patch of woods and hills that run for miles in the other direction before arriving at the popular tourist town of Saugatuck. Thus, the woods and dunes are bookends to this sleepy cottage community, which may be what draws residents back to it every summer.

The kind of seclusion the town affords, without being too removed from civilization, is what everyone here appreciates and enjoys. People own or rent cottages from all over the United States, but the town's spirit and friendliness is pure, genuine Midwestern hospitality. Cottages are passed down from generation to generation, and the chance of an outsider attempting to purchase a little piece of this heaven is usually slim to none. During the summer months, the same families and their friends gather here for any weekend they can escape from the routine and monotony back home, wherever that may be. The reasons are obvious and plentiful: the outdoor barbeques, the endless stream of parties and cocktail hours, the volleyball games, the water, and the thin slice of beach God himself seemed to carve out for this cottage town.

Some people could even mistake this little niche for paradise.

Tonight, however, no one will make that mistake.

An old man is slowly being pushed in his wheelchair at the end of the sidewalk when he holds up a decrepit hand. The male nurse attending to him halts the wheelchair without a word. They remain in the shadows near the back of the beach, silently and impassively absorbing the view around them. The old man, his scraggly gray hair blowing in the wind, examines the scene before him. Most of the cottagers sit with their backs to him, failing to notice the old man who was once considered one of the most powerful men in the world. Several people might even argue that this still remains the case.

The old man's hard, glowering eyes survey the surroundings and he emits a small shudder, but it is not caused by the cool breeze blowing off Lake Michigan. For no one on this beach knows what this man knows. No one could possibly comprehend the sinister plans that are in store for all of them. And no one could possibly be aware of the terror that will strike this peaceful scene in only a few short minutes.

Geneva, Illinois – Evans Military Base

First Sergeant Jonathan Kaley has not seen anything like it before. Private Rushmore summoned Sergeant Kaley to his station to show his supervisor exactly what he had discovered. On the screen before them appears a very faint but noticeable signal coming from the depths of Lake Michigan, approximately 150 miles northeast of their location. It is not a mayday or call for help, but similar to the *ping* associated with sonar radar. They could hardly speculate what the signal is doing in the middle of a lake that comprises 22,178 square miles, holding the title as the largest freshwater lake within the United States.

"Rushmore, what am I looking at right now?" Sergeant Kaley asks.

"I don't know, sir, but if I can speak frankly, that signal is coming from out of nowhere," Rushmore responds.

"A glitch?" Kaley wonders aloud.

"I don't think so, sir," Rushmore answers.

"How did you even find it, Private?"

"Sir, one of our birds was doing a routine flyover," Rushmore explains, "when it located the signal and zeroed in on it."

Sergeant Kaley stares at the screen, trying to decipher what it could possibly mean. It takes him little more than a few seconds to decide this is something for the colonel.

"Rushmore, punch in those coordinates and send them to my station. I have to make a call to the man upstairs."

"Right away, sir," Rushmore complies.

Kaley makes like a bat out of hell for his station, picks up the phone, and taps a few numbers. After several seconds, he is connected with Colonel Malcolm Fizer.

Colonel Fizer is a man who does not care for small talk or chitchat. He wants any situation report as quickly and clearly as possible. He is a military man through and through, and this characteristic resonates in his stern, demanding voice.

"What is it, Sergeant Kaley?"

"Sir, I've got something very unusual down here," Kaley responds.

Not sure of any forthright way to explain it, Kaley simply details what they have found.

"It appears that, um...well, sir, we discovered a signal of unknown origin coming from the middle of Lake Michigan."

"I'm already quite aware of the situation, Sergeant," Fizer replies evenly. "We received a call from the Pentagon not more than five minutes ago. Apaches have been dispatched and it ceases to be our responsibility."

"But, sir, from where have these choppers been dispatched if-"

"It is no longer our responsibility, Sergeant," Fizer abruptly cuts him off, "and I hope that makes it perfectly clear."

Kaley knows that Fizer is a somber man, but the tone of his voice sounded borderline threatening.

"Yes, sir-"

The phone clicks before Kaley even has a chance to affirm the colonel's statement.

Sergeant Kaley hangs up his end with a nagging

sense of things left unfinished. He is a man who typically follows orders without question or doubt, and he has always maintained a rigid belief in the military's chain-of-command. Conversely, he has also never been one to acquiesce easily or fails to complete a task or challenge presented to him. His curiosity gets the better of him as he rushes back to Private Rushmore's station.

"Private, what's the status of our mysterious signal?"

"Sir, our satellite is no longer in range," Rushmore indicates.

Kaley considers this for a moment, then leans in and quietly asks, "Do we have other satellites flying over that area?"

"Uh . . no, sir," Rushmore says hesitantly, "at least not any military ones."

As a result of his curious nature and his inherent need for having closure on everything he starts, Sergeant Jonathan Kaley asks a question that will change his life forever.

"Well, Private Rushmore, what other eyes up there can we look through?"

Washington, D.C. – Biltmore Hotel

A group of gentlemen ranging in age from their late 50s to mid-80s have gathered in a large suite of the private Biltmore Hotel, located on the outskirts of Washington, D.C. They mill around in suits and ties with looks on their faces consisting of a potpourri of emotions: nervous anticipation, quiet anxiety, and even outright fear. None of them doubt, however, what is to be done tonight. None of them second-guess the nature of this bone-chilling business into which they have incorporated themselves.

A handful of the men assembled here lived through World War II, all of whom fought and served courageously during the conflict. One man in the room was on the bombing mission over Hiroshima. Several men were present when the Allied forces opened the gates of the concentration camps and witnessed firsthand the atrocities the Nazis inflicted on innocent men, women, and children. Nearly all of the men in this room were involved in the campaign considered the only war in which the United States got their asses thoroughly kicked, in a small slice of jungle in Southeast Asia.

Those who served in Vietnam were mostly colonels, generals, and admirals. They were the top brass not directly involved in the deadly jungle firefights and skirmishes that defined the war. They were vital intelligence-gatherers, whether participating in or simply sanctioning the rather brutal tactics and interrogation techniques typically only used by the most barbaric of America's enemies.

It was a war where the enemy was unseen, damn near impossible to find, and oftentimes ambiguous. Their adversaries were not merely the North Vietnamese, but hundreds of thousands of civilians on both sides of the battle lines. A child could be packed with explosives as she ran into the eager arms of an American soldier only wanting to help. Everyone was the enemy, even the innocent.

Tonight, it seems the innocent have become the enemy once again. It is neither their fault nor intention to be involved in the events of tonight, but it is simply a case of being in the wrong place at the wrong time. To these men, there is a war raging, and it has nothing to do with the battles in the mountains of Afghanistan or the deserts of Iraq. The repercussions of this war are much more grave. And it is especially these men that know the innocent are always unfairly sacrificed in conflicts and warfare. It is, they all know, the way of the world.

The events of tonight and over the ensuing hours do not merely involve America's interests. The interests these men have charged themselves with protecting are those of humanity's, and the consequences of this wager are nothing less than catastrophic.

Tonight, the survival of the human race is on the table.

The harsh sound of a cellular phone rings in the hushed room and everyone turns to look at the source. A man named Moriah takes the phone from the inner pocket of his suit coat, answers it, and listens for a moment. He gives an imperceptible nod and wordlessly flips the phone closed. He places it on the table in front of him, his eyes lowered, contemplating the news he has received.

Moriah's gaze slowly rises from the table and the men gathered in the room see a look that speaks volumes.

However, to make certain everyone knows without a doubt there is no turning back, he says slowly and deliberately, "It has begun."

TWO

Tamawaca Beach, Michigan

Sean O'Connell cherishes these weekends more than anything in the world – only the three of them at the cottage for the Fourth of July weekend. No aunts or uncles or cousins running around. No grandparents fussing over anything and everything. No schedules or classes for him.

No worries, he thinks, as they wait for the show to start.

He shares a blanket on the beach with his wife, Isabella, and their 5-year-old son, Conor. The weekend thus far could not have been more perfect. The weather has been fully cooperating, they have kept Conor entertained with plenty of boating and go-carts, and Sean and Isabella even managed a night out alone while their neighbors watched the lad. He knew coming up here for the summer would be a good idea.

Sean O'Connell is a professor of political science and history, but not the kind of history with timelines and endless dates for his students to memorize, regurgitate and then quickly forget. His teachings have the students focus on historical events from a different angle, rearranging the pieces over and over again until they form a complete picture of the players involved and their oftentimes underhanded and dubious motives. It seems too general at first, he knows, like he is using too broad a stroke on the canvas. But after a while, his students begin to enjoy this new, unconventional way of thinking, and the canvas soon becomes whatever they want it to be.

Sean uses various examples in class to illustrate his belief that the vast majority of history books contain any number of errors, omissions, and downright untruths. Indeed, one of Sean's mantras, a phrase he constantly reinforces in class, is history books should always be taken with a grain of salt.

By having his students accept this core principle of Sean's teaching, it paves the way for him to introduce an element not commonly found in a college-level curriculum, let alone any type of curriculum. It is only *one word,* but it is a word that often carries far-reaching implications. It is *one word* that seems to pique people's interest when it is written in the newspapers or broadcast on television. It is *one word,* when spoken, is like a lightning bolt that jolts the collective unconscious and forces people to pay closer attention. It is *one word* that constantly exists in the minds of anyone with a grievance against or story about the government, the JFK assassination, UFOs, the content of fluoride, the magnetic strips in U.S. currency, the belief Elvis is alive, and generally anything to do with the CIA.

It is simply *one word:* conspiracy.

There is something about the word in the American conscience that is like a five-alarm bell being sounded.

For some Americans, it is a word that causes them to feel naïve and foolish for believing in the actions and words of a government they are born and raised to trust in, and then learning it is all a lie. For others, the word characterizes how the government has functioned from the very beginning. This group sees conspiracies in every nook and cranny, behind every shadow and underneath every rock. These people believe the government holds an overly simplistic view of the public at large: ignorant, uninformed, indifferent and too preoccupied chasing the American dream to concern themselves with government conspiracies and mass cover-ups. Finally, there are those who cannot even fathom the word "conspiracy" coinciding with the admirable virtues espoused by the Founding Fathers, who believed all the information concerning a nation's leaders and their actions is intended to be scrutinized by a discerning public. For this group, it seems too outlandish for a country like the United States, which prides itself on openness and its assertion of a government *for the people,* to be involved in covert, Machiavellian plans removed from the prying eyes of the citizenry.

The word evokes various responses and different emotions, indeed, in everybody. It is a word that has become a catchphrase in today's trendy society, where words like that help explain away events in history people cannot possibly begin to understand. It is a word like that which may explain the men gathered in the Biltmore Hotel. And it is a word like that which may be used to characterize the events of tonight.

Sean was actually persuaded into teaching a summer course at Hope College in nearby Holland by his friend and mentor, Dr. Albert Rosenstein. Rosenstein claimed it was a favor to his friend on the faculty, Richard Murdoch, but Sean suspected the latter solicited no such request for this type of course at his university. Sean knows Rosenstein and he presumed the old man talked Professor Murdoch into it. Sean is acutely aware how much Rosenstein enjoys spreading his unique doctrine far and wide to all corners of the country.

Rosenstein taught Sean at DePaul University in Chicago, and the former built quite a reputation there. He has always been extremely outspoken in his views of the world, and he is not afraid to express his opinions in class or outside of it.

Rosenstein was arrested more than a dozen times in the 1960s and 1970s during various sit-ins and protests over the treatment of African-Americans and the United States' involvement in the Vietnam War. He was fervently against the war and had even been cracked over the head with a billy club from one of those overzealous police officers at the 1968 Democratic Convention in Chicago. He initially viewed the era of peace and love the hippie movement ushered in as the peak of western civilization when humanity across the globe would join hands and unite to end their petty differences. His idealism some-times far outweighed anything reality could hold a candle to. Rosenstein preached this unification doctrine to his classes and many of his students mistakenly construed his joyful lectures as encouragement to experiment with even more drugs. They misinterpreted and twisted his teachings, and believed that in order "to experience humanity at its best," the use of hallucinogenic treats would assist them in arriving at their lofty destination.

In the 1980s, he constantly derided Ronald Reagan

in his classes for his exorbitant defense spending and "Star Wars" approach to the military-industrial complex. He welcomed the era of the computer age as a force capable of uniting mankind around the world, via the Internet and email. Towards the late 1990s, however, he believed human beings were relying on computers to an excessive amount, occasionally neglecting the fact that it was human beings who created these machines and not the other way around. Rosenstein feared people were slowly and gradually turning into automatons, slave to the "almighty computer" at work and then using it as a source of entertainment when they arrived home.

Dr. Rosenstein shared his views with his students and in turn, his students loved him for telling it like it is and never pulling any punches. Not for one moment did Dr. Rosenstein believe his students too young and ignorant to think and imagine on a higher level.

One of the students who came to accept as gospel nearly everything Dr. Rosenstein said was Sean O'Connell. He already shared his mentor's distrust of government and those in positions of power and authority, and he enrolled in Dr. Rosenstein's first class at the university reflecting these views, a class called, "The Conspiracy of Government." There were no textbooks or assigned readings in the course, but rather it was rooted more in philosophy and debate than it was a class of political science.

When mysterious and unexplained connections emerged after the assassinations of JFK and his brother Bobby, as well as Dr. Martin Luther King, Rosenstein began to believe there were deeper and darker meanings behind these murders than simply the hate of one man by another. He saw a "conspiracy" surrounding these events, and underneath the surface there lied something more than what the public initially perceived.

Sean excelled in the class and he was one of Rosenstein's favorite students. When Sean started teaching, he introduced a course similar to Rosenstein's wherever the administration would allow him. And as a "favor" to his old friend in the political science department at Hope College, Rosenstein asked Sean to teach the course during the school's summer semester. Rosenstein knows his protégé has a family cottage in neighboring Tamawaca, so he asked Sean to try it for a semester and see if it takes. Thus far, his students have been quite receptive to it. That is, the eight students who enrolled for the course.

Sean is lost in this last thought when his wife breaks into his reverie, "Hey, babe, you're zoning. You okay?"

Sean comes back to Earth and looks at the blonde-brown wisps of his wife's hair dancing in the wind. He reaches up and pushes the hair away from her face. She possesses striking emerald eyes that always remind him of the commercials where the ocean is shimmering off some exotic island in the Caribbean.

"Better than okay. You need another beer?" he asks.

Isabella gives him that warm, wonderful smile that makes Sean's heart skip a beat every time he sees it.

"Trying to get me drunk?" she asks playfully.

"Of course I am," Sean confirms.

Isabella chuckles.

He turns to his son. "How about you, bud? You want a brew?" he jokingly asks.

Isabella laughs and with mock disapproval, says, "Sean-"

"Can I have another pop, Daddy?" Conor asks, as the joke zooms right over his head.

Kids sometimes.

To avoid the chance of a negative response, Conor quickly argues, "I promise I won't be up all night."

"Alright kid, you promise?" Sean asks skeptically.

"Yeah," he nods happily. "Daddy, are the fireworks coming on soon?"

"Any second they will," he says. "I'll be back in a minute, okay?"

"Yeah," Conor nods again.

Sean gets up from the blanket and begins walking towards their cottage. But first, he leans down and pecks his wife on the forehead as he passes, whispering in her ear, "I hope he's not up all night. I've got plans for us later."

Isabella grins mischievously and replies, "You're a bad boy, O'Connell. Hurry back, okay?"

"I will."

As Sean makes his way towards the cottage, he says some polite "hellos" to several people and waves to a few others. He is about to start jogging when he sees him and suddenly stops.

It is like Sean sensed him before he actually laid eyes on him. Sean peers down the sidewalk to the old man seated in a wheelchair. The man seems fragile and vulnerable, a once able-bodied man whose muscles have slackened and become flaccid. The man appears weak in every area of his body save one: his eyes.

The man's eyes tell a much different story, a story that betrays the man's physical appearance. This story depicts a man still strong as a lion, cunning as a fox, and sharp as a razor. The man's eyes scan the beach like a predator sizing up his prey. Finally, the man settles his gaze on Sean, who feels a tingle up his spine.

Jesus, Sean thinks, *I thought that only happened in books.*

Sean instantly recognizes the man from the limited number of photos he has seen of him, albeit when he was a younger man: R. Jonas Abraham.

Sometimes there are men in life whose sheer mystery evokes numerous stories and rumors to be circulated about them, whether true or not. From hired assassin to double agent, from war hero to traitor, from ambassador to Russia to atomic scientist, there is no shortage of speculation surrounding the old man. In some capacity or another, it is believed Abraham worked for the government at one time. Doing what is anyone's guess.

What is commonly known about the man is that he occasionally spends summer weekends in Tamawaca, does not have any guests or family, lives like a hermit, his health is rapidly deteriorating, and he is sitting on top of a fortune. Of course, rumors are also rampant in regards to how Abraham acquired his vast wealth.

Sean holds the man's stare for several seconds before finally turning away.

Within a minute, Sean arrives at his cottage. He opens the front gate of the porch, takes a few long strides, swings open the screen door, and enters. He heads directly to the fridge and grabs a couple of beers and a caffeine-free pop. Sean then moves towards the pantry to bring down a couple snacks for Conor.

He suddenly hears *pop, pop, pop,* which signals the beginning of the show.

Then he hears something quite unusual. It is like an airplane flying overhead, but an engine noise he has never heard before in his life. He pauses and listens for several seconds. He shuffles out of the pantry and slowly walks towards the screen door.

He opens the door and as he steps onto the porch, he is greeted by a sound louder than any possible firecracker. He feels a strange sensation course through his body, as if an unseen force has washed over him. This "shockwave" knocks the wind out of him and his feet suddenly leave the ground. He is tossed over the porch railing like a discarded piece of paper thrown into the wind. He lands on a soft patch of sand bordering the cottage, but this ancillary benefit does not concern Sean in the least because the force of whatever hit him snatches his consciousness before he even hits the ground.

*   *   *

Sean does not know how long he was unconscious. His first thought is he is paralyzed and will never walk again. He quickly dismisses this notion when he wiggles his toes and pulls his legs up. Sean momentarily thinks he hears the sound of running feet, but he may have imagined it. He slowly rises to his feet and his focus immediately turns to his family.

Are they okay? Are they safe? What the hell happened?

Sean hobbles as quickly as he can towards the beach. He does not hear or see any fireworks, so the show must have ended.

But where is everyone? Why are there not streams

of people returning to their cottages? Why don't I hear people laughing or talking or...something?

There is only silence.

He arrives at the beach and stares, shocked, unable to comprehend the sight before him. There is not a soul to be found. The beach is deserted and all the people are... gone. Stranger still, the beach chairs, towels, blankets, coolers, and cabanas all remain, as if everyone suddenly got up and left.

In the next ten seconds, Sean hears two distinct sounds that take different periods of time to register in his mind. The first is the unmistakable sound of helicopter blades, a noise gradually growing louder.

He initially has trouble placing the second sound, but then he turns and looks down the sidewalk. He sees Abraham's overturned wheelchair, the wheels squeaking as they slowly turn in the wind.

THREE

Sean O'Connell has always possessed a rational streak despite the constant urge to distrust the "facts" as they are presented to the general public. He believes in conspiracies, this is true, but he also believes they do not happen everyday and especially at a time like this. His mind churns as he hears the approaching sound of a helicopter or possibly helicopters. He tries to focus and thoroughly examine the scene unfolding before him.

Sean is, as it appears, alone on a beach, where only several minutes (*right?*) before there were close to a hundred people — laughing, playing, enjoying the holiday weekend.

And now...no one. Not a goddamn soul.

What happened to my family? Where have they gone? Are they...

He does not feel it necessary to complete the thought, one that would assuredly bring undue pain and anguish.

Sean considers his options, but his mind is like putty, a useless mass unable to function correctly. The light from "Big Red" continues to forlornly scan an empty beach and a quiet lake. Beyond the gigantic lighthouse, Sean hears the approaching helicopters, meaning more than one.

A rescue party? But who here needs to be rescued? And from what?

Suddenly, the helicopters appear from behind the lighthouse. He spots four, possibly five choppers, in a single file fast approaching the beach. His first emotion is relief at the sight of other human beings, thankful for the moment he is not the only person left on the face of the earth. His relief quickly dissipates and turns to dread when the choppers begin dropping objects from their hulls as they coast over the beach.

The first impact lights up the night sky and snatches the breath from his lungs when it connects with the beach. His legs become rubbery and he starts to run as fast as he can away from the falling bombs. A second, third, and fourth one strike the beach, one after the other, creating huge craters and sending massive amounts of sand jettisoning into the air.

Sean is at a full sprint now as their spotlights comb the beach. The spotlights bounce off the beach and the cottages in a chaotic whirlwind of light, not readily apparent what they are trying to illuminate.

Sean is not inclined to guess, so he continues to run as fast as his legs will take him along the sidewalk. Nearing the last cottages on the south end of the beach, he spots one with an upraised porch and ample room to hide underneath. He veers off the sidewalk and dives under the porch of the cottage, narrowly avoiding the spotlight of the lead helicopter.

The birds continue their bombardment of the beach,

and following their first run, they turn around for what appears to be an encore. After a few seconds of silence, the echo of the blasts reverberating over the water, they resume their barrage as Sean stares in disbelief.

What is happening here? Some twisted training experiment? A kind of terrorism exercise for the military? Am I dreaming this? Have I dozed off while waiting with my family for the fireworks to begin?

He does not think so – primarily because he feels a throbbing pain in his head and his chest heaves in anguish.

It never hurts for real in your dreams, does it?

There does not appear to be a pattern to the placement of these bombs. They seem to be dropped randomly at various intervals along the beach.

So what purpose do they serve?

There is no apparent enemy or target on the receiving end of these nasty little bundles. The only destruction they seem to perpetuate is to displace a few tons of sand and thus, leave behind massive, blackened craters intermittently along the beach.

The helicopters complete their second run and begin to turn around.

Are they preparing to unload a third set?

Sean's question is quickly answered when the helicopters pull up and hover around twenty feet above the beach, as if contemplating whether it is safe to land. They gradually descend onto the surface of the beach, each one picking a spot several hundred feet from the previous one's landing area.

Within seconds after touching down, five or six figures disperse from each aircraft and sprint up the beach. They appear like a miniature invasion force, but who or what they are attacking is a mystery. The fifth and final helicopter lands nearest to Sean, and this one is close enough for him to see the whites of the figures' eyes. In fact, this is all he *can see* because each figure wears a mask that covers their face and neck, leaving only a small slit for the eyes.

It is obvious to Sean these men are soldiers, for he, too, had been a soldier once, a long time ago. Fresh out of high school Sean joined the Marine Corps, a choice his father encouraged and even cajoled him to do. His good friend had enlisted in the Army, and Sean thought the military was something else to do, a better alternative than cramming for exams and writing 20-page papers in college. It was a confusing time in his life, still stuck in the throes of adolescence, not knowing which direction fate planned for him. He was not too keen on academics initially, nor did he have a passionate interest in any particular subject.

Sean survived boot camp and he loved every minute of it. He was a good soldier, in fact one of the best in the whole platoon. The competitive fire that was always on the back burner during his dull, meandering years in high school was suddenly and inexplicably lit. Sean wanted to be the very best in every facet of the Corps, and he nearly was. It was his ability to excel at every aspect of basic training that brought him to the attention of his superiors. It was his superiors who believed they had found the perfect Marine for the perfect job, and they assumed they could use and control him to satisfy their own whims.

They were wrong.

He left the Corps with a dishonorable discharge and

it was here, in one of the greatest military institutions ever conceived, the seeds of doubt were sown in him forever about what the government, or any authority for that matter, has to say.

After the Marines, he returned home to Chicago and registered at DePaul University for fall classes. He figured with a dishonorable discharge on his record, however unjustified it might have been, a college degree would be an absolute necessity if he wanted to succeed in life. He obtained dual degrees in both history and political science, completing his undergraduate studies in only three years.

Sean came under the influence of Dr. Rosenstein early and often, enrolling in several of his courses each year. He learned from Rosenstein, while at the same time Rosenstein learned from him. They developed a relationship unlike that of teacher and pupil, but rather one of friendship. They enjoyed constant, late-night bull sessions about everything involving the government and everything else that did not. Eventually, with a wholehearted trust Sean believed the man deserved, he revealed to Rosenstein what had been asked of him by his superiors, and his refusal to do so that caused him to be dismissed in shame.

Indeed, Sean knows what it means to be a soldier, to release a certain degree of control over one's own thoughts and actions. He is fully aware how easily a soldier's morals can be trampled in the process. He also knows he never wants to have that helpless feeling again. Sean stares at the figures storming their way up the beach and he knows what kind of men they are: the kind who he had once been.

They move and look like professional soldiers, but any

amateur watching them could arrive at such an obvious conclusion. It is the little things Sean notices that tip him off. Specifically, their ability to generate *absolutely no sound* as they creep along the beach. They move like ghosts, phantoms, nearly unseen in the darkness. They do not require hand signals or walkie-talkies because they know and can predict each other's movements. These soldiers have worked together before, perhaps hundreds of times. They all possess laser targeting on their automatics, but the tiny red dots are not illuminated like in the movies. These men are not about to let their enemy know they are coming.

Sean suddenly realizes, with a sinking feeling and a knot in his stomach cinching tighter by the second, that he may be their lone enemy tonight.

He tries to devise his next move, but he is unable to construct a coherent plan of action in his mind. His brain feels cloudy, like he is trapped in a bad dream, making it difficult for him to think clearly or even rationally.

The soldiers gather steam as they approach the sidewalk separating the beach from the cottages. Their boots shuffle over the concrete sidewalk and finally, they reach the first row of cottages. In groups of three or four, they begin to enter these beachfront homes.

The group of soldiers from the last helicopter moves directly towards the cottage he is hiding under. He waits anxiously for a moment, holding his breath in his throat, terrified they spotted him dive below the cottage. He fears they will haul him out from beneath the porch and whisk him away without an explanation, unconcerned that he may have a few questions of his own.

The soldiers are practically on top of him now, no

more than fifteen feet away. They point their weapons in his direction when suddenly, they veer up the cottage's front stairs and quickly traverse them, the loud pounding of their boots on the wood above him rumbling in his ears.

Sean lets out the shortest of sighs.

He watches distressingly as the soldiers begin razing the cottages next door: banging down doors, knocking shutters off their hinges, busting windows. He hears crashing glass and heavy thuds as the men move above him in what sounds like a tango with an elephant. Each cottage appears to be receiving a deluxe redesign.

The soldiers seem to be searching for something or someone, but what or whom? Are they looking for...survivors?

The word courses through his body like an electric shock.

Is that what I am? A survivor?

Immediately, what he has survived and why are questions that begin to pinball around inside his head.

Do the soldiers know I survived? Is that who they are looking for? For me?

Sean compels himself to drop all the guesswork and devise a plan to blow this scene as quickly and quietly as possible without alerting the GI Joes. Approximately a hundred yards south of his present location is a path leading into the woods, which should afford Sean a comfortable security blanket until he can determine where he needs to go. There are miles of woodlands, nearly all the way to Saugatuck, a town around 25 miles south of Tamawaca. The woods would provide cover and possibly shelter if he is forced to hole up for the night. It seems to be his best option at the moment.

The problem lies in reaching the path without being seen. Streetlamps dot the sidewalk at various intervals along the beach, supplying more than enough light for him to be spotted. Sean decides it is a risk he is willing to accept.

The soldiers appear to be rapidly working their way from the beachfront cottages to the cottages further inland. He will simply have to ally himself with the shadows, which should offer a small measure of camouflage, until he can reach the path. His best chance is now, before they return to their helicopters.

Sean starts to ease out from underneath the porch when he suddenly stops. A lone figure casually ambles up the beach, dressed like the other soldiers, but different in a way. If Sean has to guess, this is probably the man in charge. He does not carry an automatic weapon like the other soldiers, only a Colt pistol with a pearl-colored grip in a holster at his side. The man's nonchalant demeanor suggests the utmost and supreme confidence in his leadership and that everything, despite appearances to the contrary, is under control.

The man arrives at the sidewalk and strides purposefully towards something. Sean cranes his neck around the side of the porch to watch, coming dangerously close to exposing his head to the light from a streetlamp. The man bends down at the foot of Abraham's overturned wheelchair and grabs an object from the back pocket. Sean notices the object is not much larger than a cigarette pack as the man straightens up and continues walking towards the back row of cottages.

Sean thinks momentarily about Abraham and whether the man upon whom so many legends and rumors are based played a role in the drama unfolding here tonight. The coincidence seems uncanny.

There is no time to think about that right now, however. Sean needs to exit this scene and do it fast. He glances around to determine if the coast is clear to find no soldiers or their shadows lurking about. He immediately starts sprinting towards the path.

His arms pumping and his legs running full stride, Sean is a Marine again: back in boot camp, negotiating the obstacle course. He feels like he can fly, as if he is running on air. He is going to reach the path. Sean has shelved his strategy of cautiously moving within the shadows and agrees with the great mathematicians that the shortest distance between two points is a straight line.

He is twenty yards away, fifteen, ten, and then...

Whack!!

Sean is leveled by the opposing team's linebacker, who he did not even see, let alone hear.

He sees stars for a moment as he lies pinned on the sand, a heavy weight sprawled across his body. He quickly clears his head and assesses the situation in a heartbeat.

The man hoists Sean off the sand and attempts to wrangle his hands behind his back, as if to handcuff him, but Sean's reaction is too quick for that. He painfully twists one of the man's arms out away from them, and with as much force as he can muster, slams his elbow backward, connecting squarely with the soldier's jaw. The blow does not break the man's jaw, but it unquestionably inflicts some damage. The man actually appears more stunned than hurt, for perhaps he thinks this fleeing man is simply an ordinary civilian, running scared and feeling helpless.

Sean surprises him again by pulling the man's head close and turning him around so that Sean is directly behind him. He thrusts one arm across the soldier's throat and the other across the top of his head and he begins to twist.

There is so much raw emotion coursing through Sean that he can no longer control himself. He wants answers and he wants them *now!*

"Where are *they?*" Sean whispers menacingly in the man's ear. "What happened to them?"

The man emits a strangled cry. Fearing he will alert the others, Sean makes one final twist, snapping the man's neck.

The man falls limp to the ground. Sean quickly drags the lifeless body towards the edge of the path where the woods begin. He covers the man as best he can with the available branches and leaves around him, and then scurries up into the hills. He hastily scans the surrounding area for signs this episode has been witnessed, but Sean does not see anyone in the vicinity.

Someone up there still likes me, he thinks.

Sean moves like a soldier again, like the men on the beach only minutes before. He is absolutely furious at himself and the man he killed. He did not want to hurt him, but he felt he had limited options under the circumstances. It was a matter of survival, of soldierly instincts suddenly awakened. His emotions burst forth as if a dam had broke, allowing all the rage and hatred to pour out. His fury is a result of the confusion engulfing him. What he has witnessed here tonight is not intended for his eyes. Indeed, he does not know if what he has seen is intended for anyone's eyes.

Sean knows he must escape from here and find someone he trusts. He cannot go to his parents' house in Chicago or to any other relatives. It would risk placing them in mortal danger. He knows two men he can trust with his life in a situation like this and—

KABOOM!

Another explosion from the beach rips through the night air, causing him to jump. A moment later, he hears a sound from the road below that snakes around the small town. He struggles through the dense woods and underbrush, trying to make as little noise as possible, and arrives at the edge of a hill, where he looks down upon the road.

Sean spots three large, dark trucks rumbling down the street towards the beach. Each of them possesses a green canopy behind the cab of the truck, masking their cargo. Neither Sean nor anyone else could imagine the horrific contents the trucks are carrying, let alone their true purpose. To the majority of people, they would think it the most grotesque, twisted, utterly contemptible thing they have ever heard. To a small minority, it is simply business as usual.

Sean turns and begins to make his way, *like a ghost,* through the darkness.

* * *

When he was informed of what occurred on the beach, he wept in agony.

They had not been warned! Something must have happened.

The tears of sadness that ran down his cheeks, however, no sooner turned to tears of joy when he was told the man – without his family – escaped from the beach and fled into the surrounding woods, like a mouse ducking the predatory cat. A slight feeling of hope blossomed within him and he quietly applauded.

FOUR

Colonel Malcolm Fizer is a tidy man, a man that does not care for loose ends, like Jonathan Kaley. Unlike Sergeant Kaley, Colonel Fizer knows when to obey orders – *always*. There are no ifs, ands, buts, gray areas or room for interpretation in the military. There is only the strict chain-of-command. This is a chain that can never be broken or circumvented, a chain that is the backbone on which the brass in the military relies upon and has complete and utter trust in. It is a foundation so solidly built upon for hundreds of years that no one man is above it. Not a four-star general or an infantryman, and certainly not Sergeant Kaley.

Colonel Fizer likes Jonathan Kaley because he is a dedicated soldier and believes in the righteousness of the United States military. On the other hand, Kaley is also unafraid to speak his mind to his superior officers or second-guess their judgment. It has certainly put him in hot water on more than one occasion, which explains his current assignment at Evans.

Kaley was in the Army intelligence business for years,

first as an analyst and then, after receiving reconnaissance and combat training and being schooled in stealth warfare, as an operative in the field. He earned high marks from his superiors in all areas of these missions: planning and organization, execution, objectives attained. There was only one aspect that seemed to rankle the top brass more than anything about Kaley: his constant questioning of orders. Regardless of what the orders dictated, Kaley always seemed to believe there was a better way of doing it. Namely, his way. Despite the fact that he was often right, this still did not justify Kaley's actions in the eyes of his superiors.

Although the brass viewed Kaley's hesitancy in carrying out certain orders to be bordering on insubordination, they put up with him because he was one of the best and he always seemed to achieve his mission objectives. Nevertheless, his superiors did not take too kindly to Kaley's brashness, and their tolerance of him was rapidly coming to an end. By that time, they were simply looking for an excuse to kick his ass to the curb.

Then, they found their opportunity. Kaley and several of his colleagues were conducting training exercises with a Special Forces squad based out of Georgia, a group that made Kaley and his team look like a bunch of librarians. The Special Forces squad was showing Kaley and his men new stealth techniques, as well as the latest in military gadgets and hardware.

On the third day of these training maneuvers, the Special Forces squad brought Kaley and his team to a small island off the coast for what they believed to be a P.O.W. rescue operation exercise. Instead, Kaley's team arrived to find a group of enemy combatants, *real enemy combat-*

ants, who had been in the custody of the military since shortly after 9/11.

The patriotic fervor that gripped the nation after that fateful day had a different effect on the men in this Special Forces squad. Their patriotic zeal had turned jingoistic, which happened to a number of Americans during this time, although they may be reluctant to admit it. Every man with dark, Middle Eastern features and every woman who wears a *hijab* is instantly an enemy, real or imagined. The men in this squad saw only red when it came to *these people,* and they were determined to extract confessions, terror plots, or more names from them, whether the prisoners knew anything or not.

By the time Kaley's team arrived, it appeared that many of the enemy combatants had already been worked over. What was worse, however, was that the Special Forces squad seemed to take a truly perverse pleasure in these "interrogations." This was not a good cop, bad cop routine - this was strictly bad cop. After one of the soldiers broke a prisoner's nose, another soldier tried to break it back the way it was, to no avail. Questions were asked sparingly, as an afterthought to the actual beatings, as if they needed an excuse to use the prisoners as human piñatas. No matter what the answers, it seemed inevitable that they would be greeted with a violent response.

Then, the Special Forces' men started berating Kaley's team for their hesitancy, their shock and awe at the brutal beatings, and even questioned his team's patriotism. They called Kaley and his men candyasses and pussies, and lectured them that this is the way the world works now: everyone is a terrorist until proven otherwise.

And to find each and every terrorist, you have to beat it out of them.

Finally, Kaley was ordered by the squad's commander to obtain the coordinates of a terrorist camp operating in the mountains of Afghanistan. If the man was not forthcoming with the information, force was necessary and authorized. Kaley refused, arguing that he was unfamiliar with the intelligence they were referring to and he could not be ordered to interrogate a prisoner on matters he had not been briefed. Furthermore, Kaley asserted that he would not use force on an unarmed man unless absolutely necessary. This provoked the ire of the commander, and he began echoing his soldiers' sentiments about what the real world is like now and how all Americans need to take off the kid gloves. He gave Kaley one last chance to interrogate the man or risk the prospect of a court martial. Again, Kaley refused.

The commander stared at him, his face a mask of red and his blood boiling from Kaley's refusal to follow an order from a superior officer. The commander nodded at one of his men, who approached the prisoner and loomed menacingly over the man. The soldier looked back at Kaley and smiled. He grabbed the prisoner's arm and without asking a single question, broke the man's arm over his knee, causing a horrible cracking sound, followed by the prisoner's agonizing scream. Out of pure instinct, Kaley roared towards the soldier who broke the prisoner's arm and knocked him nearly unconscious with one punch.

The commander attempted to court martial Kaley for his "unprovoked" and "unwarranted" attack, as it was described, but a member within the top brass knew Kaley's value as a soldier and thus, a court martial was prevented. However, Kaley was removed from Army intelligence and any further missions, and he was demoted from Sergeant Major to First Sergeant with the understanding that he would likely never rise above this rank. An additional indignity was heaped upon him when he was given a supervisory role at Evans, a position typically occupied by a Staff Sergeant, a full three ranks behind a First Sergeant.

Kaley, however, has never questioned this or complained. He loves the military and it, in turn, still loves him. Colonel Fizer certainly can respect Sergeant Kaley's sense of duty and purpose, but Kaley disobeyed a direct order from a superior officer and this cannot be tolerated, especially not again. He has placed his life and the life of Private Rushmore in more danger than he could possibly imagine. They witnessed something that was not supposed to have been witnessed *by anyone.*

Fizer partially blames himself for the untenable situation he has put the Foundation in. Upon ordering Kaley to stand down regarding the signal discovered in Lake Michigan, Fizer assumed with good reason that the order would be followed and that would be the end of the matter. Fizer should have known better.

Sergeant Kaley is a bulldog, tenacious in pursuit of answers to his questions. Indeed, the man craves information and he is not one to drop something at the first sign of an obstacle. He does not like to be stonewalled or bullied, a trait that has already had disastrous effects on his military career.

The signal should not have been discovered in the first place, a fact that continues to baffle Fizer. Nevertheless, he does not believe he is to blame. He has more important things on his mind than monitoring what his subordinates are doing. It was only after a substantial amount of time elapsed before he thought to review Sergeant Kaley's and Private Rushmore's keystroke log.

The keystroke-logging program was developed several years ago and today nearly every computer under military ownership contains the program. Essentially, a computer equipped with the program can detail each keystroke entered by the user during a specified time period and produce a readable report for a supervisor to review. The report serves a two-fold purpose: first, it informs the supervisor if the appropriate steps and guidelines were followed in the event of an emergency situation; and second, for security reasons, it lists everything that the soldier looked at, printed, copied, downloaded, recorded, or otherwise reviewed during the shift.

Nearly an hour after Kaley and Rushmore's shift ended, Fizer finally thought to review the logs and discovered that something appeared to have been downloaded from a non-military satellite to a disc on Rushmore's computer, which can only be done with permission from a superior officer. Needless to say, the hot water Kaley is dipping his toes in seems to be downright scalding.

Since the satellite does not belong to the military, it would take considerable time to determine from where the imagery was downloaded. More importantly though, Fizer has absolutely no idea *what* was downloaded and copied to a disc, and perhaps devastatingly, *where* the disc is now. When Fizer attempted to summon Rushmore to his office, he was informed, to his horror, that Rushmore requested a weekend pass, claiming a family emergency to his company commander. The company commander's best guess is that Rushmore is headed home to Fort Wayne, Indiana, but he admitted that Rushmore did not actually specify.

That little shit, Fizer thought, *he could be going anywhere. He could go AWOL with whatever he has in his possession, or worse yet, to the media.*

Fizer started to become frantic, contemplating what he should do, actually considering whether he could withhold this piece of information from the Foundation. He knows what their immediate reaction would be – that he had fucked up, and he is incapable of handling the massive responsibility that comes with moving into a higher position of power within the group. More time ticked off the clock before Fizer finally realized that he did not have a choice. If whatever Kaley or Rushmore has in their possession is brought to light and the group discovers that he knew all along, Fizer would be finished, and he is not thinking merely about his career. The colonel reluctantly called and informed Moriah what happened.

Surprisingly, Moriah remained calm, asked several questions regarding Kaley's and Rushmore's whereabouts, and simply stated that the necessary arrangements would be made. Moriah informed Fizer that he would see him soon and hung up.

What a damn shame that Private Rushmore and Sergeant Kaley will be dead by morning, Fizer thinks.

Like all good soldiers though, Fizer prefers to believe that Kaley would take enormous pride in knowing that he died for the greater good, to protect our nation and better yet, mankind.

What more could a devoted soldier want out of life?

*   *   *

Initially, they received the good news first. The vessel had been flown successfully without detection and it "picked up" its passengers without incident.

Unfortunately for the Foundation, a couple pieces of rather disturbing news piggybacked their way onto the good news. It was confirmed that one of their soldiers had been killed, but this could easily be written off. What concerns Moriah is that a fish has slipped the net. As far as they know, it is only one fish, but this, in Moriah's mind, is one too many. They have not yet ascertained who the lone survivor is, but the person who killed one of their soldiers certainly possessed some type of hand-to-hand combat training. The blow that snapped the soldier's neck was not a second-rate, bush league choke-job. It was a swift and lethal blow intended for one thing and one thing only: instantaneous death.

Moriah suspects who the sole survivor is, but he does not even want to mention his name until it can be confirmed. Moriah wonders if the doctor was able to deliver a warning to him beforehand, but why would the consummate family man leave his family behind?

It does not really matter. It would not be long before they establish which one of their intended victims has escaped and where he or she might be going. All they have to do is determine from the master list who is unaccounted for and then identify their closest contact points.

Doubly unfortunate, the bad news seems to travel in pairs. The second piece of information that failed to sit well with Moriah was Fizer's revelation that something was downloaded from a non-military satellite at Evans by one, possibly two, of Fizer's men. Now, the disc, or *discs,* need to be recovered, and the men...well, the men need to be located and...dealt with.

Moriah knows that Fizer initially failed to review the keystroke-logging program at Private Rushmore's station. Otherwise, why had it taken so long for the colonel to inform them of this crucial piece of information?

Moriah anticipated snags and obstacles along the way, but not caused by members of his own group. Moriah occasionally asks himself how Fizer managed to slither his way inside the Foundation in the first place, but for now, more immediate concerns appear to be pressing.

They need to stay on schedule and now, it seems, they *must* recover some wayward evidence. For that, Moriah calls in a couple teams of "specialists" to handle the situation. Moriah gives them two names and they ensure him that it will soon be taken care of: Kaley and Rushmore will be pleading for a quick death when they are through with them. While the statement is haughty and a little over-the-top, this reassures Moriah that the evidence will soon be theirs, and the men will soon be a memory, bringing a brief, mischievous smile to his face.

The Pentagon

"...authorities say that a terrorist bombing..."

"...speculation of Islamic fundamentalists..."

"...the symbolism is heavy to strike at innocent Americans on Independence Day..."

"...vows that the monsters responsible will be brought to justice..."

"...several bombs were detonated to guarantee no survivors would make it out alive..."

The group sits in a dark conference room where the

only light is provided by the glow of a half-dozen television monitors and several dim overhead lights. They listen to the news reports that are broadcast over and over again, each one recycling what the previous report described. Their faces are sallow and drawn, displaying little emotion except one of utter disbelief. The majority of the men and women seated around the conference table look completely stunned, in a state of shock that this could happen again on American soil, knowing that each one of them has failed in one way or another. There are two men in this room, however, who know the truth of what happened tonight, and they make certain to appear as the others in the room.

General Theodore Parker compulsively tugs at the corners of his salt-and-pepper mustache as he silently stares at the TV screens, studying the various scenes that unfold on each one. General Parker is a man like Colonel Fizer, men who believe in the strict rigidity of the military and an unwavering faith in the chain-of-command.

Parker's father named his son after the great war hero and former president, Theodore Roosevelt, after reading a biography on the renowned "Rough Rider." Parker's father greatly admired the bull-of-a-man for his courage, honor, cunning, and no-nonsense attitude, from his days as police commissioner of New York to his years spent in the Oval Office. Although not related, it seems that General Parker inherited some of the very same attributes from his namesake that his father so greatly appreciated.

General Parker lived through three American wars and emerged from each one more highly decorated than the last. He caught the tail end of the Korean War in 1953 at the tender age of eighteen, earning a Bronze Star for bravery. In Vietnam, he remained in the midst of the war for almost the entire duration. He served three "official" tours of duty, was wounded four times by enemy fire and twice caught shrapnel from land mines. He arrived in Vietnam as most Americans first did in the early 1960s: strictly as a military advisor. At least, that was what the rest of the world was led to believe.

General Parker was part of a small group of American soldiers, along with several CIA operatives, who were funded by both the South Vietnamese and United States governments to run special operations behind enemy lines. Their primary goal was to cause disruption and chaos, to try and weaken the people's faith in Ho Chi Minh and the tenets of communism he posited. No one can recall to this day whether the South Vietnamese requested the United States' presence in their fight against the North, or America took it upon itself to volunteer in the crusade against communism, a nefarious ideology circling many nations around the globe at the time.

Regardless, the Americans arrived in Vietnam in the early 1960s to help stop the spread of the evil empire, but it would take over a decade and the loss of 50,000 men before they realized that they had failed and their mission would not be achieved.

It is known for certain that America's primary objective upon their arrival was to simply advise the South Vietnamese on military strategy and basic warfare principles. It turned into something more, however, something that perhaps the U.S. itself escalated.

Parker was part of a group that included not only CIA operatives and military "advisors," but also South Vienamese military and several guerilla factions opposed to Ho Chi Minh. The South Vietnamese were a motley bunch, a ragtag assortment of shady, untrustworthy characters with questionable interrogation techniques and oftentimes unreliable intelligence. The group committed unspeakable acts that could never be revealed to the American public or the international media. If any of the group's missions became known, the backlash it could have caused would have made the anti-war movement a hundred times stronger than it was. The doves would have had enough ammunition, so to speak, to nearly guarantee that American soldiers would not be stepping away from their own soil for a very long time.

But that did not happen.

Their missions remained top secret, even from them until it was absolutely necessary to disseminate the mission objectives. The group managed to cause major disruption in North Vietnam and there seemed to be a brief spell of outrage at the government from its citizens, but it was to be short-lived. A small blip on the radar screen of populist unrest in North Vietnam. The country's citizens were rural people who did not involve themselves in politics and warfare. It was only after the Americans arrived that the people felt they had been pushed into a war of survival.

One night, four Americans were captured in the dark of night near Hanoi, the capital of North Vietnam. Their avarice had gotten the better of them as they attempted to strike where it would hurt most. General Parker had been on the mission, but he managed to escape, the only one lucky enough to do so.

The four Americans were tortured and interrogated for days, which slowly turned into weeks and then months. The North Vietnamese press were given copies of signed confessions that the Americans had given, detailing secret missions financed by the South Vietnamese and the United States. The "signatures" were illegible, forgeries no doubt, but the damage would soon be done.

The North Vietnamese were careful not to parade the captured Americans around in front of any television cameras, photographers, or journalists, Ho Chi Minh's reasoning being two-fold: first, by not flaunting their "prize" to the rest of the world, he knew the United States would claim that the North Vietnamese government was not, in fact, in possession of American captives. The United States would assert that the North Vietnamese had not captured American soldiers behind enemy lines because indeed, there were no Americans supposedly fighting behind enemy lines. U.S. soldiers were present acting only within the official capacity as *military advisors*. Therefore, the obvious effect Ho Chi Minh foresaw was that if the U.S. military was conducting operations in North Vietnam, they would cease immediately for fear of additional American soldiers being captured behind enemy lines. Perhaps weighted more heavily, it could lead to a very embarrassing situation for the United States on the diplomatic front and on the world stage for a war the Americans had no right to be involved in.

The second and less obvious reason was that Ho Chi Minh saw no purpose in igniting the fury of the American public by putting on display four of their own, barely holding on to their lives and desperate to be rescued. This would certainly raise the level of sentiment and eagerness for war in the consciousness of the American people. Ho Chi Minh obviously did not want every American man within fighting age enlisting to go to war against his nation because he allowed his pride to get the better of him. Little could he know that in the years to come, many of these so-called "fighting age" men would burn their draft cards and flee to Canada to avoid fighting in the upcoming war, a fortunate and unforeseen variable that would benefit the North Vietnamese.

In their response, the American government denied the existence of the captured men, secret missions behind enemy lines, or the signing of any confessions, but nevertheless, the North Vietnamese once again believed in the strength of Ho Chi Minh for staring down the United States.

Soon after, a cryptic message was sent from Washington, D.C. to their "advisors and agents" in South Vietnam, demanding the termination of any unauthorized operations that were planned in North Vietnam.

For Christ's sake, Parker thought at the time, *all the missions were unauthorized as far as the U.S. government was concerned, especially when they went wrong.*

They were to "cease and desist all activities that may jeopardize the lives of American soldiers or intelligence agents" and "remain only in the capacity as advisors to the South Vietnamese military." And that was it. The captured men were left out to dry.

Parker cabled Washington a dozen times, demanding, then pleading, and finally begging for a rescue attempt of the four men. He devised several different rescue missions that he guaranteed would retrieve the men from Hanoi without causing any kind of political fallout or embarrassment to the United States. But time and time again, as expected, his requests were emphatically denied.

He even briefly considered conducting a solo mission,

but he knew that without assistance, it would essentially be a suicide run. Parker was outraged, first at his government, then at himself and the captured men, and finally, the North Vietnamese. He came to realize that all soldiers assume certain risks, and they know the risks they take are dangerous, sometimes fatal. Whether the men had cracked under questioning was trivial because they died defending the flag, defending the world against communism, the evil force that it was at the time. They were heroes, unrecognized at that, but heroes nonetheless. And Parker dedicated himself to also being a hero, an unacknowledged one like the captured men.

When the United States "officially" entered the war, Parker fought like a man possessed. His sole mission was to kill and destroy everything in his path. He had no conscience and no time for mercy. He led Special Forces troops on slaughter-filled rampages of the Vietcong that lasted weeks. He burned down dozens of villages, no matter if they were North Vietnamese or South Vietnamese. He did it all for the four men who would never be recognized by their government, whose deaths would be denied until every politician on Capitol Hill was blue in the face from saying that these men never existed.

They existed to Parker, in his mind and in his heart every day, knowing that it could have been him rotting along with them in that shithole. The same thoughts course through his head almost each and every day since then:

What would I have done?

Would I have folded under questioning?

No fucking way.

The next major conflict for the United States was the Persian Gulf War. While it was Stormin' Norman

Schwarzkopf who attained all the glory and basked in the limelight of the press, it was General Parker's strategy that brought a swift and merciless victory for the Americans. He took charge, as he always does, disregarding fame or adulation to ensure a quick and decisive victory and bring the dictator Saddam to his knees.

General Parker played a major role advising Schwarzkopf in positioning of troops and glaring weaknesses in the Iraqi army. It was his experience with warfare that gave the Americans the ultimate edge, along with a couple thousand "smart" bombs. He emerged from the war fully decorated once again and he soon became a five-star general. Several years thereafter, he was appointed to the Joint Chiefs-of-Staff and in the last few years, ironically, he arrived full-circle. He now commands the title of "special military advisor" to the Pentagon and once again, he seems to be taking charge, this time on orders from the President himself.

General Parker rises from his chair in a body that has inarguably grown old, but has certainly not broken down. He remains fit and muscular for all of his seventy-five years and he can still intimidate a whole room simply by walking through the door. He begins moving around the conference table, simultaneously sizing up the situation and the men and women in the room.

"Well, ladies and gentlemen," he begins, "what occurred here tonight is one of the most callous and cowardly acts I have ever seen. Make no mistake, every act of terrorism is the desperate action of cowards, of enemies who are afraid to come out of the shadows and show themselves, people who hide from the very fight that they are trying to stir up. They strike at the innocent because it is not their way to be involved in a so-called 'fair fight.' The innocent are easy targets, ducks in a shooting gallery."

General Parker has the full attention of the room now, with all eyes glued on him. He is like a preacher in the pulpit whose voice begins to rise with each new word, each new condemnation. It is as if you expect one of his listeners to rise up and cry out, "Praise Jesus!"

But they do not. They remain still, motionless, giving General Parker the respect he expects and, indeed, deserves.

Parker stalks around the large, oval table and points around the room, looking each person in the eyes.

"I want a promise from everyone here today. I should not have to ask it, but I will. I need a promise from each and every person in this room that they will not stop, they will not give up, until we have caught these despicable human beings and brought them to justice. Only then will this reprehensible act be avenged, and the dead will be able to rest in peace."

He pauses, looks around the silent room, and receives solemn nods from each and every individual. Not a word is said but Parker sees it in their eyes. He nods as well.

He sits down in his chair and looks at the faces around the table.

"Good," he says confidently, "now let's get started."

FIVE

Jonathan Kaley is pissed off. He is raging mad and with good reason. He knows with absolute certainty why those men came to his house tonight, and frankly, he is not surprised at their intentions, only at the swiftness of their response. It is Kaley's own fault for letting his guard down, for not assuming the worst after he and Rushmore witnessed something that was probably not intended for anyone's eyes.

Curiosity certainly does kill the cat, he wryly thinks.

Rushmore is his responsibility and without even thinking of the repercussions, Kaley has put Private Rushmore in serious jeopardy, and now, as is evident, mortal danger.

But how could I know? How could I possibly know what the two of us would see?

Kaley *does know* that the men sent to his house tonight were professionals. They had killed before and they believed they were going to do it again. They did not plan on Sergeant Kaley, however, a black belt in the martial arts and a man whose temper is equaled by his ferocity when threatened. They certainly fucked with the wrong man tonight.

Kaley floors the battered military-issued jeep like a madman through the streets. He fully realizes that this is not the smartest thing to do, but he is returning to Evans to check on Rushmore, knowing that he must get to him before "they" do.

When their shift ended several minutes after the "incident," the two of them departed the operations center and went their separate ways, not speaking to one another or to anyone else about what they had seen.

After Kaley asked Rushmore if they could zero in on the signal with another satellite, Rushmore located a satellite owned and operated by a global communications firm. In order for most corporate-owned satellites to keep their birds in space, they not only pay an astronomical fee to the U.S. government for the right to do so, but they must also make available to the military all passwords and access information in the event of an emergency. The information is stored in an enormous database that is supposedly impenetrable, but Private Rushmore is one of the best at finding backdoor codes and access to alleged high-security networks. To their surprise, they realized the military is unbelievably lax and sloppy in maintaining the structure of their enormous mainframe.

Besides, the unwritten rule is that "if it is in the sky, it is part of the military's pie." Once Rushmore gained access to the satellite, they noticed the signal from Lake Michigan had disappeared. They found something else, however, something much more extraordinary.

The signal, which only moments before was directly in the middle of the lake in a stationary position, was picked up approaching land on the southeastern side of Lake Michigan. Their quick calculations showed that the signal traveled approximately 150 miles in the span of a few seconds. Nothing man-made could traverse that distance without killing every human inside from the *g*-forces. Furthermore, once it approached land, not only did the signal disappear, but *everything* disappeared from the satellite's view. Rushmore explained that the satellite did not appear out of range, but rather it seemed that the satellite could no longer transmit, as if somehow it had been jammed.

Less than four minutes later, the satellite was fully operational and it suddenly pinpointed several new moving objects, but the initial signal was no longer present. These objects were distinct in that they were identified as five Apache helicopters, the same ones Kaley assumed Fizer was referring to. It seemed suspicious that these choppers were dispatched to an area over a hundred miles away from where the signal was initially detected. Kaley did not think Colonel Fizer possessed the prescient ability to know where the signal was headed before it had even moved. The colonel evidently slipped on that banana peel.

The helicopters approached land and according to the satellite, low-level blasts could be detected as they dropped something along the shoreline. The satellite detected no human presence when in fact, there were two witnesses to what occurred on that beach, one of whom had seen everything.

None of this mattered as much to Kaley though as the fact, which Rushmore was quick to point out, that according to their bird in the sky, it had detected a massive human presence along the shoreline where the signal was approaching moments before the satellite went down. When the satellite began transmitting again within several minutes, the large human presence had disappeared, which seemed downright unexplainable to Sergeant Kaley.

Where had they gone? How could they all have vanished in such a short period of time?

Kaley ordered Rushmore to record the activity to a disc as soon as they gained access to the non-military satellite, and Rushmore made a copy for each of them. While it is inherently risky to have documented evidence of Kaley's insubordination, he also knows that what they were witnessing was extraordinary, even if it is utterly inexplicable. A record of the activity only seemed logical. Little could Kaley know that what they had witnessed and the documented evidence of it would, in the long run, cause more harm than good. The consequences, however, did not weigh heavily in his decision at the time.

What continued to gnaw at Kaley was Fizer's quick assertion that the situation was being handled no more than a few minutes from the time the signal was initially detected. This suggested something more to Sergeant Kaley, something insidious, underhanded and worse yet, something planned.

Kaley ordered Rushmore to keep his mouth closed and not to utter a word of this to his buddies or to Colonel Fizer. Their shift ended at 10:00 PM central time, less than a few minutes after the incident, and they did not speak to one another or to anyone else as they casually departed for their respective homes. Kaley rented a ranch house not far from the base and Rushmore lived in the barracks at Evans.

Evans had not yet erupted in the chaos that would ensue upon hearing news of a "terrorist attack" on American soil. Kaley knew better, however, and so did Rushmore, that this "attack" did not appear to be related to any terrorists or extremists, but something entirely more evil and cunning. Exactly what they possess, or what they could do with it at this point, neither of them know. They do know that what they have is, without a doubt, intrinsically dangerous.

Kaley turns into the driveway that leads to the front gate of Evans and flashes his identification card to the MP, a man named Daltry. Kaley can only hope that he does not appear too nervous or jittery in front of the MP. He is sweating buckets from a mixture of anxiety, his recent physical encounter, and the Midwestern humidity, which does not seem to dissipate even at night. Kaley's agitated appearance does not appear to sound any alarms as the MP likely has other things on his mind.

"How are you, Daltry?" Kaley casually asks.

A telephone rings inside the guardhouse and the other MP, a new guy Kaley has never seen before, goes to answer it.

"A little shocked, sir. You hear what happened?" Daltry asks.

"Yeah, I did," Kaley answers.

Kaley tries to remain calm as he looks with one eye towards the guardhouse. The base beyond the gate is abuzz with activity as soldiers scurry from one place to another.

"What's been going through the rumor mill around here?" Kaley asks.

"Mostly just guesses, sir," Daltry answers. "Al-Qaeda at the top of the list, naturally, but nothing substantiated yet."

Kaley absently nods his head, probably focusing too much attention on the other MP, when Daltry asks, "You back on duty?"

"Well, actually, I-"

Kaley stops in mid-sentence when he catches the other MP subtly glance at him while holding the phone close to his mouth. Kaley reads the man's lips as he says a couple of quick "yes sirs" and hastily puts the phone down. Kaley estimates he has no more than fifteen seconds before both MPs have their weapons pointed at him, informing him that he is under arrest.

As quickly and as casually as he can, Kaley asks, "Hey, you seen Rushmore around anywhere?"

"Actually, sir, Private Rushmore was granted an off-base pass for a couple of days. Just before the shit hit the fan around here. I think he went to the big city," Daltry offers.

Kaley cannot decide if Rushmore is the smartest s.o.b. in the world for getting the hell out of Dodge or the dumbest for leaving and probably never coming back, an AWOL nut these same MPs would have to track down.

With one last glimpse at the other rapidly-approaching MP, Kaley says, "Thanks, Tim. You boys keep cool now."

Kaley shifts the stick of the jeep into reverse, slams his foot on the accelerator, and the vehicle lurches backward in a cloud of dust and dirt as he skirts the side of the driveway. In the blur of it all, he sees an open-mouthed Daltry standing there as his partner grabs him by the arm and points at the jeep.

Kaley twists the wheel around and steps on the brake, causing the vehicle to spin out and nearly tip over. He shifts the stick into first gear in one fluid motion and punches the accelerator while easing his foot off the clutch. Kaley's heart skips a beat as the jeep buckles, the typical precursor to the vehicle stalling and worse yet, stopping. The jeep buckles again and then starts to pick up speed.

Kaley sharply exhales as he hears the faint shouts from the MPs as they tell him to stop. He has more important things to focus on, like finding Rushmore in one of the largest cities in the country.

*   *   *

The Foundation is quickly learning the craftiness of the formidable Sergeant Kaley, and to underestimate him is to do so at your own risk. Kaley managed to best the "clean-up" squad sent to his home, leaving one man dead and two others severely injured. His whereabouts are unknown and furthermore, the evidence has still not been recovered.

Now there are two fish, possibly three if they include Private Rushmore, all potential witnesses to an event so horrific and utterly merciless that if any of them are to be implicated-

No chance, as Moriah realizes his thoughts are beginning to run away from him. There is no one who can possibly connect any of them to what occurred in Tamawaca tonight.

We are untouchable, Moriah thinks.

And the thing is, he is right. None of the Foundation members can be linked to the events of tonight or over the next 36 hours. Covert plans and secret missions are nothing new to the group, and indeed, they have a multitude of experience in ensuring they are not connected to something that could lead to the group's exposure or worse yet, downfall. While the scope of what they have planned tonight and over the next 36 hours may be on a much grander scale than anything they have ever undertaken, and the stakes are greater than anything that could be imagined, the group members are certainly not ignorant to the risks they take and they never falter when it comes to protecting themselves.

Despite these risks, they do not consider their business a chore by any means, but view it as both a privilege and an honor. In their eyes, they are the true Americans, the ones who bleed red, white, and blue. They know that what they do is something that no Joe Sixpack would have the stomach or the brains for. They know that to be the best, you have to anticipate what the enemy will do and plan for every possibility and contingency, prepared to counteract at a moment's notice. Most importantly, however, you have to be utterly ruthless. You must have sharper instincts and a smaller conscience than most, a standard requirement that each member of the Foundation possesses.

Upon their shoulders rests the burden and the duty entailed in maintaining the greatest country that ever was and will ever be. The latter is what the Foundation has charged themselves with looking after and upholding for the remainder of their lives, a solemn responsibility that can never be thwarted.

Which is why it gives Moriah pause to think of the two men whose disenchantment with the Foundation and knowledge of its more unsavory activities has become a serious liability. Their very existence is a constant threat to expose and destroy the group that has labored in obscurity for nearly a century making the country the superpower that it is. The Foundation does not want these two men hanging over their head any longer.

As soon as this affair is over and hopefully, after its success has been realized, the reward for one man's service will be a swift bullet to the back of the head. The search for the other man has not yielded any results in 40 years, a fact that continues to haunt the group's leadership, despite their almost certain belief that he is dead. Of course, being "almost certain" is not the same as actually laying eyes on a body and confirming what they believe to be true. For Moriah, it is better to avoid thinking about the men altogether.

After the call came through that the mission was under way, the men scattered like cockroaches when the lights come on. They went back to their significant others, some of them returning to empty homes and others heading off to work, knowing that they would be needed there as soon as word hit of the "attack" at Tamawaca.

It is only Moriah and a man named Bellini now, alone in the hotel room at the Biltmore. They received the mixed news and passed it on to the others. Needless to say, no one was pleased with the bad news. In a highly volatile situation such as this one, however, mistakes are to be expected and even anticipated. They know how to tie up loose ends, which is one of the group's specialties.

Bellini shakes his head, causing his jowls to move from side to side, which makes him appear like he is attempting a Tricky Dick impression. He is a man who loses his temper often and with great gusto. He should have been dead of a heart attack long ago as a result of his explosive temperament and penchant for artery-clogging foods.

"Where do you think Kaley is headed?" Bellini bluntly asks.

"You know as well as I do that wherever he goes, he'll be found soon enough," Moriah reassuringly responds.

"Soon enough may not do it, Moriah-"

"Well goddammit, Paul, what else can we do?" Moriah asks in exasperation. "We have people all over the country looking for him, he can't get very far."

Bellini pauses and shakes his head again. "How could this have happened? You said the men sent to his house were the best. You said they'd take care of it."

"Well, they didn't," Moriah snaps. More calmly, he continues, "For now, we have to stay on an even keel. The next twenty-four hours are crucial to maintaining the mission and seeing it through to its completion. That is our sole priority right now and it will continue to stay that way. The fish are our second priority."

"Your fish," Bellini spits.

Moriah's phone on the table rings and he quickly picks it up.

"Yes?"

Moriah listens intently, digesting every piece of information as it comes to him, his face a mask, emotionless, not giving anything away. Without a word, he sets his phone down. Bellini is about to burst, waiting for that first word, which seems to him like an eternity.

"That was Gleason. Well, we know who our escapee is."

"Yes?" Bellini says, expectantly.

Confirming what he already suspected, Moriah says matter-of-factly, "It's our old friend, the conspiracy professor and ex-Marine, Sean O'Connell."

Bellini lets out a gush of air as if he has been sucker-punched in the stomach. In a voice barely above a whisper, he says, "Jesus . . ."

"And how's this for a kick while you're down?" Moriah asks.

As if pausing for dramatic effect and possibly to see if Bellini can survive this bombshell, Moriah lets it fly.

"O'Connell and Kaley used to be best friends."

". . . . . . .Christ."

Chicago, Illinois

Around this time, Private P.J. Rushmore is sitting in a blues bar called *Kingston Mines* in downtown Chicago on Halsted Street, a place he and a couple other guys frequent on their occasional jaunts into the city. The establishment is separated into two gigantic rooms, with a large stage and bar in each one. There is a method to the madness, of course, for as one band completes their set in one room, the act in the other room fires up as soon as the last chord has been strummed next door. Nothing but blues played every night into the wee hours of the morning. And although the cover charge can occasionally be exorbitant, it remains a great place to kick back and enjoy a few cold ones with the boys, and hopefully, a few select ladies.

But Rushmore is not thinking about that right now. He is not thinking about the cover charge or the loud, raucous music blaring throughout the bar. He is not thinking about the ladies around him or the alcohol that seems to be flowing like water tonight. He feels like he is being watched and, unfortunately for him, he is correct on that count.

Two men, as ordinary and nondescript as two human beings can be, stand at the back of the bar, watching and waiting for Rushmore's next move. They do not drink, their heads do not bounce to the music, and they sure as hell do not take their eyes off of Rushmore. They have the place covered front and back, with another two-man team waiting across the street from the bar's entrance. As soon as they see an opportunity, the young private is theirs. If it is necessary to eliminate his cohorts to capture the private, this is collateral damage that can easily be afforded.

As his friends move towards the stage, Rushmore drifts towards the bar.

"You coming, Rush?" one of his buddies asks.

"Yeah, in a minute, I gotta take a leak," Rushmore responds, nodding towards the back of the bar.

Rushmore casually looks around, attempting to study every face, looking for anyone who seems to be watching him or paying too much attention his way. Everyone seems to be talking with one another or looking up towards the stage, dancing and clapping along as the lead guitarist begins one of the many lengthy solos he has embarked on throughout the night.

Then there are two faces Rushmore spots who do not seem to be enjoying themselves like the rest of the patrons. They seem oddly out of place, like nuns in the middle of a fraternity party. He makes eye contact with them, two rather large men standing at the back of the bar. Rushmore quickly takes inventory and notes that neither of them holds a drink and the music certainly does not seem to be the focus of their attention. The men do not glance away from Rushmore, as if to avoid detection, and their piercing stares feel like they are boring a hole right through his brain.

Rushmore quickly looks away towards a small television hanging in a tiny alcove above the bar. The television is on mute but the screen shows a reporter standing in front of a beach, motioning towards it. Rushmore sees small patches of embers glowing at various points in the background, dotting the landscape. He sees medical personnel running around desperately as the camera slowly pans over the beach. Although judging from the looks of it, they are far too late.

There are tattered clothes lying about, burnt cabanas, the requisite small doll with a scarred face. Rushmore immediately feels a strange connection to the scene played out on the TV screen, a sensation that he has been there before. Then it hits him: *the mysterious signal, the shoreline, the mass disappearance of people.*

He can feel his heart beating faster and a knot forming in his stomach when the camera comes to rest on the most indelible of images. Row upon row of bodybags line the beach, their contents fresh and unmistakable.

Suddenly, the band stops playing, the people stop dancing and clapping, and one of the bartenders turns up the volume on the TV and tries to call for silence.

"Hush up over there for a second! Hush up!" he shouts.

The noise level of the place suddenly fades from a cacophony to several conversations asking what is going on, until finally, silence seems to envelop the room.

The people gather around the bar, transfixed by the images on the TV.

Another 9/11?

Not again, people groan.

It is too much for Rushmore. He feels nauseous, as if he is going to be sick. Although the bar is not air-conditioned and the abundance of ceiling fans has done nothing to ward off the July humidity that has seeped in, Rushmore feels like his whole body has been dipped in an ice bucket. A cold sweat begins to coat his skin and he feels the blood leaving his face. He starts to make his way towards the restrooms in the back of the bar when he suddenly feels his legs go weak.

Rushmore realizes why a split second later as he looks behind him and sees a syringe exiting his right buttock. He stares up at the two men he spotted not more than a couple minutes ago, who suddenly have their arms wrapped tightly around him, gripping him as if he is caught in a vice. Before Rushmore can even resist them, let alone utter a cry for help, he senses all feeling rushing out of his extremities, and the only thing that keeps him from falling is the men holding him up on either side.

A young woman notices Rushmore practically falling over and asks, "Is he okay? You guys need some help?"

One of the men responds icily, "He's fine. We're just going to take him home."

These would be the last words that Rushmore would hear as he drifts off into darkness, which, soon enough, would be his permanent home.

*   *   *

Sergeant Kaley slams his foot on the brakes as he comes to a screeching halt in front of an orange-canopied bar where a pair of Chicago police cars sit. Something tells him that he has finally struck pay dirt as he sees a couple of soldiers he recognizes from Evans speaking with a police officer outside of a bar called *Kingston Mines.*

Something also tells him that he may be too late. Kaley throws on his hazard lights, springs from the jeep, and hustles toward the group of men.

He addresses one of the police officers. "Excuse me, Officer, may I have a minute alone with my men?" he politely asks, gesturing towards the two men the officer is questioning.

"And you are . ." the officer asks.

"First Sergeant Jonathan Kaley, United States Army, sir," he responds, adding a quick salute for good measure.

The officer takes a once-over of Kaley, looks at the other two men, and finally relents.

"Yeah, go ahead, but we still need to ask these guys a few more questions, Sergeant."

"They'll be with you in no time," Kaley assures the officer.

The officer walks away and Kaley waits until he is busy with someone else before he turns toward the two soldiers, who offer him a sharp salute.

He returns the salute and asks them, "Was Private Rushmore with you guys tonight?"

"Sir, are you okay? You have blood on your forehead," one of them notes.

He reaches up and feels the caked blood just beneath his hairline.

"I'm fine," he says dismissively.

They look at him uneasily.

As if to reassure them, Kaley says, "Don't worry, it's not mine. Now listen, Boyd and Rogers, right?"

They simultaneously respond, "Yes, sir."

He urgently asks, "Where is Rushmore?"

"We don't know," Rogers responds.

"He was with us for most of the night and then, in a heartbeat, we didn't see him," Boyd chimes in.

"It was right after the news broke on TV about the terrorist attack," Rogers offers.

"Fucking bastards," Boyd mutters.

"Sir, did you hear about it?" Rogers asks.

Kaley nods solemnly, "I did, Private. But, listen, I really need to know right now about Rushmore."

"A lady said she saw him," Rogers reports, "that he was helped out of here by two big guys wearing black leather coats. But we didn't see anybody who looked like that. She said he looked pretty wasted."

"But it didn't seem like he even drank that much, sir," Boyd offers. "And she said he looked like he was struggling with them for a second, like he didn't know them or something."

Pondering this information, Kaley begins to think out loud, "Leather coats in July . . ."

He allows the thought to hang there for a moment before continuing his questioning.

"So, what did you guys do next?"

"We called the cops," Rogers says.

"Two guys in black, leather coats did not sound like people Rushmore would take off with, sir," Boyd notes.

"We thought they might have robbed him, sir," Rogers says, "maybe beat the shit out of him and left him out back."

"We looked in the alley behind the joint, sir," Boyd states, shrugging, "but we didn't find him."

Kaley contemplates their story for several moments, eyeballs the two men, and asks them something just to be sure.

"You boys aren't covering for him, are you?"

Both of them shake their heads "no."

"He didn't take an extended leave of absence, did he? Maybe he cracked and went AWOL?" Kaley asks, mining for any scrap of information.

Both emphatically respond, "No, sir," in quick succession.

"There's no way, sir," Rogers says. "Rushmore ain't that kind of guy, and me and Boyd will vouch for him."

Having been in the intelligence business for years, Kaley likes to think he knows when someone is lying or being less than forthright with him. By all appearances though, these two men seem to be telling the truth, although he almost wishes they were lying, for Rushmore's sake. Two unknown and unidentified men taking Rushmore for a stroll does not sound promising.

Shit, Rushmore was my responsibility and I might have put him directly in harm's way, Kaley thinks. He suddenly feels sick to his stomach thinking of the young private's fate, cursing himself for how careless and rash he acted at Evans, not for one second considering the possible consequences.

But how could I have known? he reminds himself. *How could I have known what we would see?*

"What did the police say?" Kaley asks, motioning towards them.

"We can't officially file a missing persons report until

twenty-four hours have passed, sir," Boyd says. "But we gave the cops a description and they said they'd keep an eye out."

"Good," Kaley nods. "Now you boys better get back to Evans on the double, and let them know about Rushmore."

"Yes, sir," they both nod.

Kaley leans in and lowers his voice an octave, "If anyone asks back at Evans, I was never here and you never saw me tonight. That's an order, understood?"

Kaley's voice is firm and deadly serious. One after the other responds, "Yes, sir."

"Good," Kaley nods.

He turns and starts to walk towards his jeep when Boyd speaks up, "Sir, one thing though."

"Yeah?" Kaley asks, turning around.

"Well, sir, Rushmore looked awfully fidgety for a guy who just got some R & R."

Curious, Kaley quietly asks, "What do you mean?"

"Well, sir," Rogers says, "what Boyd is saying is that Rushmore looked 'bout a shade whiter than grandma's thighs. He kept looking all around, real paranoid-like."

"Yeah," Boyd adds, "like he was being watched or something."

Kaley nods solemnly, cursing himself again for the mess he has gotten them in.

"Yeah," he says somberly, "well, let's just hope he'll turn up soon, huh boys?"

They both nod.

Kaley feels another pang of guilt course through him as he realizes that the prospect of finding Rushmore, let alone alive, seems to be rapidly dwindling.

Kaley solemnly nods again, pats them both on the shoulder and heads back to his jeep. He jumps in with his stomach turning cartwheels, and guns the accelerator for destinations unknown.

*   *   *

Sean O'Connell peeks through the window from outside the home and immediately does not like what he sees. The inside is in absolute shambles, with obvious signs of a struggle. There are upended chairs and a table, a broken bookshelf, and a cracked mirror. There is a streak on the wall that could be a bloodstain. He closely scans the room, but sees no sign of anyone lurking about. Sean does not like what he sees because this is his friend's house and he knows that Jon Kaley is a compulsive neat freak.

After his escape from the beach, Sean trekked through the woods for over an hour before deciding it safe to emerge. He hated to take advantage of the trusting nature of the Michiganders, but he did not feel he had many options at that point. He boosted an old, beat-up Camaro sitting in someone's driveway, the keys teasingly dangling in the ignition. Sean made the trip to Kaley's house in a little over two hours, practically a record considering the distance. He abandoned the car several blocks away in a supermarket parking lot and continued the rest of the way on foot to Kaley's pad.

Sean creeps around towards the rear of the house and finds that the back door is slightly open. He opens the screen door and kneels down for a closer inspection of the lock, but sees no sign of forced entry. If the intruders chose this as their entry point, they left no marks, a certain sign of a professional at work.

Who the hell did Kaley get himself involved with? Sean thinks.

He knows Jon does not gamble and thus, that eliminates any angry bookies or their associated muscle arriving to claim a debt. Sean immediately discounts drug peddlers or gangsters because it simply does not mesh with Kaley's persona. He is a fucking Boy Scout, a do-gooder, someone who would help an old lady across the street. He would not be involved with low-lifes like that, Sean is certain of it.

Sean enters the house and conducts a thorough search of the kitchen, the bedroom, and most of the rest of the one-story. The kitchen looks as if it was cleaned yesterday. Knowing Kaley, it probably had. The bedroom, too, appears undisturbed. The sheets are made and perfectly creased at the corners, leading Sean to conclude that if Kaley was interrupted in the middle of the night, they did not catch him while he was sleeping. The only other part of the house that appears out of the ordinary is the counter in the bathroom, where Sean finds a small streak of blood. Besides that, everything is normal, or as normal as can be considering the living room is a total disaster area, as if a twister ripped through this area of the house.

Sean stands in the middle of the living room and assesses everything, attempting to pry the smallest piece of information from any of the objects in the room. As if simply by standing amid this chaos, the scene that played out here will eventually reveal itself. When Sean, at last, realizes that he is not a vessel for ESP or able to glance back in time, he frustratingly sighs and shakes his head. He is about to leave when he notices a faint light coming through a crack in a closet door directly off of the living room.

Sean cautiously approaches and pushes the closet door open to find that it is, in fact, no longer a closet, but rather Kaley has converted it into a small home office. The room is cramped, with no windows, bookshelves occupying three of the four walls, and a small desk. On top of the desk are a computer and a tiny lamp, which emits the light he saw from the living room. Sean also notices that the computer monitor is on, but the screen is blank except for a small American flag floating across the top, an obvious screensaver for a man like Kaley.

Sean moves the mouse and the computer hums to life, followed by the screen slowly defining itself as it comes into focus. The desktop appears with several file folders and the basic Windows applications.

He reads some of the file folders: "Contacts," "Military 1," "Military 2," "PJ," and "Command Structure."

Sean clicks on the file marked "Contacts," and instantly, a box pops up prompting him for a password.

Shit.

Knowing the intricate security measures Kaley likely established to protect against "unauthorized" eyes viewing something he does not want them to, Sean is about to abandon hope of finding anything useful on the computer when he notices at the bottom of the desktop a small box. The box is labeled, "PJ," and it is open, minimized at the bottom of the screen.

"What the hell is this, Jon?" Sean says out loud.

He clicks on the box and it opens up. At the top is a heading: "Personal Journal."

The cursor is flashing at the end of a sentence, waiting for its next command. The previous entry was last night, July 4th, only several hours ago. Sean begins to read:

July 4, 2011 11:58 pm—What is it that we have witnessed tonight? Something horrible I imagine. Something I hope our government is not behind, and yet I have this terrible suspicion that it is the very institution I unquestionably serve that has committed an act I am unable to understand. How else to explain the fact that F knew so quickly of the situation, and steps had already been taken in response?

Innocent Americans have been taken or killed, by what or whom I cannot fathom. The news reports have started to trickle in and they are all saying that it is a "terrorist attack." I am afraid that what I have witnessed tonight along with R was no terrorist attack, and furthermore, what we have seen may place us both in extreme danger. There is evidence of what we have witnessed, or at least evidence of something, but I fear there is no culprit that can be brought to justice for this . . .

I hope my friend didn't go to the beach this weekend

they're here

Sean rereads the journal entry and the same chills inhabit his skin now that did the first time he read it. The second to last line even references Sean. Although he has not spoken to his friend in several weeks, Kaley knows that Sean and his family typically spend the Fourth of July holiday at the beach house in Tamawaca.

Kaley saw something surrounding the events at Tamawaca Beach, something "horrible" he imagined.

That means the military is somehow involved, right? How else would Kaley know about what happened there?

Sean's mind flashes to the image of the soldiers storming their way up the beach.

Who are "F" and "R"? What was the situation "F" knew about and the rapid response to it?

The fact that Kaley wrote that "innocent Americans" had been "taken or killed" and he suspected the government, specifically the military, was responsible, make the situation seem all the more surreal. Kaley does not appear convinced it was a terrorist attack, an opinion that Sean is in complete agreement with. Certainly Kaley and the mysterious "R" were not knowing participants in whatever occurred. If anything, it seems that what they have seen could get them both hurt.

But what had they seen? What evidence do they have?

And then the ominous last line . . .

"They're here."

Obviously, Sean can figure out what this means based on the current condition of Kaley's home. Unfortunately, since there are no bodies, Sean cannot determine the outcome of what subsequently ensued.

Sean slams his fist down on the desk, creating a loud, cracking noise that sounds like a gunshot in the empty house. Sean's temper begins to flare as he thinks of the possibility of the *United States government* behind the events of last night. It seems inconceivable that the American military would be involved in the disappearance of his family and over a hundred other people from the beach last night. Still, he thinks of the sleek Apache helicopters and the soldiers storming the beach and it suddenly does not seem so far-fetched.

One thing Sean is certain of is that Kaley was interrupted. His friend knew he was in danger and yet he still wanted to leave a record of it in case someone stumbled onto his journal.

Suddenly, something else occurs to Sean, a distant memory from his childhood. When he and Jon played "soldier boy" in the woods with the other kids on the block, it always seemed that it was the two of them versus everyone else. As a result, the two of them devised a secret system whereby they used a subtle marker that indicated they were still "alive" and had not been captured by the other team. When one of them found the marker, he picked it up and placed it at another strategic location where he believed the other might see it, with the top of the marker indicating which direction he was headed.

Sean scrambles up from the desk and begins looking around for it. He checks the floors, the counter top in the kitchen, the bedroom, and the bathroom. He looks around the office once again, but to no avail. It is possible that Jon forgot about the marker, too. After all, Sean's memory barely conjured up the forgotten child's game.

Then, Sean glances at a picture on the wall of the two of them on graduation day from high school. Such young, vibrant faces ready to go out and tackle the world, like nothing can stop them. They appear as carefree as two kids can be with an uncertain and unknown future stretching out before them.

Sean approaches the wall, less focused on the picture than the frame itself, which is slightly askew. Knowing Jon, even after a brutal fight, he would probably adjust the frame to ensure that it is straight. Sean lifts the frame to look behind it and a huge grin ripples across his face.

The marker.

It is not green like they always used in the woods and it is certainly not the real thing, but rather a drawing. A crude drawing at that. Sean can understandably sympathize with his friend's artwork. Sean stares at it and knows that Jon is alive, for now.

He allows the frame to fall back over the marker, a shamrock that has been hastily sketched on the wall using, at the time, what was probably the best available material: blood.

Sean only hopes it is someone else's.

SIX

The Pentagon

General Theodore Parker tries to rub the weariness from his eyes as he sits alone in the same conference room in the Pentagon where the group gathered the previous night. The televisions that occupy one side of the wall are muted now as they no longer depict, ad nauseam, the grisly pictures of death and destruction from the night before. The cameras that pan over the beach now display a serene scene, a surreal calm, with the sun breaking over the beach as Lake Michigan's waves slowly amble up the shore, like delicate ghostly fingers that quietly leave their mark and then are quickly washed away, soon to be replaced. The reporters point and gesture over the long stretch of sand, giving the same, sad eulogy that can never possibly do justice to over a hundred lives lost in what seems to be the breadth of an instant.

Parker slowly opens his eyes and focuses on the televisions, but only for a moment. He seems to stare past them, as if by looking through them he might catch a glance of what happened on that beach and why.

Last night, upon hearing news of the attack, his mind began to race with possible perpetrators, and the group reinforced his initial suspects: Islamic fundamentalists, Muslim radicals, al-Qaeda, a rogue faction of the North Korean military, and on and on. There seemed to be no end to the list of potential enemies the United States has made in the past few years, a fact that several in attendance subtly blamed on the current administration's international policies, which in turn caused more grumbling and finger-pointing. Parker quickly quashed any discussion of the current administration because he does not care if certain policies were the root cause of the attack. He simply wants to find the culprits responsible.

In truth, there were no real answers that materialized at last night's brief bull session. Only more questions.

Theories were posited and dismissed, possible motives tossed back and forth, and ideas both practical and extreme were presented. One person even suggested that maybe the intended target was simply a single individual who was present on the beach, which was greeted by several skeptical guffaws. This seemed too outlandish to even consider, let alone worth time to investigate. For anyone who knows General Parker, however, *everything* and *everyone* would be explored to the fullest extent possible, with no theories or ideas off-limits or taboo. No one would be above suspicion, including fellow Americans. At the mention of this thought, the entire room bristled, not caring to dwell on the ramifications such a scenario, if true, would have on the public consciousness.

It was certainly bad enough, many in the room believed, that Timothy McVeigh and Terry Nichols leveled the Alfred Murray Federal Building in Oklahoma City without the American intelligence agencies so much as catching a whiff that something was amiss. But for Americans to be the primary suspects once again, after 9/11 and all of the alleged security upgrades, the backlash would be fierce. Furthermore, it would show the rest of the world that the United States is unable to even monitor their own people, let alone terrorists around the globe. The whole administration, along with the military and intelligence communities, would be roasted on an open flame by the press. The same question would be posed without mercy:

How could you have let this happen, *again?*

General Parker, however, is not afraid to ask the tough questions or explore unpopular theories. And he did, all throughout the night. He lambasted his colleagues on everything from suspicious passport identification to how tight the security is on the Canadian border. Nothing was out-of-bounds and he made certain that everyone in the room understands the rules of the playing field, which, essentially, contains only one rule: there are no rules in this game.

After an exhausting night of questions fired back and forth and theories bounced off the walls, the truth is that they have no clearer picture of what happened last night than when they started. Too much speculation and conjecture without a solid link or motive.

Parker dismissed them all a short while ago, disgusted with himself and his colleagues, knowing that their collective fatigue was not doing them any favors. He has no new information to offer the President, no quick leads or prime suspects. Actually, there are several suspects, but these, he would acknowledge, are the most obvious ones.

Now, alone with his thoughts, Parker begins to form an idea out of the void of nothingness that has occupied the room for the last several hours.

Something does not feel right to him. There was no warning and not even the slightest bit of intelligence that suggested an attack on American soil over the holiday weekend. No informers, leaks, anonymous calls or letters. No misinformation or misdirection, absolutely nothing. Obviously, for a terrorist act to be successful, the element of surprise is a crucial component. However, usually some type of data, however cryptic, is gathered, processed, digested every which way, then converted into usable material and disseminated to every federal agency, top military brass, anti-terrorist unit, state police department, sheriff's office, security guard, and rent-a-cop to look out for.

Even with 9/11, there were subtle hints and clues beforehand that may have been critical to preventing the attacks had the various American intelligence agencies been more forthcoming and cooperative with one another. If this information had been compiled as a whole, it is possible that someone could have predicted that there was something looming on the horizon.

Of course, hindsight is always 20/20 and it is easier to assign blame to whichever American agency is convenient. In this case, the FBI, CIA, and NSA were all accused of possessing information that could have prevented the attacks, and they received the brunt of the criticism, justified or not. No one on God's green Earth, however, could have guessed what was to transpire that fateful Tuesday morning, except, of course, the lunatics who concocted such a plan.

Conversely, who could have predicted that the enemy

would strike a peaceful, sleepy cottage town in such an audacious manner? Although the scope and destruction was on a vastly smaller scale than 9/11, Parker did not differentiate between the numbers: an attack on American soil is an overt act of aggression and therefore, an act of war.

Still, it does not make sense to Parker or his colleagues. They had mulled the motives that seemed inherent to every terrorist act, but in this case, they could not produce one that seemed logical considering the chosen target and location.

Was it simply to show the American people that no one is safe? That everyone must choose a side? And that no one, not even children, can stand on the sidelines? Was it purely a symbolic act? Was the objective to target innocent Americans on their proudest day as a people and as a nation?

If that was the message, it had been heard. And, as Parker thinks with utter contempt, it would be answered in full.

Parker hears a sharp knock on the door that snaps him from his reverie. The man pauses for a moment to be certain that Parker is finished with his solitary brainstorm, and then he quickly walks into the room, a slight bounce to his step.

This is the man who acts as Parker's aide-de-camp, his right-hand man, only without the right hand: Lieutenant Colonel August "Augie" Hermann. Augie served under Parker in the Vietnam War and was one of the toughest and bravest soldiers Parker ever commanded. What Parker soon learned as well is Augie's uncanny knack for the espionage and intelligence trade. His ability to gather information and analyze it with equal swiftness is unparalleled to any other individual that Parker has worked with. Augie seems to maintain his own network of spies and informants, and he has a singular ability to care for and groom each one to his liking. He was, and still is, the ultimate Gepetto.

In addition to his abilities in the realm of intelligence, Augie also has a special talent for interrogation techniques, focusing primarily on the psychological aspect of an interrogation rather than the physical, coercive style preferred by some. It is truly a scene to bear witness to, and Parker takes a kind of gleeful satisfaction in watching Augie "do his thing," so to speak.

Augie proudly trumpets the theory that pain is a mental state of being. In other words, if you think something is going to hurt and expect it to hurt, it is going to hurt. If you can detach the pain from your mind, if you can, in essence, mentally detach your nerve endings, then there is no pain because it simply does not exist for your brain to comprehend. It is a difficult concept to grasp, and many dismiss it as existential garbage, but Parker quickly became a proponent after watching Augie "work" in Vietnam.

On more than one occasion, Parker watched as Augie was able to pry crucial pieces of intelligence from high-ranking officers in the Vietcong without, remarkably, resorting to violence or torture. In one particular instance, Augie politely informed a Vietcong officer that if he did not receive the information he sought, he would be forced by his superiors to sear the skin on the man's back. If the answers were still not forthcoming, Augie gently explained, the torture would continue. He intended to work his way down the prisoner's back and around, cutting a path that would eventually arrive at the man's now extremely shy genitals.

Augie lit a welder's torch and placed the flame within inches of the officer's face for the purpose of searing, so to speak, the image of the red-hot flame in the man's mind.

Several seconds later, when Augie had not yet received an answer to his question, he slowly walked around behind the officer and placed it into the man's back. The officer started screaming as he smelled burning flesh and instantly coughed up the intelligence they needed.

The officer did not know at the time, although he would sheepishly learn later, Augie employed a chunk of ice in the small of the man's back to represent the torch, while he lit a piece of bovine meat to produce the aroma of burning flesh. For added measure, and with a touch of irony, Augie instructed a medic in Vietnamese to put ice on the prisoner's wound.

To the utter amazement of observers at these interrogations, Augie's theory was proven correct: it is not the pain itself, but the idea of pain, the thought of harm being inflicted to the physical body that sets the mind racing. It is the mind, ultimately, that tricks the body into believing that severe harm and pain is being wrought despite the benign sensations the body feels. Augie is certainly not averse to more aggressive forms of interrogation, but in many cases, he simply knows which subjects will crack with the mere threat of physical harm.

Unfortunately, more aggressive forms of interrogation were used on Augie when the second prong of his theory was proven correct, if only to himself. Given a choice in the matter, Augie would have preferred to not be the subject this time around.

He was captured behind enemy lines on a mission near the Laotian border, and he remained in a P.O.W. camp for several weeks before he and several others managed to escape. The entire duration he was there, he did not issue a single scream when he was mercilessly tortured for information. Hardly a grunt either when they took his right hand.

When Augie was found, he was near death from a staph infection and blood loss. The wound had been shabbily covered with dirty bandages, and the doctors thought the infection was so severe, he might lose the whole arm. Augie kept the arm, however, and he survived.

He also knew the exact coordinates of the camp where he was held and when he was fully recovered, he and Parker returned to retrieve his hand and let his captors know that he was doing just fine.

Parker places his hand over his eyes and looks down. Muffled, he says, "Tell me something good, Augie."

Augie holds a manila file folder in his prosthetic right hand and states, "Nothing very concrete, sir, but it is pretty interesting."

Parker's head shoots up as he gives Augie a curious look, "Yeah?"

"The forensic team has been combing the beach all night and are still looking, but they found something and sent it on right away," the excitement in Augie's voice not initially registering with Parker.

He places the folder on the table in front of Parker as the latter snatches his reading glasses from his pocket, opens up the file and begins scanning it.

Parker reads the paper in front of him and rereads it, and then slowly looks up at Augie.

"Radiation?"

Augie beams as he nods his head, "Several of the cottages that sit on the beach contain heat marks on the wood, obviously from being within the blast radius. And underneath the marks, they found minute traces of radiation."

"From the bombs?" Parker wonders.

"The lab boys don't seem to think so, sir," Augie responds.

"Why not?"

"The radiation was unlike that found in man-made bombs, sir."

Augie lets this sink in for several seconds. A quizzical look crosses Parker's face as he tries to grasp the meaning of this information.

"Sir, they seem to think that it is a type of radiation never seen before," Augie says excitedly.

Parker stares at his subordinate for a moment, removes his glasses, and starts, "Are you telling me . . ."

Augie finishes the thought for both of them.

"Invited or not, sir, there was another guest at the party."

He pauses, and adds, "Human or...otherwise."

SEVEN

Chicago, Illinois

The flashing blue and white lights of the squad cars reflecting off the water clash against the pale glow from the morning sun. The colors produce a shimmering explosion of light that causes one to shield the eyes when looking directly at the water. This is exactly what Detective Eddie Pryzchewski, Homicide Division, does as the sound of heavy machinery hums in the relative calm and silence of the early morning hour.

Eddie received the call about an hour earlier at the station from a nurse walking home from the graveyard shift. Earlier in the night, as instructed, he had issued an all-points bulletin (APB) on an olive green jeep, possibly a military jeep, and the call appeared to be a hit according to the nurse's description. Unfortunately, the jeep is not occupied by the man they are looking for, and furthermore, it is currently floating upside down in the Chicago River.

Eddie was certain to collar the inquiry before either of the other detectives on duty volunteered. Under the guise that he was bored with the current workload piled high on his desk and in need of action out in the "field," neither detective raised a hand in protest or otherwise objected. At the early morning hour, they were more than accommodating in letting him fish a scrap of junk out of the Chicago River. They told him to pick up some decent coffee and breakfast on the way back to the station. They figured it would only be another headache from a mountain-load of paperwork and most likely, no real witnesses. And to the other detectives' chagrin as they would later learn, no body. A dead-end case waiting to happen which no sane detective would want a part.

The blue-and-whites of the Chicago Police Department arrived on the scene nearly simultaneously with Eddie.

He instructed the officers to cordon off a small area to preserve evidence and keep onlookers at bay. The department would be able to save some tape on this case, however, as bystanders and rubberneckers seem to be rare in this part of the city. The jeep was found in an industrial section of Chicago, surrounded by old factories, dilapidated warehouses and not much else.

A few blocks away is a set of housing projects where the nurse happened to be walking to when she spotted the top, or rather the bottom, portion of the jeep protruding above the surface of the river. The vehicle was pinned against the side of an embankment where the water is extremely shallow, due to a very dry summer. The woman considered scaling down the side of the embankment to determine if there were any bodies, but she thought better of it when the slope appeared far too steep to successfully negotiate. She then called "911" on her cell phone and alerted the police to the location of the jeep. She even waited for the police to arrive, which she should be commended for considering that she recently completed a nearly 14-hour shift. One of the patrolmen ran down the basic list of questions with her after arriving on the scene.

Smokestacks can be seen a couple hundred yards away billowing out the day's first products, whatever they may be, as Eddie stares down at the jeep. He called an old friend of the department's to help extract the jeep from the river.

"Lou's Hauling Service" is a general term used by Lou to denote that his business handles any sort of towing, pulling, hauling, dismantling, resurrecting, or blow-torching that may be needed. Lou markets himself as a specialist, and indeed he is one of a kind in his area of "expertise." The department calls on him in cases where they need a little extra power and it seems unnecessary to rouse the local fire department for assistance. In fact, a fire department unit was about to be dispatched when Eddie called and informed them that they would not be needed. Apparently, the early morning hour caused more than a few individuals to be agreeable, perhaps even a little apathetic.

Lou appears indifferent as he pulls what looks to be an olive green jeep from the water, which matches the description Eddie was given. Lou uses a special crane attached to the back of a huge truck that is capable of hauling up to ten tons of weight. The crane slowly raises the jeep above the water and Lou gradually directs it over towards the embankment, where land takes over for the river. Lou chomps on an unlit cigar that could have been in his mouth for the past few months, when he sees, along with Eddie, what is stenciled in faded, white letters across the side:

U.S. ARMY

Bingo, thinks Eddie.

Got the car, but unfortunately from the looks of it, not the man. Maybe the owner was kind enough to leave behind the item they are looking for.

Eddie slips on a pair of plastic latex gloves as the crane delicately places the jeep on the ground. Water cascades from several orifices as the jeep once again comes to its natural, upright position.

Lou hurries over with a bounce in his step as he trudges towards the jeep, his considerable girth swaying back and forth. The letters on the side of the jeep have obviously gotten Lou's blood pumping, something Eddie certainly does not need. The less people who know about this, the better. He did not want firemen to assist at the scene because the Chicago Fire Department have their own spokesmen, separate from the police, who tend to divulge any information to the media that they can, whether it is interesting or utterly mundane, such as a military vehicle found abandoned in the Chicago River. If other people start becoming involved, it has the potential to become a circus that Eddie cannot control.

Eddie approaches the vehicle, appraising it like an antiques dealer might examine a priceless, family heirloom. He circles it several times, certain to eye each and every part of the exterior, looking for...well, anything.

"Looks like da Army got some bad coordinates," laughs Lou.

Eddie nods and says, "A little off course I would say. Thanks for your help, Lou."

"No problem there, Eddie," he responds. Lou reaches

out for the door handle and says, "We going to take a look inside-"

"Don't touch anything, Lou," Eddie barks.

Lou snaps his hand back as if he received an electric shock and looks at Eddie apologetically.

By way of explanation and because it sounded a little harsher than he intended to, Eddie offers, "It's evidence."

Lou nods knowingly and continues to stare at it, like a child looking through the front window of a toy store. He wants so badly to go in and play with everything, but his parents will not allow him.

Eddie opens the door and does a cursory inspection of the interior. He looks in the back and in between the seats. He looks in the small glove compartment and beneath the front passenger seat. He checks the compartment in the middle between the front seats and finds... absolutely nothing.

Eddie starts to become disheartened when he spies near the bottom of the gear shift a torn piece of fabric. The fabric is stuck under the bottom portion of the gear shift, wedged underneath the plastic. Eddie gives the fabric a couple of tugs before it is finally released.

He lifts the fabric into the light of day, noticing that it appears to be the dark olive green of an Army uniform, practically matching the color of the jeep. Eddie runs his fingers over a small stain on a portion of the fabric.

He looks underneath the steering wheel, near the pedals, and he notices a reddish-brown stain, which he also moves his fingers over. The liquid is all but dried, but it still leaves a faint residue on the tips of his gloved fingers. He is almost certain what the substance is.

Eddie lifts his head up from beneath the steering column when the sun, barely above the horizon, seems to catch something under the driver's seat that reflects its rays. The rapid flash of light that streaks across his eyes allows him to spot a small item attached to the bottom of the seat.

Eddie lowers himself farther into the jeep and peers under the seat, certain he is not imagining things or tricking his brain into believing that something is there. Sure enough, something is there.

He reaches for the item and yanks once, then twice, and finally, on the third tug, the item is released from its clutches.

Eddie holds it up to the morning sun, scrutinizing it more carefully. It is a small, round disc in a plastic container, with a clear baggie taped tightly around it. He studies it for a moment before concluding that amazingly, it does not appear to be inundated with water.

He quickly clears out of the jeep and takes a few steps away from the area. A couple of the officers glance at him, curious as to what he has discovered. Eddie ignores them and takes his cell phone out of his inside pocket and punches in a number he has memorized.

There are a couple of rings before a brisk voice answers.

"I think I've got something you might be looking for," Eddie says triumphantly.

"You mean someone?" the voice on the other end responds.

"No sign of a body yet, but it appears that there is a fairly recent bloodstain on the inside of the jeep," Eddie offers, hoping this might appease the man on the other end of the line.

There is a pause for several seconds.

"You have the disc then?"

"Yes, it's intact," Eddie responds.

"Get it to me immediately," the man demands.

"Yes, sir."

"And get a sample of that blood," the man adds.

"You got it," Eddie responds, not the least bit perturbed at the unusual request from the man on the other end.

*   *   *

Moriah hangs up the phone on his end as he contemplates the recent news for several minutes. Moriah believes that whatever the disc contains, it is something that Kaley would never part with unless his life depended on it.

And maybe it did, thinks Moriah.

Perhaps half their problem had been solved by street punks looking for a joyride, or Kaley was more seriously injured than initially believed in the struggle at his home, or maybe his car simply had a bad transmission. Whatever the case may be, Moriah is pleased to learn of the recovery of the disc, but he needs to determine its contents immediately.

The search of Private Rushmore turned up nothing and thus, Moriah still does not know what Kaley and his subordinate witnessed at Evans. And they still need to find Kaley, whether he is dead or alive.

Moriah focuses back on the present situation where now, it is time for the other half of their problem, Professor O'Connell, to be solved as well.

EIGHT

Evanston, Illinois

The homes that line tree-shaded Ridge Road are some of the most beautiful and ornate homes in the entire state of Illinois, not to mention some of the oldest. The houses' stately appearance and perfectly manicured lawns suggest a neighborhood stocked full of rich, upper-crust, conservative citizens. On the contrary on at least one count, the town of Evanston is one of the more liberal strongholds in the state. Due in part to the nearby campus of Northwestern University and a significantly large Jewish population, the people who live in this town that borders the City of Chicago tend to sway to the left at the voting polls.

It is because of this liberal atmosphere and a kind of indescribable cozy, small-town feel that caused Dr. Albert Rosenstein to choose to live here over thirty years ago. Dr. Rosenstein's home is one of the more modest dwellings on the street, but nonetheless spectacular in its architecture and appearance.

Some may question how Rosenstein can afford a home

in the high-end, upscale part of town on a college professor's salary, and two words immediately spring to mind: academic publishing. Rosenstein is a machine when it comes to detailing the thoughts and research that occupy, respectively, his mind and his time. Although typically not a lucrative form of income, when dozens of universities around the nation employ one of your books or your writings are used as a supplement in over two hundred college courses, the money seems to flow in quite freely. Rosenstein does not tend to spend money on lavish items and his vacations are few and far between. The only thing he seemed to spend money on was his wife, when she was alive.

Dr. Rosenstein has lived alone for the last several months, having been widowed by his wife a few days after their 45th wedding anniversary. The big "C" allowed them forty-five years together, but there was no chance it would give them forty-six. She was everything to him and many secretly wondered if Rosenstein might soon join her, having succumbed to a broken heart. There were always whispers of a miscarriage here and there, but besides those lost souls, Dr. Rosenstein and his wife never raised any children.

He wanted to sell the house after she died in an attempt to flee from all the memories and good times he had with her here, but it was not to be. After rethinking it, it seemed more appropriate to keep those special moments alive by remaining in their house together. Although it had startled him on several occasions, he imagined as he stepped through the door after work that he could hear her humming softly in the kitchen or laughing with someone over the phone. For Rosenstein, the echoes of her beauty still resonate throughout the halls and rooms of their home, a constant and reassuring reminder that she is still here with him.

Dr. Rosenstein mourned his wife's death and then something unusual happened: he thrived. He dove head-first into his classes and his teaching and felt like he was starting all over again. He lectured more fervently, his voice boomed more loudly, his research became more intense, and the projects he produced for the world of academia were astounding, mind-expanding disserta-tions that numbered hundreds of pages. It was as if he had breached the subject of mortality with the passing of his wife and he suddenly realized that he needed to accomplish everything he could before his number is called as well.

Some of Dr. Rosenstein's work garnered true believers and followers, while other pieces of work alarmed the stauncher, conservative-minded members of the academic world. Dr. Rosenstein's penchant for claiming just as easily that JFK's murder may have been the result of a bet Frank Sinatra made with a member of the Mafia, to his theory that the government placed chemicals in the water supply to keep people docile and therefore, more prone to accept the status quo, he never failed to gather his share of critics and admirers. The former tended to ignore or refute the fact that the theories and hypotheses Rosenstein posited in many of his research papers contained, at the very least, circumstantial evidence to support them, even the most outlandish. Evidence and proof are elements Rosenstein can never bring himself to skirt or disregard. Indeed, the two questions he constantly poses to himself and to others remain steadfast:

Is it possible? Can we prove it?

As Sean threads his way through some light woods that lead to the back of Rosenstein's home, he considers this notion of proof. He wonders whether he will find evidence of his family's whereabouts or any indication of what happened to them at Rosenstein's home. The chances are slim, Sean realizes, knowing that Rosenstein in all probability did not leave any clues for him on the kitchen table. But since Sean has already tried one of the two men he trusts with his life, it is time to call upon the other.

Sean is thinking this when suddenly, a feeling of uneasiness sweeps over him. His instincts are obviously not as sharp as they used to be, considering that he should have smelled that man on the beach a mile away. But a feeling in his gut immediately kicks into overdrive and he has no choice but to listen to it. He crouches low to the ground and carefully watches where he steps.

Before departing from Kaley's house, Sean borrowed several items from his friend's miniature war closet. After rummaging through it, Sean bogarted a pair of field binoculars with infrared capabilities, a pair of hiking boots, two 10-inch hunting knives, face camouflage, a compass, a canteen, rope, a couple of road flares, and an old .22 that may fall apart upon firing. Sean knows that Jon almost certainly maintains a small cache of more specialized weapons located somewhere in the house, but Sean had as good a chance of finding them as he does of finding Jimmy Hoffa. Regardless, Sean figured that if the same people who invaded Kaley's house were involved in what transpired on Tamawaca Beach, it is better to have a shitty sidearm than no sidearm at all.

Sean quietly makes his way through the last group of trees that borders the backyard of Rosenstein's property, careful to remain covered by some underbrush. He peers into the house like a predator surveying his prey. Unfortunately, at the present moment, he is not certain which category he actually falls into.

He carefully scrutinizes the entire rear of the house, scanning every window, checking for any movement. After a few moments, Sean finally acknowledges that he does not see anything.

Of course, he reminds himself, *that does not necessarily mean there is no one around.*

To be certain, he waits several more painfully agonizing minutes, as if there is a clock whose second hand is reverberating through his head, pushing him to *hurry,* telling him that his family needs him.

Sean does not see any movement inside Rosenstein's home and he does not hear any suspicious sounds that would suggest unwelcome visitors. Finally, he decides that neither he, nor his family, can wait any longer. One man he trusts is on the run and the other man is his only hope. The cover of darkness would be preferable, but this is simply a reminder that we do not always get what we want in life.

There are two stands of trees on opposite sides of the backyard that run nearly the length of it until they reach the house. The good news is that they are large, old oak trees, offering plenty of cover to hide behind. The bad news is that they are separated by at least 25 feet from one another.

Sean takes a deep breath and decides it is time to move.

He slips over towards the first oak tree leading out of the woods and ducks behind it. He moves quickly from the first tree to the next, with an eye on the house at all times. His breathing is steady and under control, likely owed to a rigid and vigorous workout regimen that keeps him in excellent physical condition.

Sean steals another glance towards the house as he prepares to scurry to the third tree when he looks down for the briefest of moments and notices something unusual. Mere seconds before stepping on them, he sees a pile of discarded sunflower seeds.

Sean slowly raises his head and there, perched nearly 40 feet above him, sits a man and his gun. A semiautomatic gun, in fact, wrapped around the side of the man's body.

You gotta be fucking kidding me, thinks Sean.

He had always been taught in the military that if the enemy is near, do not leave a trail of breadcrumbs in your wake. In other words, the smell from a burning cigarette or the whiff of a man's aftershave can disclose your position in a heartbeat and can be the difference between the element of surprise and winding up with a tag on your toe. A pile of sunflower seeds, a wad of tobacco, or even a small collection of recently-gnawed fingernails on the ground can tell a keen enemy where you are and where you might be going. In case they do not already know, the enemy also realizes that you are a complete idiot.

Sean crouches low and hugs the tree, looking up at the unsuspecting man in disbelief. The man scans the surrounding area through a pair of binoculars in the direction that Sean emerged from the woods no more than a couple minutes ago. The scout must have missed him by pure luck, and Sean figures that his guardian angel is earning his wings today.

With a hunch that the man is not alone or on a bird-watching safari, Sean looks towards the opposite side of the backyard. Around 30 yards away, Sean sees another man perched at virtually the same height in a tree. The man is turned to the side in his roost, with his back slightly to his partner, scanning the terrain in the opposite direction.

Sean instantly realizes that he is not going to be able to waltz into Rosenstein's house with ease as it initially appeared. There is most likely someone watching the front of the house, too. As far as Sean can see, the only way in entails first dispatching these two housesitters.

Sean notices a silencer on the man's weapon above him and instantly begins to formulate a plan. The plan, of course, looks nearly flawless in his mind, but even the most perfectly laid plans cannot possibly quantify the variances of human behavior. Sean envisions the plan working smoothly because all of the pieces fall into place for him, a subjective bias that can result in unforeseeable and unpleasant results. Nevertheless, his options are limited, and his mind urges him to take action immediately.

Sean steels himself for the task ahead, mentally and physically preparing himself for the fight and the rush of adrenaline coupled with it. He prays his skills have not significantly diminished to the point of handicapping his chances, or this could be over soon after it begins.

He removes one of the knives from its sheath that he "borrowed" from Kaley and takes aim at the man above, focusing tightly on the man's chin. He takes a few seconds to adjust to the awkward throwing position he finds himself in, and then he slowly exhales. He unleashes the hunting knife with as much velocity as he can muster. The knife produces a low whistle as it flies through the air and then suddenly meets flesh.

The knife connects with its intended target, making the briefest of sounds, like an angel's kiss, as Sean likes to think of it. There is a short pause as it takes the man's brain several seconds to register the serious harm that has been inflicted on his body. The man starts to fall and weakly attempts to catch a branch on his way down. Amazingly, he is able to grasp a branch for an instant before it snaps and he plummets to the ground. The man hits the ground with a *thud* at Sean's feet, who quickly snatches the gun from around the man's back.

Now that was definitely loud, Sean thinks.

The man on the opposite side of the yard turns at the sound of a faint noise behind him. He looks at the tree directly across from him only to find that his partner is no longer there.

Do we have visitors?

He clicks his walkie-talkie and urgently whispers, "Jimmy, what the hell-"

Before his sentence can be completed, a bullet rips through his head, flinging the man back against the tree. The bullet impacts with such force that it appears the tree is holding the man in a bizarre death grip, rather than allowing gravity to follow its natural course and sweep the man to the ground. The man is cradled in between several thick branches, as if the tree itself has adopted the man into its fold.

There follows a crackle of static over the man's radio and then a voice, "Eagle Eyes One or Two, do you copy? Over."

There is a pause as the voice repeats, "Eagle Eyes, do you copy? Over."

Still nothing.

Then, in a barely audible whisper: "This is Eagle Eye One, O'Connell is here, over."

Two men inside Dr. Rosenstein's home glance out between a set of blinds towards the backyard, giving Sean the visible targets that he needs.

He stands several feet away from the back of the house, towards the side in order to provide a measure of cover for himself. He holds the radio in one hand and the semiautomatic in the other, and he introduces both men to the latter within seconds of them peeking out the window.

Sean fires a burst from the semiautomatic and the muffled blasts of the weapon are quieter than the sound of the windows shattering as both men fall to the ground in a storm of glass and blood.

Good, Sean thinks, *one of them is still alive for questioning.*

He had a sharp angle on the man furthest from him and appeared to only wound him.

Within moments, Sean is inside Rosenstein's home, quickly surveying the scene. One man is clearly dead, while the other man is squirming towards a pistol several feet away from his outstretched hand.

Sean hurries towards him and kicks the gun away from the man. He sits squarely on the man's chest, bringing his full weight down upon him. Sean uses his knees to pin the man's arms at his sides. The man groans and squirms in agony as the weight of Sean's body only exacerbates the pain of his wounds. Blood has already begun pooling around them as it slowly spreads along the floor.

Sean holds a knife under the man's chin as the semi-automatic dangles around his back.

"Where's my family?" Sean demands.

The man, through blood-soaked teeth, sneers, "Fuck you, Professor."

Sean pushes the knife in deeper as it slowly penetrates the man's skin. The man exhales sharply, followed by a stifled grunt. A spot of blood has begun to form around the area.

"For a second time, where's my family?" Sean asks through clenched teeth, prepared to push the knife through the top of the man's skull.

Suddenly, Sean's heart drops as he hears an all too-distinct *click,* followed by, "Don't bother asking a third time, Mr. O'Connell."

Sean's head snaps up to see a solidly-built man standing a few feet away from him, holding a pistol aimed at his head. The man apparently emerged from behind the wall that leads to Rosenstein's study, although Sean did not hear the man make a sound.

Sean looks down at the man on the floor, who has a befuddled expression on his face as he stares upside-down at his would-be rescuer. Sean wonders if the look is confusion or actually fear.

Sean presses the knife in deeper.

"You shoot me and odds are my muscles will produce one final spasm, causing this knife here to go right through your man's throat like I'm slicing through butter. So why don't you put the gun down-"

The shot rings out like a church bell, and Sean's face is instantaneously covered in blood.

It takes a few moments but finally, Sean looks down in shock to realize that he was not on the receiving end of the deadly bullet. The man on the floor was the unfortunate recipient and nearly half the man's skull went along with it.

"Not much more to bargain with, is there?" the man calmly asks.

He is fucking crazy, is Sean's first thought.

Anyone who would eliminate one of their own simply to improve their negotiating position has to be crazy. The look this man possesses, however, is one of steely determination and ice in his veins. There is a kind of controlled ruthlessness evident in the man's eyes, as if he has the potential to snap at any moment. Conversely, he is able to balance this chaotic element with a calm and cool demeanor.

As if reading Sean's thoughts, the man asks, "Do you think I'm crazy, Professor? For killing one of my own men?"

Sean remains still, displaying his own icy calm. Panic and fear are his worst enemies right now, and he tries to maintain some semblance of rational thought in the face of a pistol being pointed directly at his head. Sean clutches the knife and calculates mathematical equations like distance and velocity, but keeps returning to one core principle: he is not Superman and he is not faster than a speeding bullet.

"He's not really mine, in any real sense of the word," the man remarks.

An odd comment, Sean thinks.

"Where's Rosenstein?" Sean casually asks, as if he is asking about the weather.

"The same question I had for you," the man replies. "What are you doing here and why are you looking for Professor Rosenstein?"

The man pronounced the "stein" as "*stine,*" with a long *i* instead of a long *e.* Obviously, the man does not know Rosenstein very well if he cannot even pronounce his name correctly.

Sean is not thinking about phonetics at the moment, however, but rather what he can do to escape this jam. If he can stall the man a little longer, perhaps a neighbor with a good set of ears heard the shots and breaking glass and called the cops. A siren may cause the man to flinch for just an instant. That is all Sean would need.

Ignoring the man's question, Sean says, "I've seen you before, somewhere," trying desperately not to sound like he is stalling for time.

The man gives Sean a hard stare and answers flippantly, "Is that right?"

"Yeah, weren't you-"

"Well, Mr. O'Connell," the man interrupts, "you can try to figure it out on the way to our destination. We may even find ourselves on the same side at that point in time."

The last part of the man's sentence sounded awkward to Sean.

That point in time.

It sounded so formal, robotic even. There is something...different about this man, something Sean cannot put his finger on.

"I doubt that, especially when you've got a gun pointed at my head," Sean replies caustically.

The man's façade remains calm, steady, and cool. He does not seem to notice the anger in Sean's voice.

"At the very least, you may make a good bargaining chip, Professor," the man states matter-of-factly.

"Bargaining chip?" Sean repeats.

The man curtly orders, "Cut the strap on the automatic with your knife, drop it, turn around, and get on your knees."

"Why don't you tell me where my family is?" Sean asks, trying a different tactic. Maybe the man will bite.

"I do not like listening to the sound of my own voice, Professor, and I do not enjoy repeating myself," the man replies menacingly.

The man does not even give Sean a nibble.

"At least tell me where we're going," Sean pleads, trying to sound desperate and afraid, as if he is ready to throw in the towel.

The man never seems to lose his temper, but his irritation is becoming apparent. It is almost do-or-die time. Sean's only chance is the antique .22 in his back waistband.

"Professor O'Connell," the man says simply, "I do not intend on harming you, not yet at least. However, if you remain uncooperative, whatever force I may apply will be justified."

The man's voice is so utterly detached, emotionless, and ultimately, merciless, that the hair on Sean's neck begins doing cartwheels.

Sean holds up his hands as if in surrender, "Alright, I'll go with you. But if I come with you without resistance,

I want assurances that I will be told where my family is."

The man smirks, which is quickly replaced by the stone face. "I do not believe that you are in a position to make demands, Professor, and I could not care less what happened to your family."

The tone of the man's voice brings a chill to Sean's bones and a small lump forms in his throat. He quickly swallows it away and the melancholy feeling that momentarily washed over him is replaced by pure anger.

Sean nods his head in resignation. He cuts the strap on the semiautomatic and it falls to the ground in back of him. He drops the knife and stands above the dead man's body.

The man's gun hand is trained on Sean with every move he makes, exposing no chinks in the armor. Nevertheless, the prospect of emerging from Mr. Ice's captivity alive down the road does not seem to be a viable alternative. Sean has to make his move *right now.*

He takes a large stride to his right and kneels on the floor. He starts to turn around to face away from the man. In one motion, Sean reaches for the .22 at his back, snatches it out of his waistband and raises it in the general direction where the man is standing.

He squeezes off several rounds while at the same time rolling to his left behind an end table. The man simultaneously returns fire as Sean feels a burning sensation across the side of his leg as he attempts to roll out of the path of the oncoming bullets.

The brief volley of gunshots ends as quickly as it began, with the house now filled with an eerie silence and the smell of gunpowder.

Sean peeks around the side of the table before quickly

pulling his head back in case the man is waiting for him with another barrage of gunfire. The man is no longer there. If Sean has to guess, his foe ducked into Rosenstein's study and is using the wall that separates the two rooms as protection.

Sean glances to the side and sees the swinging door that leads to the kitchen several feet away. He fires several rounds in the direction of Rosenstein's study in order to provide cover, and then he hustles through the door and into the kitchen.

After settling beneath the counter against a row of cabinets, he curses himself for wasting the bullets when he does not have a large enough reserve to spare even one.

Sean examines his leg to find a slight tear in the pants where a small bloodstain has formed. It appears as if the bullet only grazed him, and the pain is easily manageable as a result of the adrenaline pumping through his veins. A more thorough examination and care of the wound will have to come later. Survival trumps any concern over a scratch at this point.

He slows his breathing until it is under control and considers what his next move should be. He has a gun with less than a handful of bullets and after a quick inventory of the kitchen, several sharp cutting knives.

Better than nothing, he figures.

Sean inches his way along the cabinets, keeping his gun trained on the kitchen door the entire time. He arrives beneath a small rectangular block where several knives of various lengths are sheathed. He reaches up and extends his hand toward them when, at that moment, he sees a faint, green glow radiating from the kitchen wall adjacent to the room he has just exited. The green glow casts a familiar light to him, a light he feels he has seen before.

A moment later, there is a high-pitched whine from the adjoining room and then, the kitchen appears to implode in a jumble of wood from the cabinets, granite from the countertop, and steel from the kitchen sink.

Sean is knocked off his feet and lands on the other side of the kitchen as pieces of debris crash down around him.

Within seconds of landing on the kitchen tile, he realizes he needs to gather his bearings immediately. His gun was tossed somewhere along with the other debris, and his only weapons appear to be several jagged pieces of wood lying nearby. Sean's ears are ringing, like the persistent drone of an alarm clock buzzing in each one, but he hears nothing else. Sean flails his arms like a man caught in an enormous wave, trying to find his way upright.

Suddenly, he feels the presence of someone else in the room.

He slowly turns around and sees the man standing several feet away from him. The man is no longer holding a gun, but something else, an object he has seen before, a long time ago. A small green light glows at the end of a device that looks similar to a track and field baton.

The jungle, Sean thinks as a flood of memories come rushing back to him.

The man does not smile or give Sean a look of triumph, but simply stares at Sean as if he is a bug waiting to be squashed.

Suddenly, the man cocks his head, as if listening to a sound off in the distance.

A police siren?

Sean could use any distraction at this point.

The man stares at the ceiling as a look of puzzlement covers his face. Even with his impaired hearing, Sean not only starts to hear something, but feels something as well, a slight rumble that seems to course throughout the house.

An earthquake? In Illinois?

The prospect of that occurring at so fortuitous a time seems unlikely to Sean.

The man continues to look around when finally, his focus turns back to Sean. As if suddenly remembering his target is wounded a few feet in front of him, the man advances towards him.

Sean, with whatever fight remains in the reserve tank, prepares to spring up and give the man everything he has left. He tightly grips a jagged piece of wood and is about to lunge at the man when suddenly, a sound like steam being released from a pipe reverberates throughout the entire house.

It feels like someone is rattling Rosenstein's home back and forth as several vents discharge some type of mist, which blankets the entire kitchen. The mist thickens into a fog that quickly envelops them, shrouding them both in the mysterious substance. Sean immediately loses sight of his adversary as his vision extends no more than two feet in front of his face.

The first thing that strikes Sean is that it is extremely cold, like the sub-arctic winds that gust through Chicago for nearly a third of the year. The mist takes his breath away, a familiar feeling when stepping outside in the middle of January or immersing oneself in a frigid lake. Sean notices tiny ice crystals forming on his arms. Temporarily forgetting about the man, Sean instinctively lashes his arms out in case the man is directly in front of him. He hits nothing but air.

Sean hears several muffled sounds from outside the kitchen. He decides to avoid becoming a stationary target, and immediately starts moving cautiously towards the kitchen doorway while he stays low to the ground. He reenters Rosenstein's living room and notices that the mist has practically encased this room as well.

Where is he?

Sean moves towards the center of the room to determine if the semiautomatic or the knife are in the same spot where he dropped them. He blindly feels around and does not find the gun, but his hand touches the extremely cold blade of the knife, which he gathers up.

Sean looks around in confusion as he suddenly realizes that the dead man is missing. He stares at the spot the body occupied only moments before and he sees nothing but empty space. The only thing that occupies the spot now is a circular, charred hole. There is a wisp of smoke above the hole and a pool of blood surrounding it. Sean looks toward the area where the other body was lying and he sees the same thing.

He stumbles out the door and into the backyard, finally emerging from the mist that occupies Rosenstein's home. The heat and humidity actually quell the goose bumps that inhabit his entire body.

Sean takes a few steps away from the house and stares disbelievingly towards the backyard. The man cradled like a baby in the branches of the tree is gone. Sean looks to the area where the other man plummeted from his perch, only to find the spot vacant as well.

They are gone, vanished, like the people from Tamawaca Beach. Like his family.

The man is nowhere to be found, either.

Where the hell did he go? Where did the bodies go?

Sean turns around and gazes into the house, wondering what the mysterious substance is being pumped from the vents in Rosenstein's home. It does not appear to be affecting him at all, but at this point, it may be too early to tell. Whatever it is, it certainly saved his hide by causing his adversary to flee. How the rest of the welcoming party disappeared is a question Sean cannot answer.

At last, Sean hears the sound of distant sirens, *reinforcements about to arrive in the nick of time*, he wryly thinks.

Sean starts to make a beeline for the woods when he does a double-take into Rosenstein's living room, something catching his eye.

He hurries back towards the house as the sirens grow louder. He stares at one of Rosenstein's bookshelves, the mist gradually starting to clear.

There, on the top shelf, above a large book titled *Government Conspiracies and Cover-Ups*, is etched something. It appears almost neon-like through the mist. Sean quickly memorizes it, dashes from the house and exits the same way he arrived.

NINE

Evans Military Base

General Theodore Parker respects Colonel Malcolm Fizer for his skill as a commanding officer and his rigid adherence to the military code of honor and discipline. In Parker's eyes, Fizer is a top-notch military man cut from the same cloth as himself, and a fierce believer that everything the U.S. military stands for is nearly as good and as sacred as the word of God.

General Parker also thinks Malcolm Fizer is a sneaky little prick who always seems to be following a different agenda. Parker would aptly characterize Fizer as "power hungry," and that is an appetite for some people that can never be satiated. Parker views Fizer's aspirations stretching beyond the boundaries of the military, as if his standing in this institution is not quite good enough or a valuable source of pride for him. To Parker, a rank of colonel in the United States Army is an extraordinary achievement, a level that many career officers would be pleased as punch to reach. It seems that Fizer, however, measures himself outside of this arena, against something or maybe someone higher than him. General Parker tends to feel that Malcolm takes his rank for granted, and on more than one occasion, the general sensed that Fizer possesses both a disdain and an unwarranted pretentiousness for the position, as if his rank is below him.

Parker only hopes, and occasionally prays, that the colonel's ambitions do not lie in the world of politics. As is readily apparent within several minutes of meeting the man, Fizer borders the thin line between "far right" and "radical right," and he seems closer and closer to stepping beyond that line everyday. Anyone who pumps money into the military-industrial complex is a personal hero to him, and one would certainly not find Fizer lobbying for more social service programs on behalf of the poor and needy.

"Hello, Malcolm," Parker says, as he accepts Fizer's outstretched hand.

The rotors from the helicopter begin to slow as General Parker and Lieutenant Colonel Hermann disembark and are greeted immediately by Fizer on the tarmac outside the main administration building. Evans is abuzz with activity as soldiers rush from place to place, crates are loaded onto waiting trucks, planes are fueled, and drills are conducted around the exterior of the base. No one seems to pay attention to the newly arriving officers as Parker and Hermann look around at the surrounding activity. Although last night's attack might have left everyone a little spooked, you would not know it by looking at the men and women at the base. The troops appear completely focused on the duties before them, oblivious to anything outside their scope of concentration.

That is good, Parker thinks. It shows that their superior officers are acting calmly and are equally focused, avoiding undue panic that can trickle down and cause the men and women under their command to follow suit and lose sight of their responsibilities. Then Parker lays eyes on Fizer and looks him over, and his initial thoughts take a sharp U-turn.

"A pleasure, General," as the two men briefly shake hands. "Welcome to Evans, sir."

Fizer quickly nods at Augie, "Lieutenant Colonel Hermann."

Augie responds with a swift, "Sir."

Fizer turns back towards Parker and indicates for them to follow him, and he briskly walks towards the main building. The general notices that Fizer appears slightly agitated, perhaps even a little flustered. Considering the circumstances, this is not extremely unusual. However, considering Fizer's typically calm, detached, and even cold manner, it does seem a bit out of character for the colonel.

"As you can see, General," Fizer explains over his shoulder, "we're in a heightened state of alert as a result of the terrorist attack last night. All passes of leave have been revoked, and every man and woman stationed at this base are present and accounted for."

Fizer pauses to see if this pleases the general, but Parker remains silent.

They arrive at a door that Fizer swipes with a card. The door opens in an instant, revealing a long, bleak corridor. Again, Parker notices that Fizer is fidgety, as the latter shifts uneasily from side to side.

"General, I only received word here about twenty minutes ago that you would be paying us a visit. I'm still a little uncertain as to how we can help," he says hesitantly.

"General Marshfield must have informed you already that none of our birds were overhead at the time-"

The general cuts him off, "General Marshfield did relay that information to me, yes, Colonel. But we are interested in seeing what our satellites might have picked up after the fact, as well as your staff's response to the attack, if that's alright by you, Colonel?"

"Certainly, *sir*," Fizer responds, an almost imperceptible edge to his voice. Almost.

They arrive at an elevator that Fizer swipes with his card and the doors open.

As the elevator car ascends, Augie feels that the tension can be cut with a knife. He is acutely aware of the dislike the two men share for one another, but he has never determined the exact point of origin for this animosity. Augie wanted to ask the general about it, but he did not want to pry or pressure him into disclosing this if he did not feel comfortable doing so. Augie figures that if the general wants him to know, he will tell him. Augie has always believed, however, that it is not as simple as Fizer's envy of the general's lofty position of power, or the general's distrust of Fizer's true intentions. There is more to this story, something that goes beyond simple dislike for one another.

The elevator doors open and Fizer leads them out onto a platform that extends the length of a massive room, which appears large enough to house a dozen fighter planes. The platform provides a bird's eye-view of the room, whose main source of illumination comes from an enormous screen, which is roughly twice the size of a movie theater screen. Instead of one large screen, however, five separate screens that display maps, coordinates, and hundreds of lines that crisscross the topography of the earth cover the wall. Several areas around the world are highlighted on the maps in different shades of blue, red, and green.

Occupying the floor are dozens of booth-like stations facing these screens, where soldiers busy themselves with their respective assignments. The room is quiet, but there is an unmistakable sense of purpose that can be felt as the soldiers' duties and responsibilities have taken on a deeper meaning due to recent events. Their focus and concentration is totally and completely on the tasks at hand, and they all realize that the time for mourning is over.

Fizer motions to the room below, "This is our hub of operations, General. We monitor and control satellite movement in our particular region, track domestic threats, such as militias and paramilitary groups, and occasionally, we'll handle interrogations of any illegals trying to get in from Canada. We also ensure that no other nations are trying to get a free peek behind the curtain, so to speak."

Fizer seems momentarily pleased with his succinct, yet thorough explanation, but Parker's impatience quickly begins to show, as the purpose of his visit does not include the standard elementary school tour.

"Colonel, that's all very interesting," Parker says sardonically, "but what I want to know at the present time is . ."

Parker points toward the sky.

". . how and why, for the amount of birds we have up there, not one got a glimpse of the attack or anything preceding it. Can you tell me that?"

Fizer gathers himself as if Parker has levied a personal insult at him. "Well, General," he explains, "our satellites have certain rotations and, particularly over the States, we have what we call 'black patches.' These are areas that have no satellite coverage whatsoever, and it can last from a few seconds to several minutes during a given day.

"Obviously, in more desolate parts of the country, such as Montana, the Dakotas, the deserts of Arizona, these black patches are a little more lengthy because the way the satellites are programmed. We do not care to waste the taxpayers' money on looking at absolutely nothing if we don't have to.

"Now," Fizer continues, "in a place like Tamawaca, it's not isolated by any means, but it's also not exactly bustling with activity. Simply put, General, it's an off-the-beaten-path cottage town and does not rank high on our priority list for domestic threats. Now, the Upper Peninsula in Michigan is a different story, as there are several camps for militia groups in that area and-"

"Well, maybe that's why they chose it," Parker interjects. "An isolated town, celebrating the Fourth of July like thousands of small towns across the nation. Families, innocent Americans, enjoying the holiday. Who would have thought, or predicted, it could be a major target for a terrorist attack?" Parker asks.

The question was asked rhetorically, but Fizer feels he needs to acknowledge the general in some way.

"Uh...yes, sir," Fizer manages. The scene of apple pie and small town Americana that Parker paints is something the colonel can do without. He had not really paused to think about the families or the actual people involved, and he does not really care to start now.

Parker seems disgusted at the colonel's lack of empathy at a time like this, and he says rather belligerently, "Colonel, just tell me what our satellites *did* pick up."

Fizer gives the general a hardened stare and says with a touch of animosity in his voice, "Certainly, *sir.*"

Fizer walks toward a small box stationed on a railing that encircles the platform and he punches a button. "Private Santos, will you cue up our satellite recording of last night's activity. Put it up on the big screen for General Parker."

A voice responds through the speaker, "Right away, sir."

Fizer walks back towards Parker and Augie as several seconds pass. The large screens on the wall suddenly go black as the whole room is bathed in darkness except for the glow of computer screens and small desk lamps located at various stations.

Then, on the screen appears the continental United States as seen from above the earth.

"This is what was first recorded by our satellites," Fizer says.

An area suddenly becomes highlighted on the map, indicating the area around Lake Michigan northwest of Indiana. Large red letters in the upper left-hand corner read:

WARNING
THERMAL ALERT DETECTED
WARNING
INTERIOR EXPLOSION

Underneath these letters are listed longitude and latitude coordinates of the area highlighted. In the lower right-hand corner is the military time to the millisecond. The recording occurred at 9:51 PM central time, or 10:51 PM eastern time.

The satellite's view continues to focus in as clouds and static intermittently mask the clarity of the picture.

As Parker and Augie stare at the screen, Fizer explains, "Our satellites have been programmed to pick up what we call 'hot areas,' or areas where large explosions, inordinate amounts of gunfire, or anything nuclear has been detonated. Excluding nuclear blasts, which are extremely rare, there are hot areas all over the world, and when the satellite closest picks up a 'hot' area, it instantly and automatically re-routes itself in order to take pictures for us of what is going on at that particular location.

"Unfortunately for us," Fizer sighs, "the satellite that was closest to the hot area at Tamawaca is a satellite we call, 'Plymouth Rock,' which is how old I think it is."

Fizer smirks in his attempt at humor, but Augie and Parker fail to share in the levity of the situation. Parker stonily asks, "And Plymouth Rock did not get any pictures for us?"

"No, sir, she did, just not very good ones," Fizer responds. "First of all, the satellite did not pick up the explosions immediately, but after some time had elapsed. By the time she recognized the hot area, re-routed, and zoomed in, all the action was over. Second, there was a lot of cloud cover that night, and-"

"Why is the picture full of static?" Parker interrupts.

"And third, she's old, sir," Fizer says with a touch of annoyance. "The Plymouth is due for retirement. She has a limited rotation around the upper Midwest and a little sliver of the Canadian border, and that's it. To be honest, sir, there's a reason she is observing the States and not an area like the Middle East. A lot more action over there that needs monitoring than over here.

"Well," Fizer corrects himself, "usually that's the case. In my opinion, General, she did her duty, but someone within our government feels she's got a few good years left. Budget money's tight, sir, you know how bureaucracies work," he says, as if Parker is to blame for it.

Parker does not fail to notice Fizer's accusatory tone, and he shoots him an irritated look at what he feels to be an unnecessary remark. "Is that it?" he asks.

"No, sir, quite the contrary. Look," Fizer says enthusiastically, pointing towards the screen.

The satellite moves in a little closer, which causes a greater degree of static on the screen, but the cloud cover is suddenly nullified. A large beach can be seen with several fires scattered throughout. The satellite captures the waves of the lake slowly clamoring up the beach and then retreating. There are dark shapes that dot the landscape like cacti that pierce the barren expanse of a desert. Only a few moments pass before Parker and Augie realize what these shapes represent, but both would certainly agree that they would have been better off if they had not. As every soldier remains motionless on the floor below, not even the sound of a person breathing can be heard, another phrase erupts onto the screen:

NO HUMAN LIFE DETECTED
UNABLE TO ASSESS NUMBER OF CASUALTIES

Augie glances at the general, who is stone-faced, transfixed by the images and words on the giant screen.

The first time he ever saw the general cry was when Augie had been lying on his back in the jungle, clutching at the stump where his recently severed hand used to be. Augie had been praying for death at that point, and hoping against hope that it was God's face taking mercy upon him. But it was not. It was General Parker, looking down at his pupil, cradling his protégé in his arms, and his eyes were somehow filled with the contradictory emotions of revenge and compassion. A single tear had formed in the general's eye upon finding his missing charge after Augie escaped the POW camp.

Now, for only the second time in all the years Augie has known the general, a solitary tear forms in one of the general's eyes, pausing there, not wanting to stay and yet, unable to be released. As it was in that jungle so many years ago, so it is now that if looks could kill, every person in the room would be dead. Revenge always seems to trump everything else in the world.

*　　*　　*

There is an atmosphere of quiet and reserve that seems designated specifically for wakes and funerals. A feeling that it is inappropriate to speak too loudly, or smile, or even cough. This is the mood that envelopes Fizer's office as the three men are lost in their own thoughts after viewing the destruction that was wrought on their countrymen and women, brought to them via satellite. Though the satellite had not captured the actual attack, it is enough to view the aftermath, to see the outlines and shapes of bodies strewn across the beach. It is enough to picture a festive scene with families and children only moments before, and then…chaos, death, carnage.

Parker is not a man prone to use grief and regret as a crutch, an excuse to not continue, to not get the job done. People who wallow in sorrow, who feel guilty because they are alive, who beat their breasts and implore God, "Why not me?" and think, *If only I could have been there*, seem to have no idea how utterly idiotic the idea sounds. To blame or fault yourself for being alive or to believe that an event such as this would have changed in some dramatic fashion had you been there is completely ludicrous. For Parker, he does not have the time for such inconsequential and trivial ruminations.

Feeling sympathy and pity for the innocent people that were slaughtered like lambs last night has its time and place. That time and place is not here. Parker has been handed the reins of finding the evildoers responsible for this attack, and being distracted with feelings of sadness would only sidetrack him from finding them. In Parker's eyes, the goal is to seek and capture, if not destroy. He could care less if the perpetrators ever saw the inside of a courtroom for their crimes. Parker would be more than honored to punch their one-way tickets in this life so that they can quickly catch up on their next life in hell.

A man knocks on Fizer's office door, and Fizer says impatiently, "Come."

Private Thomas Anderson salutes, enters quickly and says, "The disc the general requested."

"Well, Private Anderson, as you can see, the general is right in front of you, why don't you hand it to him," Fizer tersely says.

"Yes, sir," Anderson embarrassingly responds.

Augie speaks up, "Actually, I'll hold it for the general, Private Anderson."

"Very good, sir," Anderson says, as he hands the disc to Augie.

As Fizer is about to dismiss him, Parker takes a step towards Anderson, as if sizing him up.

"Tell me, Private Anderson, how long have you been stationed at Evans?" he asks.

"Two years, sir," Anderson responds.

"Is that right?" Parker asks, more to himself than to Anderson. "So you're familiar with standard operating procedure in a scenario like last night's?" Parker poses.

"Uh, yes sir, fairly well, sir," Anderson says, glancing at the colonel.

As if asking where the latrine is, Parker questions, "So, Private, what do you think of the relatively slow reaction time of our satellites last night?"

Fizer's ears suddenly perk up as if he is a deer that just heard the hunter step on a twig. Anderson glances again at Colonel Fizer, who obliges him with a hardened stare that says, *Watch where you step, boy.*

Parker catches the brief exchange between Fizer and Anderson and continues to wait on the latter's answer.

Anderson, for the first time since stepping into the room, looks uncertain of himself and his footing. He stammers, "Well, sir, I'm not in a . . um, I mean, I wouldn't know by my, um, whether our-"

"Private Anderson!" Parker sharply bellows. "I didn't ask for a dissertation on all the ways to sound like an asshole. I asked for your thoughts on our satellite coverage last night."

Anderson sheepishly lowers his head and turns a slight shade of tomato, biting his lip and trying not to make eye contact with anyone in the room.

"Private, answer the general's question," Fizer orders.

With all the strength he can muster, Anderson blurts, "Sir, I thought our coverage of the terrorist attack last night was as embarrassing as getting caught by your mom firing the cannon with your wick in your hand…sir."

The room remains silent for what seems like an eternity to Private Anderson. He had heard the term before, but now he thinks he understands its meaning: he had committed a serious faux pas. He nervously glances at the general, who nods his head slowly and, despite the circumstances, a slight grin crosses his face.

"Thank you, Private, for your honesty," Parker says.

Again, it appears that Fizer is about to dismiss him when Parker asks Anderson, "Private, can you tell me why it was so poorly handled?"

This time, Anderson avoids looking at Colonel Fizer, already well aware that he is treading on dangerous ground.

"Sir, if I may speak frankly?" Anderson implores.

"Of course, soldier," Parker responds.

"General, if I'd been monitoring that territory and a hot area was recognized, I would have called a blitz, sir, to let everyone in the room know, as well as the closest orbiting satellites know, that a major hot spot had been detected."

"A blitz, Private?" Augie asks.

Anderson turns to Augie, "Sir, a blitz is like an APB the cops use for fugitives or stolen cars, things like that. You know, an all points bulletin?"

When Anderson realizes that everyone in the room seems to know what an APB is, he continues, "Basically, it alerts everyone who is monitoring domestic satellites, including personnel at other military installations, that a hot spot has been detected, its location and coordinates, and basically informs them to point their satellites at the area. Sir, the purpose ultimately is to get as many pictures as possible, and worry about what the hell it is later."

"And this blitz was never called, Private?" Parker asks.

"No, sir, not to anyone's knowledge," Anderson responds, quickly glancing at Fizer.

Both Parker and Augie catch the sideways glance.

Parker, purposely addressing Private Anderson, says, "So, the only pictures we have are from Plymouth Rock, is that right?"

"As far as I know, sir," Anderson indicates.

"And she's an old bird, isn't she?" Parker says, which sounds more like a statement than a question.

"Yes, sir, she's definitely a grandma. Not like the newer KH-11 satellites, sir."

"Yes, I recall hearing about them recently, but would you mind refreshing my memory?" Parker asks. "It's not what it used to be."

On more reliable footing now, Anderson explains, "Certainly, sir. The KH-11's have special lenses specifically designed for satellites. They have the ability to pass through the haze and pollution that covers the planet, as well as the ability to see directly through clouds, inclement weather, practically anything, sir. I wouldn't be surprised if one is reading my thoughts right now, listening to me babbling like an idiot."

Parker chuckles, "Very good, Private. Not at all."

There is a moment of silence as Parker pauses, and again he purposely directs a question towards Private Anderson, "Who was in charge of that territory last night, son?"

The composure that Anderson attained a moment before instantly vanishes and is replaced by a look of trepidation and anxiety. Anderson glances at Colonel Fizer, who also tenses at the question, appearing as stiff as a block of wood.

Anderson's uncertainty returns with a vengeance. "Well, sir, that would be, um-"

Fizer speaks up, "That would have been a Private Rushmore, sir."

"Well, bring him here immediately, Colonel," Parker orders. "I want to speak with him."

Fizer cautiously responds, "Well, sir, that's not possible."

"And why is that, Colonel?" Parker inquires.

Fizer appears fidgety again. "General, Private Rushmore has been missing since last night. He was last seen by a couple of troops at a bar in Chicago. He has not been heard from since," Fizer says, a touch of regret in his voice.

Parker slowly digests this information and says dramatically, "That's quite troubling, isn't it?"

"Yes, sir, it is," Fizer acknowledges.

"Any ideas?" Parker asks.

Fizer slowly shakes his head, "None, sir. Rushmore was issued a pass and-"

Augie quickly speaks up, "Pardon, Colonel, correct me if I'm wrong, but didn't you say that all personnel had been recalled to the base and are accounted for?"

Fizer gives Augie a look that would make the Devil weak-kneed. "Do not interrupt a superior officer, *Lieutenant Colonel*," Fizer snaps.

"The question still stands, Colonel," Parker says.

Fizer stares at the general, further incensed that Parker has failed to admonish his assistant. A major breach of military etiquette occurred when Lieutenant Colonel Hermann interrupted Fizer in the midst of a subordinate. Parker should have reprimanded Hermann immediately and instead, the general had allowed it to occur and worse yet, chose to further embarrass the colonel in front of one of his men.

Fizer collects himself despite this breach in etiquette and explains, "Rushmore was issued a family emergency pass, General, and despite the fact that all of these need to be approved by me, as you can imagine, there was a lot of confusion around here last night, and I was not immediately available to approve the pass.

"Rushmore took advantage of the situation, General, and decided instead to get drunk at a bar with his friends, but I can assure you he will be found," Fizer says adamantly.

After a moment's silence, Parker argues, "Despite that, Colonel, it's a little distressing to learn that the one man who was monitoring the exact site of a terrorist attack is now missing, and on top of that, he failed to call in a 'blitz,' I believe is how Private Anderson put it, which sounds like standard operating procedure."

"Well, actually, sir," Anderson interjects, "that really would have been his supervisor's call."

Fizer's heart skips a beat as he inwardly winces

at the comment. Private Anderson is certainly having a difficult time keeping his mouth shut.

"Who was Rushmore's supervisor last night?" Parker asks.

Anderson looks towards Fizer, seemingly becoming aware that he has said too much at this point.

Fizer says softly, "That would be First Sergeant Jonathan Kaley, who, at the present time, appears to be AWOL, sir."

A look of shock registers on Parker's face as he attempts to find the words, "Private Anderson, thank you, you've been helpful. Dismissed, son."

Anderson nods, clicks his heels together, and salutes the general, who curtly returns the salute.

"Yes, sir," Anderson says as he quickly leaves, grateful to be fleeing this boiler room.

Parker turns to Fizer and with a look of pure outrage, forcefully says, "Well, Malcolm, it seems you've managed to keep a few important items from us so far. Would you care to share anything else before we find out about it from someone else?"

TEN

It is a little early for Halloween, but Sean figures he has earned the celebratory rights prematurely this year. In case "they" are looking for a six-one, 200-pound man with black hair, blue eyes, and a four-inch scar that runs down the side of his neck, "they" are not going to find anyone who fits that description around here.

With some cheap cosmetic help and assistance from a costume store, Sean has become, in the restroom of a Quik Mart, a changed man, in every sense of the word. The alteration is not mind-blowing, but it certainly belongs in the realm of the dramatic. With the exception of his height, the aforementioned characteristics of the wanted man have been replaced: he now appears as a 230-pound man with blond, ruffled hair, brownish-black eyes, and no longer sporting a scar down the side of his neck. Added to his new look is a solid two days' worth of stubble on his face, which is only getting more defined. He is finally satisfied: he appears nothing like the man whose face may soon be tacked on post office walls and television news programs everywhere.

As he looks at himself in the mirror and examines his new makeover, he thinks, *Isabella might not even recognize me.*

As this thought passes through his head, a noticeable tremble courses through his body, and Sean starts to shake almost uncontrollably. He attempts to stifle the sudden emergence of his nerves, but it becomes nearly overwhelming. He has been running on pure adrenaline for the last twelve hours without a wink of sleep since the night before last, he had eaten nothing, drank but a small amount of water, and he had almost no time to ponder the fate of his wife and baby boy.

Where are they? Would I ever see them again? Are they.... dead?

Sean feels dizzy as a combination of sleep deprivation, the fading of his adrenaline energy, and the morbid thoughts passing through his head give him a feeling of weightlessness, rubbery legs, and an unavoidable collapse of his body and shutting down of his mind. He tries to focus on the task at hand, but it suddenly seems daunting and insurmountable. Everything else seems insignificant compared to the devastating thoughts that seem to completely invade his mind, recurring over and over again.

If they are alive, he does not know the first place he would look to find them.

If they are dead, then I want to be dead, too, Sean thinks, as his legs buckle at the knees.

Along with this fatalistic thinking arrives one additional thought, this one more helpful to his predicament.

The sequence on Rosenstein's wall, I know where I've seen it before!

Sean takes a small measure of comfort in this victory, and a tiny step, he hopes, that can lead him to his family, wherever they may be.

Sean stumbles away from the mirror and into one of the stalls, locking the door behind him. He retches once, then twice, and when he realizes that he has nothing to refund, he plunges to earth with a guttural wail and hits the ground, unable to stave off the overwhelming rush of fatigue that engulfs him.

*   *   *

Sergeant Jonathan Kaley turns the DePaul University baseball cap around on his head as he peers through the slats in the railroad car. The *clickety-clack* of the train wheels against the track continue their monotonous chant as the train, at a leisurely pace, rolls across the countryside. The boxcar feels like a furnace on this steamy, summer afternoon as Kaley wipes from his forehead the seemingly never-ending stream of sweat that pours into his eyes like a waterfall. The baseball cap is practically soaked through with perspiration, rendering the new school colors a shade of midnight blue or even black. The salt from the sweat burns his eyes, leaving them raw and irritated as he constantly rubs at them with the palm of his hands, which are also slicked with sweat.

Kaley wears civilian clothes now, which he pilfered from a closed store late last night in a secluded part of Chicago. The Boy Scout, of course, got the better of him, as he left more than enough money to cover the cost of the clothes and the broken window pane in the back of the store. The gesture in such a rough part of town would probably lead his pursuers to the store, but he could not help it: his conscience seems to have its own conscience.

These same clothes stick to him like barnacles to the bottom of a ship as the perspiration continues to cascade out of every pore on his body.

Nothing interesting, Kaley thinks, as he scans the plains and prairies that blanket the Midwest like a layer of skin. Anyone remotely familiar with the Midwest region knows that large, flat expanses of land are the norm, while fascinating scenery to behold by train or car is a scarcity. Kaley notices the heat waves rippling off the land and pities the farm animals he sees, unable to find a sliver of shade or a spot in the barn to escape the merciless, sauna-like conditions.

Kaley wipes his brow again and gulps a swig of water from a canteen he salvaged from his jeep before plunging it into the murky waters of the Chicago River.

I loved that jeep, too, thinks Kaley, *what a fucking shame.*

But it was, without question, necessary. After dispatching the uninvited guests sent to his home the previous night, Kaley understood all too well that what he had witnessed was not intended for his eyes. Or for Private Rushmore's, whose life Kaley now fears had been taken with a lot more ease than their attempt to take his. Kaley had inadvertently put Private Rushmore in this situation, and he feels a twinge of guilt every time he thinks about him. So Kaley tries not to think at all, but this is easier said than done.

Kaley relives last night's decision over and over again, mulling over the choice of leaving well enough alone or ordering Rushmore to find a different satellite to track the signal. Though it may have cost Rushmore his life, and soon enough Kaley's as well, he does not stray far from the belief that he would have done the same thing 99 out of a 100 times. He wanted and indeed needed to know what was going on. There was something about the manner in which Colonel Fizer instructed him regarding the Apache helicopters that seemed odd.

How could the Pentagon have known so quickly about the signal? And they just happened to have Apache helicopters standing by to investigate?

Granted, the Pentagon maintains more sophisticated and high-tech equipment than Evans, but the fact remains that the signal was discovered in an impossibly remote part of the country.

The middle of Lake Michigan?

It seems to Kaley that the Pentagon had to be actively looking for something specific in that area in order to actually find it. So the question becomes:

How did they know to look for anything at all?

Additionally, the fact that a group of Apache helicopters were dispatched within a couple minutes of first contact seemed practically unthinkable. *Where were the Apaches dispatched from? Evans is the closest military installation to the coordinates, so how did the choppers get out there? And so quickly?*

The whole thing reeks of something devious and something...*planned.* Kaley keeps returning to this one word as it continues to bounce around inside his head. He has the unmistakable notion that something had been set in motion last night, an event masquerading as a terrorist attack, the true purpose of which is something else entirely.

Adding to his justifiable paranoia is what Rushmore and Kaley had witnessed on that screen, or believed they had witnessed. What they had seen and what they could infer from it, however, might be two very different things. The satellite's picture was slightly distorted, but what it had transmitted was something that seemed utterly inexplicable. The signal from Lake Michigan had moved and it had moved quickly. Rushmore's calculations assured Kaley that the source of the signal was nothing that could have been man-made, at least nothing Kaley is presently aware of. After the satellite went offline for several minutes and returned, over a hundred people had disappeared, replaced soon thereafter by five Apache helicopters. Then, numerous low-level blasts were detected and the satellite subsequently drifted out of range of Tamawaca, and the scene before them vanished.

But what had actually happened on that beach? What had approached the area at such a fantastic speed? Where had the people gone and why do I have a difficult time believing that terrorists had anything to do with what happened at Tamawaca? And what the hell were the helicopters doing?

One thing Kaley is certain of is that their objective was not search and rescue.

Kaley moves away from the door and sits down in a heap in a corner of the boxcar. He quickly realized his jeep would be a red flag to whoever was after him, and therefore, a liability. Dumping it into the Chicago River like a scrap of junk was intended to throw the dogs off his scent and make them believe that something "unfortunate" befell him. This, along with a positive identification of Kaley's blood type on the floor of the jeep, would hopefully buy him some time to create significant distance between him and his pursuers.

Kaley looks down at the sweat-drenched bandage wrapped around the palm of his hand, the area where he made his tiny incision. After rethinking it, he concludes that he should have made the cut in a far more strategic place. Although the wound is small, his hand aches and he has a difficult time making a fist. Kaley reminds himself that he needs to change the bandage fairly soon to avoid infection, especially in this heat.

As he lies there, mulling over the events of the past few hours, Kaley wonders about his friend. He knows that Sean is staying at his family's cottage this summer, but was he on the beach last night? Did he see what Kaley and Rushmore saw? Did he see more? Is he even alive? And what about his family?

The thought had crossed Kaley's mind on more than one occasion that Sean and his family were part of the "pack" of people who suddenly and mysteriously disappeared within a matter of minutes from the beach last night. But Kaley, ever the optimist, maintains hope that his friend is alive and kicking. And in the slim chance that Sean comes looking for him at his home, Kaley was sure to leave a small sign behind, a signal that he is alive, too – for now. Kaley simply hopes that Sean remembers to look for it.

As a multitude of thoughts continue to race around inside his head, Kaley begins to feel a massive fatigue settling around his bones. A combination of the stifling heat, the events of the last few hours, and his mind at its wits end are all starting to take a toll on him. He was able to briefly catnap when he first caught the freight train pulling away on one of the many railroad tracks that snake in and out of the city limits. It was a solid hour of sleep before the intense heat of the new day startled him awake, and the paranoia began settling in.

Since then, a disheartening feeling continues to nag at him. No matter what distance he puts between him and his pursuers, they will soon come to realize that nothing tragic has happened to him. He did not have a fatal car accident, nor was he car-jacked while waiting at a stoplight. He did not fall asleep behind the wheel and accidentally plunge his car into the depths of the Chicago River. Jonathan Kaley is very much alive, and he knows that the people looking for him will soon find this out as well. And, as he pulls a small item from the pocket of his pants and stares at it, they will also realize that he still has evidence of a fragment of what occurred last night. Indeed, Kaley holds no illusions that the disc tells the whole story, but certainly a portion of the story, a portion that can already debunk the version being disseminated to the public about the attack. To avoid that from happening, it appears that his enemies are willing to kill to obtain it. And now, Kaley is willing to do the same.

He stares at the small disc in its case and holds it up to eye-level.

This, he thinks, *could be my death warrant or my get-out-of-jail-free card, or possibly both.*

Kaley turns the baseball cap around again and pulls the brim down over his eyes. With this last heavy and burdensome thought, Kaley drifts off to sleep and thinks of all the nasty things he will do to the people responsible for this. And if anything happened to his friend . . .

The steady drone of the train rolling across the tracks as it heads east slightly comforts Kaley. There is only one destination that he believes will help him make sense of what occurred last night, and soon enough, it will be time to see it with his own eyes.

ELEVEN

Washington, D.C.

Moriah, Bellini, and a high-ranking intelligence officer in the Central Intelligence Agency named Michael English peer over the man that sits at the computer terminal. The man at the computer occasionally speaks over his shoulder to the three men hovering over him like vultures circling a carcass. To the three men, the man at the computer just as easily could be speaking Ancient Greek or pig Latin for as much as they understand the terminology and nuances of the computer.

These three men emerged and were bred in an espionage era that was not yet ruled by computers and access codes. Their language tends to be couched in whisperings, veiled conversations, cryptic messages and the like; not in the data, algorithms, cross-referencing, and equations that characterize the dialect of the computer. Now, it seems every piece of vital intelligence worth its salt in the spy world is generated on a computer and maintained on a hard drive, diskette, compact disc, or more recently, digital file. This, of course, has its advantages and disadvantages, but the bottom line is that one must adapt to surrounding technology. The Foundation is able to do so by retaining a full array of computer specialists, hackers, and even several tech-savvy entrepreneurs that are well-funded by the group. The man sitting at the computer before them falls into the first category, and like most of his kind, he prefers to explain every minute detail about the task at hand.

With a heavy time crunch starting to bear down on them, however, the tolerability levels have plummeted, and the impatience is evident on each man's face. Finally, one of them decides to speak:

"Jesus, Davidika, just tell us what you found," Bellini bellows. "Save the jargon for someone who gives a shit."

Davidika spins his chair around and faces the three men before him. Having become practically impassive to the typical range of human emotions as a result of employing computers as a constant companion, Davidika fails to capture the urgency in Bellini's voice, let alone the strain in each man's face. He does not discern the lines of worry that crisscross the men's faces as if a child has used their mugs for a game of tic-tac-toe. The worries and stress that people typically carry with them every day are unable to register a similar alarm in him. Of course, if Davidika were to know the cause of concern these men share, he might be anxious as well. It does not even bother him that they are currently two hundred feet below ground, in a secure, underground installation that no more than fifty people know exists. To him, it is all part of the fun of being extremely good at what he does.

The only things that do seem to fluster Davidika are computer codes he cannot break and discs he cannot read. In this particular case, neither scenario would keep him from sleeping tonight.

Davidika motions towards the computer, "Okay, well, simply put," he begins, "there are a ton of different files on this disc, each with an encrypted password. This guy was clever, he knows his computers. He took a bunch of junk satellite imagery from another source and put it on the disc, creating hundreds of files for what appears to be several seconds of some very uninteresting shots of the Canadian border.

"What takes time is figuring out the password for each file and then downloading the images," he continues. "I had to sift through each file to make sure none of them contained the stuff you guys are looking for. But after a little while, it's apparent that he used the same password over and over again, meaning that he probably ran out of time in the middle of doing this."

"You think he was interrupted?" Moriah asks.

"Well, for the first couple dozen files, he had a unique password for each one," Davidika responds. "Nothing real complicated, just a set of numbers and letters that I was able to decode through a program I wrote. But after a while, he probably just hit repeat on the password for each file because he was in a hurry."

Michael English speaks for the first time, reluctant to believe that Kaley went to this much trouble to create a bogus disc, and most likely expressing the sentiments of the other two men as well. "Are you sure there's nothing there? You checked every file?"

"Every file, man," Davidika responds, irritation creeping into his voice. "There's nothing there, or at least nothing that you're looking for."

"Well, it was hidden for a reason," Bellini points out.

"My best guess is that the purpose of it was to generate some time and create confusion as to the importance of it," Davidika posits. "He wanted us to meticulously sift through each file, each password. He was stalling for time. That was the point of it," he concludes.

"Meaning that he's still alive and he still has the real disc," Moriah says.

Bellini's voice cracks with tension as he blurts, "Moriah, he could go to the newspapers with what he's got, the TV stations-"

"He won't do that," Moriah calmly answers.

"Why the hell not?" Bellini asks.

"Cause he does not have enough evidence," Moriah states.

"He'll want something more," English says evenly.

Bellini looks at English and then back at Moriah.

"Exactly," Moriah concurs. "His case report indicates that he is a finisher, a guy who does not settle for loose strings or pieces of the puzzle. He wants the whole fucking puzzle, Paul."

Moriah pauses for a moment and then reiterates the intelligence officer's belief. "He'll want something more," Moriah says confidently.

It takes only a split second for Bellini to draw a conclusion from this statement.

"Tamawaca," Bellini breathes.

Moriah takes a few steps away from the men.

Another fucking wrinkle, he thinks.

Since the plan was set in motion, Moriah feels that they have been confronted with problem after problem, decision after decision. Moriah, of course, did not expect everything to run smoothly across the board, but he also had not anticipated this many snags. The most recent of which occurred only minutes ago with the outrageous demands of the "Sword of Allah," a well-connected and finely-tuned network of Middle Eastern terrorists that have wreaked death and destruction around the globe on behalf of their jihad. Moriah knew it was risky getting in bed with the group, but the Foundation needed an organization that contains a certain name recognition around the world, but at the same time are still looking to prove they are one of the premier terrorist organizations on the planet.

Through several intermediaries and after months of negotiating, Moriah and the Sword agreed on a predetermined fee for the latter to claim credit for the "attack" on Tamawaca. The Foundation provided them with crucial details that would confirm to authorities that the Sword was indeed behind the attack. Then, several hours after the attack was reported, as Moriah and the rest of the Foundation grew restless waiting for the group to claim responsibility, a member of the Sword contacted one of Moriah's intermediaries and informed him that the group's asking price had now been raised by five million U.S. dollars.

Clever fucking bastards, Moriah thought when he heard this new demand. The Sword knew they had Moriah between a rock and a hard place, fully aware that Moriah did not have the time to "negotiate," and that he needed the Sword more than they needed his money. Nevertheless, the galling arrogance on the part of the Sword's leadership caused Moriah to instantly refuse, informing them that a fee had already been established and the group could not go back on its word. The Sword countered that they could do anything they want, which may include revealing secret negotiations with a group of Americans regarding a bogus "terrorist attack" to the press. While there is no solid evidence to support the group's claims, this would hardly stop the media from picking up a conspiracy story and running with it. It is a can of worms that the Foundation never wants opened.

Moriah hesitated for several hours, perhaps several hours too long, thinking that perhaps the claim from the Sword was unnecessary in the overall scheme of things. But finally Moriah relented, with extreme reluctance, and wired an additional five million dollars to a bank account in Zurich. The Sword would claim credit for the attack and post proof of their involvement on a radical Islamic website, and Moriah's "witnesses" would soon come forward with their stories. Moriah had never been so angry in his life, not necessarily because of the money, but the utter insolence on the part of the Sword was infuriating. After this is over, he vowed to obtain his revenge on them, one way or another.

Moriah turns around and quickly walks back towards the men.

"I did not want to employ any more outsiders, but this is the way it has to be," Moriah says. "The stakes are too high and it is too damn risky to use our own people."

Moriah looks at the CIA officer first, "Call Sloan right away. Give her Kaley's last known location and let her pick up the scent."

English nods, "You got it."

Moriah turns now to Bellini, "I don't want to forget about our friend Mr. O'Connell. See if you can dig up Barbary somewhere. Last I heard he was south of the border. He should get along best with the professor."

"And the rest of the plan," Bellini asks, "is still running smoothly?"

"Like clockwork," Moriah answers.

"And Jericho?" Bellini inquires, a certain reverence in his voice bordering on fear.

"As far as we know," Moriah states, "he believes everything is still going according to *his* schedule."

Moriah glances at his watch and continues, "The meeting planned at the battlefield outside Spokane occurs in little more than eighteen hours, and we'll hand over our test subjects and his-"

Moriah pauses for a moment, looks at both men while trying to suppress a devious smile, before finishing the sentence, "-vessel then, and perhaps show him that we now speak his language."

TWELVE

Madrid, Spain

The evening air is permeated with the scent of candles, incense, and a type of cured meat, a strange combination no doubt. The sun has sunk to the rim of the horizon, painting the sky a fiery reddish-orange tinge. The sound of music from the street drifts up and through the open windows, a concession reluctantly granted because the building they occupy is the tallest for several miles around, and their informant occupies the top floor. The ensemble below plays an old patriotic song that proclaims the strength of the Republic of Spain and its gloried, albeit bloody, history.

People have taken to the streets as the evening siesta has arrived. The sound of laughter, singing, and dancing mingles with the volume of a television in the room, seemingly competing with one another to be heard.

A man sits on the end of a bed and presses the volume button once again on the television's remote control. The violence depicted on the television becomes louder as the sound of gunshots and explosions fill the room. One might even confuse the noise from the TV with the firecrackers that echo from the street several stories below.

The man on the bed is dressed rather shabbily in light cotton pants, slippers, and a short-sleeve button down shirt that has neglected to be buttoned. His hair is long and unkempt, veering off in several directions. A patch of week-old stubble covers his face, and there even seems to be crumbs from previous meals trapped around the area of his mouth and chin. His eyes are bloodshot, but despite conveying an impression of total fatigue, he looks positively ecstatic at the spread before him.

The man sits before a table where an assortment of food has been laid out. Grease drips from his fingers and his chin as he guzzles from a goblet that holds a fine Italian wine that he, of course, specifically requested. He certainly enjoys wine from his native Spain, but he requested the Italian wine because he knew he would receive it.

The man casts an annoyed look towards the doors that lead to the sixth-story terrace, desperately wishing he could mingle and join the fun in the streets below, but he knows this is impossible. He quickly springs up from the bed before the guards can protest and he swings the doors shut with a *BANG!*

A couple of windows on both sides of the terrace doors remain open a crack, but the noise from the streets is greatly diminished.

In Spanish, one of the guards standing by the door chides, "Senor Armas, please do not make yourself a visible target to someone outside. That makes our job all the more difficult, and you're simply not worth much if you're dead."

Armas smiles at the guard. "Of course, senor, I understand," he says placatingly. "Now, would you be kind enough to fetch me a cloth from the kitchen, to wipe my hands?"

Armas smiles at the other guard flanking the doorway, who exchanges glances with his partner. They both wear the uniform of a special army unit, with pistols attached to one side of their belts and a long, sheathed sword swinging from the opposite side. Typically, they are assigned to protect high-ranking officials in the government, cabinet ministers, and other esteemed dignitaries and ambassadors associated with the Spanish government, as well as visiting emissaries. However, in this case, they are protecting a turncoat, an informer of the Basque rebels. A man who already cost several lives upon extracting him from a situation in which he almost certainly would have been killed. The Basque separatists learned of their traitor through another informer and were about to commence with some rather brutal and uncomfortable torture techniques when government agents intervened at the last moment and rescued Hector Armas, and all the secrets that he possesses.

The government stashed him in a safe house just inside the city limits of Madrid, an area considered secluded but not completely isolated in the event the rebels find him and reinforcements are needed. Because this section of the city has little to no Basque presence, however, they felt confident he would be secure regardless.

Think again.

The guard looks at Armas and nods his head, not entirely thrilled to be pulling servant duty for this puerco. The guard unlatches the door, opens it, and exits, closing the door behind him. The other guard quickly latches the door after the other one leaves, and he moves to the side of the doorway.

"He is a good man," Armas nods approvingly.

The other guard does not care to respond to Armas, remaining still as a statue.

Armas walks back to his bedside table and motions towards the food. "I cannot finish, will you eat some?" he asks the guard.

The guard shakes his head no.

"Come on, do not let it go-"

Pop, pop, pop.

The sudden eruption of firecrackers outside snaps the guard's attention away. Armas, too, looks apprehensively outside. The firecrackers sound close, a lot closer than street-level.

The guard hurries toward the doors that lead onto the terrace, but first looks through the blinds. Someone managed to toss a bundle of firecrackers onto the balcony. The guard looks from side to side and slowly opens the door, skinning his sidearm at the same time.

A hell of a throw if the firecrackers were chucked from the street six stories below, the guard thinks.

The guard gingerly steps onto the terrace, as if walking barefoot on a layer of glass, and he continues to glance around as the firecrackers carry on their incessant popping. The guard warily looks from side to side before approaching the railing at the end of the terrace. The guard peeks over the side at the people below and scans the immediate area. He sees no one paying any particular attention their way.

As Armas stares outside, his anxiety starts to fade at the sight of the firecrackers on the terrace.

Some prankster, being funny, he thinks.

Armas turns as the other guard returns with the familiar coded *knock* at the door. He turns back around to the guard on the balcony, ready to crack a joke, when the smile is quickly erased from his face. He sees what appears to be a snake, slithering down the slope of the roof towards the unsuspecting guard. The snake is black with blotches of silver on its skin, unlike anything that Armas has ever seen.

Armas peers closer and is about to call out to warn the man when the snake wraps itself around the guard's neck with a ferocity and quickness Armas has never seen before in any kind of creature.

Suddenly, Armas realizes in abject horror that whatever it is, it does not belong to the reptile family. The silver he spotted is a type of razor, and within seconds, as the weapon is given a rapid tug, the guard's head twists off like a cap on a beer bottle. The guard's head hits the ground with a *thud* and rolls towards the fireworks, which instantly engulf it in flames. The guard's body stays upright for several seconds until it can no longer defy gravity and it comes back to earth, with several geysers of blood rapidly spouting from the top of the torso.

Armas appears frozen in shock as he stares out at the terrace. He tries to will himself to move towards the door, but his legs are not receiving messages at the moment. He looks around for a weapon, but sees none in the vicinity. Urgent pounding outside the door finally spurs Armas to take action. He stumbles towards the door, reaches it, and starts to lift the block of wood that latches it.

In the next instant, Armas hears an unusual sound, as if someone whistled sharply in his ear, and he feels a sharp pain in his hand. He looks down, unable to comprehend what he sees. His right hand has been impaled on the wooden block by a long, double-sided dagger.

Armas immediately looks behind him and there, standing in the doorway of the terrace, is a tall, striking, muscular woman. She is dressed from head to toe in traditional Spanish garb and her hair is slicked back, her eyes boring into his. She stares without a sense of mercy, or urgency for that matter.

She is calm, holding another dagger in one hand and a pistol equipped with a silencer in the other hand. Armas looks directly into her eyes and sees absolutely nothing. He sees blackness against the backdrop of a blood-red sky. This horrific nightmare does not seem possible with all the joy and happiness that can be heard only six stories below.

"Dios mio," he mutters.

Armas pounds on the door and screams for help to the guards outside. He then tries to use his free hand to remove the dagger and immediately, he hears an object soar past him with another *whistle*. The woman's other dagger penetrates Armas' left hand through the palm, impaling it on the door. Armas emits a shriek that fails to pierce the din of the revelers below, but more than likely was heard by the guards on the other side of the door.

Urgent banging continues to barrage the door and numerous voices can be heard shouting on the other side. A moment later, several guards repeatedly heave their full weight against the door in a futile effort to knock it down. The door is six inches thick and made of solid oak.

The woman takes several long strides and within an instant, she is standing next to Armas, close enough to be wrapped in the fear that surrounds the man. She gets directly in his face until they are eye-to-eye and then, in a hoarse voice, she whispers, "Jorge says hello."

She stuffs a small, round object in his mouth, places a piece of duct tape over it, and yells in muffled Spanish, "Help me!"

Because of the door's thickness, the guards' ability to discern one voice from another is diminished, and they only hear the urgency of the tone.

Armas' eyes bulge and he looks alarmingly at the door. He helplessly kicks his legs at it as he struggles to scream.

Within several seconds, the woman slips out the way she came, not so much walking as gliding. She shimmies up the roof and she hears, for her, what sounds like music to her ears: the door ripped apart by bullets, along with the mark, and several seconds later, an explosion that eradicates any chance of pursuit, along with Senor Armas' head.

Tijuana, Mexico

Barbary, unlike Sloan, does not enjoy sharing an intimate "relationship" with an intended target before dispatching them. Up close and personal is not his style. Barbary prefers to imagine the surprise the person must have felt having never seen it coming, the suddenness with which he is able to summon death to their door. One minute, a person is alive and kicking, and the next minute, they are dead. So simple, and yet it remains such a powerful elixir to him. Barbary enjoys taking life in that instant, to snatch it away without the mark ever knowing what hit him. Snipings, car bombs, poison – these are some of Barbary's preferred methods. For him, there is no better rush in the world than taking a person's life who had for so long been taking it for granted.

Barbary slouches at the bar of a filthy, rat-infested restaurant, nursing a *cerveza*. These places are a dime a dozen in this part of Tijuana, and it is in a place like this where people can disappear, where they can be left alone to drink their miseries away. He lights another clove cigarette and inconspicuously glances through the screen door to the dirt road outside. Several working girls walk back and forth down the "boulevard," peddling their wares for what might amount to a can of Coke in the States. Here, everything is cheap. The prostitutes appear to be the most visible forms of human scum that occupy the street, along with the lesser-seen but always-present pimps, drug pushers, thieves, and murderers. They all are looking for something to sell, someone to con, or even someone to kill.

A pair of policemen walk by, glance in his direction and look over the other sad patrons of the place. After a few seconds, they continue their patrol, indifferent to the nefarious happenings on the street before them. They do not wear uniforms, but everybody knows who they are. They simply do not care. The cops might be looking for someone to shakedown, but finding a person around here who has any significant money or drugs on them would be an extreme challenge. Nine out of ten people in this area of Tijuana probably could not offer the officers a pot to piss in.

Barbary glances up at the mirror behind the bar. He has a sweat-soaked bandana tied loosely around his neck, and a dusty, black cowboy hat hangs low over his face. He has grown a mustache to appear like a Mexican *muchacho*, and he even added a couple of crooked, silver teeth to his grill to complete the seedy look. He begins to reminisce of how he came to be here.

Barbary was given this job by an individual with no face and no name, but the price was certainly right, a handsome fee too good to pass on. It was arranged through a friend of a friend, which is the only way Barbary works. He does not simply accept any assignment presented to him, but rather only if somebody he trusts has vouched for the prospective client, many of whom tend to be repeat customers. For all he knows, he could be getting played, a patsy in a game he is not aware of.

The man who gave him the job used no names, except one: General Luis Salador. A million dollars, one dead general, that is the deal. The fee is overly generous because the target is a high-ranking general in the Mexican Army.

The general has been causing numerous problems on the border for several influential businessmen and their respective couriers in the dope game. It is not because General Salador dislikes drugs or even because he is some type of drug crusader, but because he did not feel he was getting paid enough for his "protection." For the past eighteen months, the general ensured that certain couriers breeze through the border without any hassles or inspections. He was paid well for it, until he thought he deserved more.

After his bosses refused to increase his protection money, the general's retribution was a series of high-profile drug busts at the border. Large shipments of cocaine, marijuana, ecstasy, and heroin were seized and confiscated, creating a ripple, a small one, but a ripple nonetheless in the business of his former employers. The Mexican and American press praised the general for his actions and glorified him in the papers for his cunning and courage in capturing these despicable drug peddlers. The general suddenly reveled in the role of hero, of the indestructible crimefighter battling evil and lawlessness.

In reality, the general knew whom to arrest because they were the same couriers he allowed to waltz through on hundreds of previous occasions.

The men who operate the drug trade in this area hired Barbary because he is one of the best assassins in the world, but more importantly, he has no connection to them whatsoever. After all the media exposure given to General Salador, an untimely death would certainly bring enormous pressure and a whole assortment of questions directed at the heads of the drug trafficking, a consequence they would like to avoid. Nevertheless, it was unanimously decided, the general needs to go. *Rapido.*

They would, of course, be questioned regardless, but with airtight alibis and assurances from Barbary that it would appear to be an accident, the authorities will arrive at a dead end, lacking proof of any wrongdoing by the people under the most suspicion. The group, all of their associates, and anyone even remotely connected with them would not be within fifty miles of the "accident."

Thus, Barbary arrived in Mexico several weeks ago and began studying everything about the general: his mannerisms, his daily routine, his habits, and of course, *his weaknesses.*

It did not take long for Barbary to learn that Salador has a penchant for young whores, girls ranging in their mid- to late teens. But it is the general's weakness of indulging in a cigarette after his dalliance that Barbary would exploit. Every few days, Barbary noted that Salador or his bodyguards cruise the boulevard searching for a fresh one that strikes the general's fancy, of which there is no shortage. The place he chooses for these "dates," however, is always the same.

How very sloppy of the general, Barbary thinks. *So confident he is untouchable that he fails to alter this pattern.*

It is this arrogance and sense of invincibility that Barbary will prey on. The general's indifferent attitude has begun to infect his bodyguards, whose vigilance in protecting the general during his trysts is downright lackadaisical to begin with.

Barbary sits in this particular bar because the love nest for the general's escapades is directly next door, in a second floor shithole of an apartment that is as cozy as a prison cell. Perhaps this is what gets the general off.

Barbary has been cautious since he arrived in Tijuana, biding his time, changing his appearance every day, ensuring that no one sees him the same way twice. He had avoided eye contact with the general or his bodyguards, and he always played the part of the bitter, down-on-his-luck drifter around town. He has been waiting for the perfect time to strike.

And the time is now, Barbary's instincts tell him. *Today.*

Barbary developed his plan after learning that the owner of the bar rents cots to overserved patrons to sleep it off upstairs when they are unable to stumble home. A few nights ago, while pretending to be intoxicated,

Barbary drilled a hole the size of a macadamia nut in one of the rooms upstairs, giving any would-be peeping tom an X-rated view of Salador and his young lady *in flagrante delicto*. A touching site to behold indeed.

He had mulled a number of ways to eliminate the general and after several options were considered and then discarded, he settled on one that he thought to be the most creative and the most fitting.

Barbary glances outside as a camel-colored jeep screeches to a halt outside the bar. Salador's bodyguards instantly jump out and escort Salador and his prize into the fine establishment next door. Since Salador's picture has appeared so frequently in the papers and on TV, he has resorted to using disguises during these brief rendezvous. Unfortunately for him, Barbary is not fooled by these pathetic attempts to conceal his identity, and any moron could deduce that there are few people in Tijuana with military-issued jeeps accompanied by two burly bodyguards around town.

The walls are so thin next door that seconds after the party enters, Barbary hears muffled speaking, and even understands a few words here and there in Spanish. Next, Barbary hears footsteps hurriedly walk up a flight of stairs.

He waits about two minutes, stumbles off his barstool, and then moves towards the back of the bar and asks in slurred Spanish, while pointing towards the back:

"El bano, por favor, senor?"

The bartender annoyingly nods his head, "Si," knowing that the man had used the bathroom before, but is too drunk to remember where it is.

Barbary walks towards the bathroom in the back, but

as soon as he turns the corner and is out of sight of the bartender, he slips up a short flight of stairs hidden by a makeshift door. He quickly heads down a hallway to where Salador's "regular" room is located. The hole he drilled is at waist-level, which Barbary glances through to ensure he has the correct room. Barbary spots Salador, and then a moment later he hears a groan from the woman. This is followed by loud, rhythmic grunting coming from the general.

The woman can put on a show, Barbary thinks, as she purrs and moans with every thrust. She whispers sweet nothings in his ear, Barbary is sure, as she tells him how *grande* he is and how *bueno* he is making her feel.

Too bad the actress will not make it to Broadway.

Barbary fishes from the pocket of his pants a small, oval object that resembles a miniature oxygen tank a scuba diver might wear. The object is no bigger than a man's hand and weighs almost nothing. Barbary loves these types of toys. It is not a weapon in and of itself, but is simply a catalyst for disaster.

Barbary secures the object over the hole. The miniature tank has two tiny suction cups that attach to the wall and hold it upright. Barbary gently turns a small nozzle located at the top of the tank and a slight hissing sound is discharged. The brief noise does not come close to penetrating the lustful sounds from the next room. An odorless, highly flammable gas called deuterium, which is a heavier isotope of ordinary hydrogen, begins pouring into the room at an extremely rapid rate.

Barbary quickly exits the hallway as an orgasm reaching its crescendo grips one of the parties. If Barbary has to wager money, he would bet the squeals are not coming from the woman. Barbary quietly slips down the stairs and stumbles out of the back room while pretending to struggle with his zipper. He pulls the hat brim down over his eyes and exits out the screen door.

Remember, General, smoking kills. The explosion will destroy any evidence of the deadly tank and the cause of the blast will probably be attributed to a gas leak from an old decrepit pipe that occupies the even more decrepit building. No evidence of a bomb will be discovered and the authorities will chalk it up as an unfortunate accident.

As he casually walks down the street, Barbary hardly hears the earth-shattering explosion as he begins to count the one million dollars in his head and now, in his bank account.

THIRTEEN

The small military plane takes off from a runway at Evans Military Base, carrying Lieutenant Colonel Hermann, General Parker, Private Anderson, formerly under the command of Colonel Fizer, and the pilot. Parker explained to Colonel Fizer that Anderson is needed in an advisory capacity: since he was present and on-duty at the time of the attack, any assistance he could provide at the site would be helpful. It was an unusual request, Parker certainly knew, but he also knew that the colonel could do little in the way of stopping Parker from shanghaiing one of his charges.

Fizer did not bat an eyelash at the general's request, but the look on his face said it all when Anderson departed with the general. Parker takes a certain perverse pleasure each time he recalls the expression on the colonel's face, which closely resembled the look a newly anointed college student gives his parents when they drop him off hundreds of miles from home and wish him good luck. It was a potent combination of anxiety, nervousness, and outright fear. To the general, it was a moment worth a thousand words.

Parker and Augie sit near the rear of the plane, which Parker managed to pry from the colonel, explaining that a helicopter trip to Tamawaca from Evans was wholly impractical and would squander too much time. Parker insisted that he must get to the site as soon as possible, and he left the helicopter as collateral, promising that he would return the plane within a few hours. Fizer reluctantly agreed, fully aware that he could hardly haggle with a five-star general.

As Parker and Augie settle in after take-off, they compare notes after their unexpected visit to Evans and their meeting with the jittery Colonel Fizer.

"Lying prick," the general spits, upon unbuckling the seat belt after the plane levels off.

"No doubt about that, General," Augie responds. "I could see his nose growing. What do you think he's hiding?" Augie asks.

Parker lets out a loud gush of air as he rubs his increasingly achy head. Migraine headaches are a constant threat to strike the general at any given moment of the day. He has had them for as long as he can remember, and the dull ache now is doing little in the way of helping him think clearly.

"What worries me the most," Parker states, "is not just the lie we caught him in, but what other nuggets the colonel is hiding. Something doesn't smell right, Augie, got my bullshit radar going haywire. I just don't know what it's trying to tell me."

Augie is on the verge of responding, but hesitates for a moment, as if trying to delicately choose the right words.

The general catches his protégé's hesitancy, however brief, and inquires, "What have you got, Augie?"

With a deep breath, Augie plunges ahead, "Sir, we have to consider the possibility that Fizer is somehow involved in the attack from last night, or is covering for someone who is. There are too many things that don't add up."

Augie ticks off a list on his fingers and continues, "The base responsible for satellite coverage completely blows it, the men monitoring that particular area are now missing, standard protocol was not properly followed. It all seems to rest on Fizer's shoulders, sir."

Parker stares at Augie for a solid ten seconds before sighing in exasperation. "Jesus Christ, is this what it comes down to?" he asks, shaking his head. "A high-ranking military officer involved in an attack on his own people? It just doesn't seem to fit with what we know about Fizer."

Augie gives the general a look of puzzlement. "What do you mean, sir?"

"Well, I've known Malcolm for a long time," Parker explains, "and though he may be a sneaky little bastard, one thing I would never peg him as is a traitor. The man bleeds red, white, and blue, Augie, you know that. He's borderline radical in his leanings, sure, but I can't believe you could sell him in attacking innocent Americans on the Fourth of July, of all days."

"I see your point, sir," Augie concedes.

"Malcolm's like a typical card-carrying NRA yahoo who thinks there is only one way in life," Parker asserts, "and that's the American way. Damned if I disagree with that, Augie, but he's just too patriotic for his own good."

"Sir?" Augie asks, clearly puzzled at Parker's remark.

"Never mind," Parker says, waving his hand in dismissal.

After a few moments, Augie posits, "Maybe we're looking at this too simplistically, sir."

"What do you mean?"

"Well," Augie begins, "if the colonel is involved, then there would more than likely be an ulterior motive for the attack, right? At least from his perspective?"

Parker leans forward, "Go on."

Augie continues, "If what we have already said about him is accurate, that we could never see him involved in a plot to harm innocent Americans, then maybe there is a deeper meaning behind it. You know, like a small sacrifice now for the greater good later."

Parker half-heartedly nods, thinking that Augie's reasoning seems to be a bit of a stretch. Augie, sensing the general's skepticism, adds, "It wouldn't be a surprise the colonel has a hidden agenda in mind, sir."

"No, it wouldn't," Parker agrees.

After a few moments, Parker shakes his head, "Still, we're straying too far from the facts, Augie. We're clutching at straws, and while it's certainly constructive to brainstorm, it can lead us down some dead-end roads."

"Understood, sir," Augie says.

Parker and Augie remain silent for several minutes as each man loses himself in their own respective thoughts. Finally, Augie speaks up.

"Sir, I feel bad for even saying it, but I think I should express a thought that has crossed both our minds," he says.

The general slowly nods his head and mutters, "Go ahead."

"Well, sir," Augie begins, "with the lack of even the slightest bit of intelligence, Fizer's strange behavior, the embarrassing satellite coverage of the attack, and not even a bogus claim yet from one of the dozens of extremist, anti-American groups out there . . "

Parker nods again, encouraging Augie to continue.

". . sir, I think we need to start seriously considering the idea that this attack was carried out by Americans, and if someone like Colonel Fizer is involved, then it's possible other high-ranking officers in the chain of command may also be involved," Augie concludes.

Parker gives Augie a hardened stare and in a voice barely above a whisper, says, "You realize what you're saying, Lieutenant Colonel Hermann? That men and women we have sworn to bleed with on the battlefield are possibly behind this act? Officers who have unquestionably served this country without hesitation, who have seen it through the good times and bad? You're suggesting that they could have committed this godforsaken act? On American soil no less?"

Augie returns the stare and states matter-of-factly, "Yes, sir, I believe that's exactly what I'm saying."

Parker nods his head with a look of satisfaction, "Good, now I know I'm not the only one who's fucking crazy."

"You suspected Americans before, sir?" Augie questions, surprised.

"Let's just say I get paid the big bucks to determine every conceivable possibility, and that is certainly one of them," Parker acknowledges.

"Yes, sir."

Parker leans forward, excitement in his voice as a plan of action begins to form.

"Now," he begins, "I want you to call General Hutchinson and get one of his ballbusters over to Evans right away. This person is to act as a special liaison that answers strictly to me. Their job will be to stick to Fizer like glue, shadow the fucker, do not, I repeat, do not let him out of sight, observe his command, report anything out-of-the-ordinary, things like that. Instruct Hutchinson to tell Fizer some bullshit about making sure things are being done the right way, and so on. But make sure Fizer knows the liaison is answering only to me," Parker says sternly.

"Sir, what about General Marshfield? He won't like being cut out of the loop like that. Fizer is really one of his guys-"

"Exactly my point, Augie," Parker says sharply. "One of 'his guys.' We don't know who is involved at this point, so we need to keep it in the family. Anybody closely associated with Fizer receives limited information from now on. I've known Hutchinson for three-quarters of my life, I trust him as much as I trust you."

"Yes, sir," Augie replies.

Parker continues, "Next thing, send a couple of our best tech guys from our office to Evans, see if they can dig a little further into the satellite coverage from last night. There is something definitely strange going on there, and I don't trust that Fizer is giving us the whole story. And be sure Fizer knows that these people should have the full authority that I would have if I were there."

"Of course, General."

"And Augie, you got anybody who specializes in missing persons?" Parker asks.

"Sir?"

"Get someone from your elaborate intelligence network to find . ."

Parker glances down at a pair of names written on a legal pad in front of him.

" . . one Private P.J. Rushmore and one Sergeant Jonathan Kaley, and pull the files on both of them."

"Got the perfect man for the job, General," Augie answers.

"I suppose you don't want to tell me who, Lieutenant Colonel?" Parker asks.

"Classified, sir," Augie responds.

Augie slyly smiles at the general, enjoying the occasions when Parker tries to pry tiny pieces of information from him. Augie knows the general would never want him to compromise his sources, and Parker knows that his protégé knows this. These little playful attempts by the general are simply his natural curiosity and a result of being in the intelligence business for over four decades.

"Okay," Parker continues, "but I want to know where these men are, and whether they're alive or dead. Can your man do that?"

"He can sure as hell try, sir," Augie replies.

"Alright then, I'm taking a quick catnap. Wake me when we land, and make sure they know at HQ that we're coming."

"I believe, sir," Augie notes, "General Cozey is in charge at the site, on orders from the President himself."

"Alright," Parker nods, "give the general a heads-up of our ETA."

"Yes, sir."

"And I want a full briefing from the forensic team at ground zero as soon as possible. I want to know what those bastards hit us with."

"You got it, sir," Augie responds.

"And Augie?"

"Yes, sir?"

"See if they got a couple aspirin on board," he says, rubbing his head wearily, "my head's fucking killing me."

* * *

The first thing Sean realizes is that he is horizontal to earth, or perhaps the rest of the world has turned sideways, which would not be surprising considering the events of the last few hours. The ground feels cold and hard. He puts a hand to his face and runs it through his hair, startled at first by the crusty feel of it, thinking that he is still locked in a dreamworld. Then he quickly remembers the work was done by his own hand, and besides the fact that a career as a professional hairstylist in his next life does not appear in the cards, everything that has occurred in the last few hours comes rushing back to him in a sudden and enormous wave, bringing a mix of emotions.

The disappearance of more than a hundred people from Tamawaca Beach, including his family; the soldier he killed and his desperate escape; searching Kaley's ransacked house and finding his friend's personal journal referencing the "attack;" the shamrock marker; the near-deadly encounter at Rosenstein's home and the mysterious mist blown from the vents that caused his adversary to flee; the familiar green glow from the man's weapon; and finally, the sequence of letters and numbers etched on the wall. It was like a message or a directive of some kind.

From Rosenstein? he thinks. *If not, who else could it have been?*

Only one of Rosenstein's students from DePaul might know what the seemingly random assortment of numbers and letters mean.

Sean pushes himself up off the floor of the bathroom, his body sore and achy. The hard tile of the bathroom floor probably did not do him any favors, either. He checks the wound on his leg from the bullet that grazed him. He had disinfected the wound earlier and hastily patched it up, and though it is only a flesh wound, it still hurts like hell.

He opens the stall door and moves to the sink, again startling himself when he looks in the mirror and sees his new makeover. He splashes cold water on his face, takes a few large gulps of it, and then pats his face dry with a paper towel. He takes several deep breaths and exhales slowly. Although he had slept for probably an hour or two, he feels energized and recharged. He suddenly feels that the odds of finding his family are not insurmountable, which they seemed only a short time before.

It is time to find them.

Sean slowly opens the bathroom door, half-expecting an army of soldiers or a S.W.A.T. team waiting, guns leveled at his head, telling him *to get the fuck down on the ground!* But there is no one, an empty parking lot on the side of the Quik Mart. A couple of cars and trucks parked at the half-dozen gas tanks.

Sean wonders how long he had actually slept on the floor of the bathroom, as the sun is further west on the horizon than he initially imagined it would be. As untimely as his panic attack had been, the sleep had certainly rejuvenated him, but he does not know if he would trade it now for the precious loss of time. At first, Sean thought he would not rest until he found his family. But alas, even with the adrenaline pumping and the rage boiling inside him, it all caught up to his mind and his body, causing a massive shut-down of his faculties. If he had been in top physical and mental condition, the likelihood of that happening was nil.

Sean is only a few miles from Rosenstein's home, on the corner where the town limits of Evanston abut the northern boundaries of Chicago. Sean obtained a small satchel after picking up his makeover supplies this morning and he checks the contents once more. He still has Kaley's face camouflage, the infrared binoculars, two knives, a compass, a canteen, rope, and a couple of road flares. He accidentally left the .22 in the kitchen of Rosenstein's home in his haste to flee before the police arrived, a piece of evidence that Sean wonders if they can trace back to Kaley. He'll have to worry about that later.

At the corner, Sean sees a Chicago Transit Authority bus making its way towards the stop, where several people mill about.

What do you know, it's going my way, Sean thinks. Finally, something is.

Sean throws on a pair of shades, pulls out fare money, and trots to the bus stop. The bus screeches to a stop and he hops aboard with the other passengers, taking a seat on the nearly empty bus near the back. He again starts to think of his family, but quickly tries to suppress the morbid thoughts bouncing around inside his head.

He tries to think about something else instead, and for the time being, he accomplishes this. Over and over again, Sean reassures himself that he is going to find out what happened to his family, and when he determines who is responsible, he is going to make sure they wish they had never been born. Sean, for the first time in a long time, allows himself to feel better for the moment.

Around forty-five minutes later, Sean enters the DePaul student library and heads straight up a flight of stairs. The place is practically empty the day after the Fourth of July holiday, and it is apparent many people do not feel like studying after the events of last night. Similar to when 9/11 occurred, people confine themselves to their homes, where it is safe, glued to the constant and repetitive news coverage on TV.

Sean feels like he is on automatic now, having walked this same path so many times before when he was a student. He arrives on the second floor and swings to the left, down a long, narrow hallway. He comes to a section separate from the endless rows and rows of books that occupy the floor.

The section is marked, "REFERENCE and CLASS READINGS." The section contains materials that certain professors use in class besides the standard textbooks, as a type of supplement to the primary readings. These may include booklets, research papers, and compilations of articles written by veteran members of academia and specialists in their particular field.

Sean approaches the desk, where a young woman sits tapping away at a computer, looking equally bored and irritated at the same time.

Sean, with the most disarming voice in his repertoire, says, "Excuse me, miss, can you see if you have this item in?" Sean slips her a piece of paper with the sequence of numbers and letters that were etched on

Rosenstein's wall.

The woman lets out an exasperated sigh, as if Sean interrupted her in her attempt to find a new energy source for the planet, and she turns to him. She is somewhat taken aback at his appearance, and Sean nearly forgets that he does not really look the part of the go-get-'em college student.

Without looking down at the paper, she asks rather haughtily, "Are you a student here?"

Sean fumbles for a second, "Well, um, see, I used to-"

"Oh my god," the woman says slowly, her eyes wide with fright.

Sean's heart bounds into his throat, and he is a New York second away from booking for the exit when the woman grabs his arm and pulls him towards her.

"Professor O'Connell, do you remember me?" she asks.

Sean's mind races through the possibilities, but nothing comes to him. Unless she used to be a-

"I used to be a student of yours," she finishes his thought. "Freshman year, International Conspiracies and Nuances of Government. Oh my god, that was, like, six years ago, I'm sure you don't remember me-"

"Anita, right?" Sean asks.

Thank God for a photographic memory, he thinks.

"I don't remember your last-"

"Gladstone. I cannot believe you remember me, that's amazing." Anita begins to gush, "Oh, I loved that course. I wanted to take more of your classes, but it wasn't my major, you know?"

"I appreciate that, Anita. Listen, I was wondering if you could do me a favor."

As if Sean is not even talking, Anita continues, "I'm in grad school now, it's such a drag. All it is is reading and writing, and then more reading and writing. But I'll be done by next semester."

Sean takes her hands in his to get her attention, and says gently but forcefully, "Listen, Anita, I need something from back there." He points behind her.

"Oh, no problem, Professor, I'm sorry, I'm just rambling on, aren't I?"

"No, not a bit," he reassures her. "Here, this is the reference number," sliding the piece of paper towards her.

"I think I know what you're looking for," Anita says, not bothering to look at the paper as she hops off her chair.

She gives him a sly smile, while at the same time Sean appears utterly confused.

She giggles flirtatiously, "Did anyone ever tell you that you look adorable when you don't know what's going on? I love the hair, by the way, it fits you."

Sean begins to blush.

"I'm out of here in about a half-hour, maybe you feel like grabbing a drink?" she inquires.

"Well, Anita, I'm kind of in a hurry and…"

Sean points to his wedding band.

"Oh," she says, clearly disappointed. "I guess it wasn't meant to be then, huh?" she remarks good-naturedly.

"Guess not. Maybe in the next life," he says.

"Yeah, maybe," she says coyly. From underneath the counter, she grabs a half-inch thick black booklet with a white band that runs the circumference. It looks almost like a seal. A small, white sticker on the upper left corner of the booklet has the exact sequence of numbers and letters that was on Rosenstein's wall.

"But how did you know-" Sean begins, mystified.

"Dr. Rosenstein dropped it off for you, he said you might be looking for it," she says casually.

Now it is Sean's turn to reach out and grab her arm. "Dr. Rosenstein?" he exclaims. "You saw him? Here? When, when did you see him?" Sean asks desperately.

Anita suddenly looks frightened and Sean instantly catches himself. "I'm sorry, Anita, I . . just haven't seen him for so long, and I really need to talk to him," Sean says, trying to sound calm and simultaneously reassure her that he is perfectly sane. "It's kind of urgent," he adds.

Anita looks at him like he has turned into a circus freak right in front of her eyes. "This was a few days ago, Professor."

"Please, call me Sean," he says gently.

This seems to put her slightly at ease. "Oh, okay . . Sean."

"So this was a few days ago?" Sean coaxes.

"Yeah," she confirms, "he said you might need this or something like that."

Sean looks deep into her eyes and says, "Anita, this is very important. What exactly did Dr. Rosenstein say?"

Anita thinks for a moment and finally responds, "He said this will point you in the right direction, and to make sure you read it from front to back."

"Was that it?" Sean asks.

"Yeah," she nods. "He didn't stick around very long, he dropped this off and then he left. He said the booklet was to be given only to you and no one else. He was pretty insistent on that, I remember."

"And that was it?" Sean asks, desperate for more information.

"Well, to be honest, Sean, he looked worn out," she states, concern in her voice.

"He didn't look good?" Sean asks.

"No, he seemed real nervous, kept looking around, even kind of paranoid. Usually when he stops by, we talk for a few minutes, he hangs out, but not this time. He said he had an important meeting, and now I remember, cause this was weird."

"What?" Sean presses.

Anita stares off into the distance, trying to recollect. "He wished me good luck and said, 'God bless,' like he was leaving somewhere."

Maybe he was, Sean thinks. *But where? The same place my family went?*

"Sean . . you okay? Sean? I'm not in med school, so you can't drop on-"

"Anita, listen," Sean interrupts, as he picks up the booklet, "I need to take this, alright?"

Anita shrugs her shoulders, "Sure, Sean, it's all yours."

"Thanks, Anita. And I need one more favor from you, if you don't mind?"

"Shoot," she replies obligingly.

"You never saw me here today, okay? I never came by here and we never talked. Don't mention our little chat with any friends, nothing. I know that sounds really strange, but believe me, it's for the best. Okay?" he asks hopefully.

Anita sits down in her chair, focuses indifferently on the computer screen, and begins typing again. "Talked to who?"

Sean smiles, pats her hand, and says, "Thanks, Anita, you're the best. Take care of yourself."

Sean starts to exit the same way he arrived when Anita calls out.

"Hey, Professor?"

Sean turns around. Anita points to her ring finger, "Call me if things don't work out."

Sean nods, hoping more than anything in the world that Anita, God bless her, would never see that wish come true.

FOURTEEN

Holland, Michigan – Windmill Airfield

As the jet slowly taxies down the runway, Augie gently prods the general awake.

"Sir, take a look at this," Augie says urgently.

Parker awakens with a start and is alert within seconds, having honed his skills at sleeping in short intervals, which has been a constant of his entire adult life. The ability to arise from REM sleep, digest your immediate surroundings, and decide a course of action within moments is a skill that cannot be taught. It takes years of practice, and to be able to do it effectively could mean the difference between life and death. Parker likes to think he has mastered the art of it, but with advancing age and the tendency to never receive a good night's rest anymore, it remains an endless challenge.

Parker quickly notes that the sun is slowly approaching the western horizon, the plane is taxiing to a stop, and Private Anderson is staring ahead of him as Augie motions toward the television screen. Augie turns up the volume.

A CNN TV anchorman speaks in a clear, deliberate manner:

". . . Once again, 'The Sword of Allah' has recently claimed credit for the attack on the American people that occurred less than twenty-four hours ago. Government sources have received several previous claims for the attack, but each of those were dismissed, either because the group claiming credit was not considered a legitimate threat, or the group could not furnish specifics about the attack that have yet to be made public. But, a source close to CNN has informed us that 'The Sword of Allah' has provided enough specifics regarding the attack that the government has begun to take the claim very seriously.

"Our source cannot disclose the exact specifics that were provided by the group, but, under the condition of anonymity, he allowed us to quote him as saying, 'It appears now with almost one-hundred percent certainty that 'The Sword' perpetrated this cowardly act on the American people,' end quote.

"We go live now to the President flying somewhere over the continental United States, in Air Force One, who wishes to deliver a brief message to the American people."

The anchor's face is replaced by a headshot of the President as the steady drone of the plane's engines can be heard in the background. A stern look occupies the President's face, and he speaks in a forceful, yet hushed tone.

"My fellow Americans, it appears with utmost certainty, and after speaking to several of my closest advisors and top military personnel, that we have discerned who has committed this atrocity against our fellow countrymen and women. We cannot begin to understand their reasons, nor can we determine their manner of thinking when it comes to an act of this nature. They say it is for their religion, but I know of no god who would condone such a violent act against innocent people.

"What it comes down to is this: the hatred of one group of people by another group of people. I would venture to say that this hatred stems from envy and jealousy, and the abhorrence of everything that is good and decent in our society. They do not understand us as a people, and this misunderstanding breeds distrust and fear, and eventually, loathing."

The President pauses for a moment before continuing. When he does resume, a look of deadly conviction crosses his face.

"I wanted to make a brief statement to the citizens of this great country, and inform you, as well as our enemies, who I pray are listening, that this extremely spineless attack will not go unpunished. You will be hunted down to the ends of the earth, you will be flushed from your shelters, and you will be dragged into the light of day and revealed to the rest of the world for the shameful cowards that you are. I personally guarantee that we will never stop, we will never tire until we find every last one of you, and bring you to justice for the crime you have committed. Your day is coming, and it will be sooner than you think.

"As my colleague from Arizona said after September 11th, 'I say to our enemies that we are coming, God may show you mercy, we will not.' We have a lot of work to do, so let us continue to go about our daily lives remembering . ."

Parker turns to Augie and asks, "What took 'The Sword' so long, Augie?"

"My exact same thought, General," Augie replies.

"We need to get to the bottom of this A.S.A.P. before the President starts World War III," Parker warns.

"Right on, sir," Augie concurs.

They turn back to the TV as the President concludes his remarks.

"God bless you, God bless America, and may God bless the souls of our fallen citizens. Take care of each other, America."

*   *   *

Sean finds a secluded coffeehouse several blocks from the DePaul campus and sits down in the corner. He orders a black coffee from the waitress and scans the interior of the establishment to ensure no one is paying him any special attention. Only three other people occupy the coffeehouse, and they all appear engrossed in what they are reading or studying. There are few students around with the Independence Day holiday, and for those that are, the temptations of the city's bars and taverns are likely far too great to pass up on this gorgeous summer night. It is just the type of distraction people need at a time like this, and Sean does not blame them one iota.

Sean removes his sunglasses and eyes the booklet in front of him. He runs his fingers over the black surface as if trying to discern what awaits him inside. His stomach is churning with butterflies, nervous whether the booklet holds the answers that he seeks. His level of anxiety and worry exponentially increases each time he thinks he might be pinning too much hope on it. Sean can hardly bear the thought that his expectations could be dashed upon opening the mysterious little booklet and finding nothing that guides him in the right direction. He almost does not want to open it.

Almost.

He patiently waits for the waitress to return with his coffee before opening the booklet, not wanting anyone to catch even a glimpse of something they are not supposed to see or read, especially an overly curious waitress.

Sean thanks the woman and quickly takes a sip – steaming hot and strong, just the way he likes it. He looks at the indistinguishable cover once more, takes a deep breath, and rips off the white band that rings the booklet.

He opens it to find a small folded note attached to the first page, which is blank. He once again glances around before opening the note, and he reads:

> *Sean – If you're reading this, then Murdoch got to you and pointed you in the right direction. It also means that you and your family are out of harm's way, for now. I am so truly sorry they were in any danger to begin with, and though you probably do not understand what is going on, everything will be explained shortly. The mother of all conspiracies has begun, and I want you to witness it firsthand. This will get you started on the right path – make sure you read from COVER to COVER. I will find you along the way. There is so much I need to tell you.*
>
> *Good luck, and I'll see you soon.*
> *-Al*

Is he crazy? He certainly does not feel his family is safe given he has no idea where they are.

And Murdoch? Rosenstein's friend at Hope College?

This is the only Murdoch Sean knows, but he had not spoken to Professor Murdoch in over a week. Sean tries to recall every minute detail of that conversation, but he does not believe Murdoch pointed him in any direction last time they spoke.

Most importantly, why is Rosenstein apologizing for the danger he feels he put my family in? How could he be responsible?

The "mother of all conspiracies," Rosenstein wrote, which he wants Sean to witness firsthand.

And what is this booklet supposed to tell me exactly? How will Rosenstein find me along the way? And what will be revealed once he does find me?

Questions swirl around inside his head as he tries to decipher a greater meaning from the cryptic note. He turns the note over, not sure what he is expecting to find since he already knows it is blank. Still, he wants answers *now*, not later.

Sean flips the first blank page of the booklet and sees a white page with a title centered in the middle, along with a year recorded at the bottom of the page:

PREPARED: 1951

In the center of the page is the last thing Sean expects to see, a title that, upon reading, would cause the average person to laugh at, to mock, or to casually dismiss. It seems so utterly preposterous, and yet, the formal title lends itself a seriousness that may not be so easily dismissed.

Still, Sean feels that a very elaborate joke has been played on him, with Rosenstein acting as the ringleader. Now that the "cat is out of the bag," everyone can come clean.

It reads:

THE POSSIBILITY OF AN ALIEN INVASION & COLONIZATION EFFORT and MANKIND'S PRESENT LEVEL OF RESISTANCE

Underneath the bold title are the authors' names written in a smaller type:

Dr. Albert Rosenstein

Dr. R. Jonas Abraham

What the hell? Sean thinks. *The old man from the beach I saw only a couple minutes prior to the mass disappearance?*

Sean first recalls the man's eyes and their piercing stare, and the chill it sent down his spine. He sees those eyes flash in his head and suddenly, Sean feels as if those same eyes are watching him now. He quickly looks up, around the coffeehouse, and then outside towards the street, half-expecting to see Abraham, fixing him with that emotionless stare. No one outside, however, seems to be paying him any mind, let alone looking his way.

Just being paranoid, Sean thinks. *But still . . .*

The same old man whose life has been an enigma to the public and press, whose life has been a constant source of speculation, rumors, gossip, and innuendo, whose life has been surrounded by intrigue and mystery since as far back as anyone can remember. The same old man who just happened to be the last person Sean noticed minutes prior to the mass disappearance. And now, Sean sits before what appears to be a research paper the man co-authored with his mentor and friend. Sean does not believe in coincidences, hardly surprising considering his line of work and his methods of teaching.

But why the hell was Rosenstein collaborating with Jonas Abraham on a piece of research that seemed contrary to both men's personalities?

Rosenstein is a liberal thinker, Sean would concede that, a free spirit whose openness to new ideas and unusual concepts is an inherent trait of his character. But Rosenstein also tends to be practical as well, fiercely realistic, and not prone to wild leanings of the imagination or things that seem too fantastic to even consider. Namely, alien invasions. True, Rosenstein believes in his share of conspiracy theories and shady government cover-ups, but intrinsic to his nature, even the most absurd ideas are couched in some type of factual evidence, however roundabout and stretched the conclusions might seem.

The lone actual fact that has been gleaned from the myth of Jonas Abraham amid all the speculative stories that engulf the man is that he appears conservative, with both his fortune and in his personality. The press naturally spins this conservatism to translate to pragmatism and practicality, and several journalists, after being rebuffed for an interview, went so far as to frame the man as some kind of radical fundamentalist, leaning strongly to the right in his views. Whether accurate or not, to Sean these characteristics do not sound like the traits of a man who believes in things as outlandish as flying saucers and alien creatures.

Still, one never knows . . .

The booklet was written nearly sixty years ago, and with emerging technology in the area of space travel, as well as the approaching race to the moon against the Soviets, contemplation of an alien species or civilization may have begun to enter the consciousness of top leaders within the government. A Cold War had begun, and America's enemies were not just the Soviets, North Koreans, and Chinese, but anyone not allied with the United States, including beings yet to be heard from or seen. All potential enemies needed to be considered, and perhaps Rosenstein and Abraham's research conducted over a half-century ago was done to serve that exact purpose.

Sean turns the page and begins reading the opening paragraphs, confirming what he had suspected, and yet it still seems rather startling that such a report was ever written, let alone necessary.

The first question any man, be it a politician, a five-star general, or the average working man, has upon the discovery that alien life does exist in the universe, is actually two-fold:

First, are they friendly? And second, if they are not, can humanity destroy them?

While the former has yet to be fully answered, the latter question is the one that occupies the minds of our government's top military men today, and it is this question that forms the basis of the following research.

Can humanity withstand an alien invasion and possible colonization effort in its current state of progress?

There is little doubt that within the last several years, with the development of the atomic bomb, current experiments with the hydrogen bomb, or thermonuclear bomb, more sophisticated models of stealth aircraft being constructed, an increasing emphasis on the military-industrial complex, and spending on vastly superior weaponry compared with the rest of the world, the United States of America would seem poised to defend its sovereignty from any and all invaders, human or otherwise.

But what about other nations on the planet? Do they have the necessary capabilities to thwart an alien attack? Would it be possible for American forces to assist other nations around the globe in the event of a worldwide attack from alien aggressors? And then, in the most dire scenario, what if the United States cannot counter an invasion? To contemplate complete annihilation as a very real possibility is not an underestimation at all, in these researchers' minds.

Sean rereads this last line and it gives him the chills to think that Dr. Rosenstein had such a calamitous view of what the future might hold for mankind. Rosenstein has always appeared to be a hopeful man who foresees nothing but infinite possibilities for the human race, never one to dwell on the more apocalyptic situations that have been philosophized and theorized by man since he (and she) began to contemplate such heady matters. Maybe Sean had not looked deeper into what kind of man Rosenstein truly was, but instead saw only the energy and vitality the man consistently brought to their frequent discussions, the unflagging optimism that the man seemed to always possess.

Sean continues reading.

With this debate arises several questions: What technology does the enemy possess? What might they have that humanity does not? And what type of physical specimens are they? Are they similar to human beings in their strengths and vulnerabilities? Do they bleed as us?

With the evidence we have procured from study and observation, it becomes fairly obvious, through even the most cursory examination, that our extraterrestrial counterparts are far more advanced than we could have imagined.

While it is difficult to determine if their society has advanced at a more rapid pace than ours, or rather their society has been in existence longer than mankind's, to determine which is the more likely scenario seems, on the surface, to be an irrelevant question, and one, whose answer, compounds its triviality.

On the contrary, the answer should be a vital part of any research conducted on this topic.

On the one hand, if the alien society has been in existence longer than mankind, then it raises some troubling questions for the theologian and scientist alike:

If God created Man, who or what created Alien?

Or, from the opposite viewpoint, if Man descended from the ape, where does the alien life form stand on the evolutionary ladder?

In terms of religion, mass hysteria could ensue upon the discovery that alien life existed before humanity. For if God created Man, and not the other way around, when did God create alien life? And did God create alien life in his own image, rather than in mankind's? Skepticism and doubt would prevail on a global level and the majority of people on Earth [four-fifths of the people on this planet believe in some form of higher being] would denounce their religions and topple one of the fundamental institutions of society.

From a scientific perspective, the questions raised are from an evolutionary standpoint, and the inevitable one that will arise is this: Is it plausible, since alien life existed before Man, that we are actually evolutionary products of an alien species? That our actual bloodline relatives can be traced not to the apes, but rather to alien life instead?

On the other hand, the scenario that is actually more frightening to behold is one in which the alien society has existed for approximately the same period of time as ours, but has advanced at a far more productive and industrious rate. This would lead one to conclude that the alien being is smarter, more imaginative, and better equipped to conquer potential enemies than humanity. Applying basic Darwinian principles, "Only the strong shall survive," humanity finds itself, for the first time on this planet, cognitively inferior to another species, and therefore, more prone to extinction. For if our race cannot keep pace with that of a far more technologically-advanced species, what is to stand in their way if eliminating us is one of their goals and in fact, is their sole intention?

The various questions that arise from these arguments can be overwhelming and far too complex for the sake of our research here. Additionally, the purpose of this project is from a strictly scientific point of view, not a sojourn into the philosophy of the beginnings of the universe and, ultimately, Man. Therefore, we must discuss the actual logistics and possibility of an alien invasion, and what chance we have to resist and defeat the aggressors.

For the next twenty pages, Sean reads in amazement the careful detail and thought process that Rosenstein and Abraham devoted to the research topic.

There are various scenarios of potential methods by which the alien species will attack. There is speculation that the largest metropolitan areas of the world will be targeted first, and the invasion will subsequently spread to outlying rural and suburban areas. Another scenario posits that the United States and the Soviet Union will likely be the first countries invaded given that they are the strongest nations in terms of military might. Countermoves and counterattacks are proposed, positioning of troops are offered, and areas where reinforcements should be solidified. There are even suggestions for how communication lines can be maintained and a functioning working government can be sustained in the event that the American executive branch is destroyed.

There are schematics, diagrams, and illustrations of enemy weaponry and ships, contrasting in sharp detail with that of humanity's. There is speculation regarding the extraterrestrials' future technological advances.

Sean takes special notice of a small, baton-shaped weapon that is sketched in the booklet. It appears nearly identical to the weapon the man was wielding in Rosenstein's kitchen only hours before. Which immediately begs the question of the man at Rosenstein's house:

Was it a man, or something else entirely?

Abraham and Rosenstein also noted that because no known life exists in the Milky Way galaxy beyond that found on Earth, the alien beings must have traveled from a great distance and at extremely intense speeds. Assuming that their life span is similar to a human being's, which Abraham and Rosenstein never confirm, they would need to travel at speeds intolerable for a human to endure in order to reach Earth from another galaxy without dying from old age as a result of the journey. Therefore, their body type must be highly conducive to space travel and thus, a vastly superior structure when compared to a human body.

Indeed, Abraham and Rosenstein make references to the physical aspects of these extraterrestrials: words like "indestructible" and phrases like "not susceptible to man's conventional weapons" crop up in the report, which suggest to Sean that everything that has been detailed in this research is not mere speculation. Abraham and Rosenstein were not dealing in opinions and guesswork, but rather they must have had an actual template to study from.

They wrote, *"With the evidence we have procured from study and observation."*

This statement certainly implies that the United States government was in possession of various extraterrestrial objects, namely an alien weapon and/or spacecraft. More importantly, they may have captured actual beings from another world. While Abraham and Rosenstein use specific details when outlining their research and conclusions, they seem to remain purposely vague as to where they are receiving their information.

But why would Abraham and Rosenstein fail to cite the evidence that expounded their conclusions?

This is a necessary and indeed, required part of any research paper that puts forth certain theories and hypotheses. Referring to established and widely-known evidence helps the reader place a certain level of validity in the conclusions of the authors of the report. A common framework of reference certainly assists the reader to trust the researchers' methodology in how they approach their subject and examine the facts before them.

Sean can think of only two reasons why Rosenstein and Abraham fail to cite their specific evidence. First, the report was prepared on behalf of individuals who were fully aware of the "evidence" the two men were referring to, and no further explanation was necessary; and secondly, they were protecting against the chance that the report would accidentally be seen by a person outside the scope of those authorized to read it. The disclosure of classified government information on the topic of extraterrestrials today would certainly cause a stir, so Sean can imagine the panic it may have caused back in the 1950s.

Still, it is vexing to read the report and remain in the dark about what, or possibly *who,* Abraham and Rosenstein are referring to.

Sean notes one final thought at the end of the paper:

Thus, once again, we arrive back at our topic question: Can mankind withstand an alien invasion and possible colonization effort? Can we survive a full-scale attack? In our shared opinion, and with great reluctance and apprehension, we must answer these questions with a resounding "No" on both counts. It is with the utmost trepidation that we report after several years of study of our extraterrestrial neighbors-

There it is again, Sean thinks.

-that their technology is far beyond the reach of humanity at the present time. We speculate that we are at least fifty years, if not an entire century away from climbing towards a similar level of advancement for human civilization. Then, the question becomes: How far along will our alien foes be?

Sean reads this last sentence with a feeling of dread that spreads like wildfire throughout his body. He cannot believe this is what Rosenstein intended for him to find. For what possible reason? Did the events at Tamawaca have something to do with what was written on these pages? They almost certainly did, but now Sean seems more confused than ever.

What is the next step?

Sean thought the booklet would lend a clue to the whereabouts of his family, but instead, his greatest fear concerning it has been realized. It has only further muddled the answer to the question of where his family is. Still, Rosenstein had meant for Sean to find it, and therefore, it must serve a definitive purpose.

But what goddammit? What are you trying to tell me, Al?

Sean stares at the last page when he notices there is one more page to the booklet. The page is blank, but Sean moves his hand over the back portion of the booklet to find a strange indentation. Sean turns the back of the booklet to see nothing but the black of the back cover. Sean glides his hand over the booklet again and this time, he knows he is not imagining it. He looks closer and notices that there, about the size of a hand, is a faintly discolored black patch that sticks up about a quarter inch from the surface of the booklet.

"Make sure you read from COVER to COVER," Rosenstein's note read.

Sean scratches and claws at the patch, and slowly, tiny black pieces begin to peel away. A pile of it forms as if Sean is trying his luck on a scratch-and-win lottery card, which essentially he is, and he sweeps the pile to the side and blows the remnants on the floor. In this snug hiding spot at the back of the booklet is a small, clear, plastic bag. Sean looks around the coffeehouse to find the establishment empty and quiet as a tomb, with the waitress no longer in sight.

He looks back down at the booklet and picks up the plastic bag. He unfurls it to reveal, written in large, green block letters:

WASHINGTON APPLES

There is a drawing of a few scattered apples, along with a short but sweet description at the bottom of the bag:

DELICIOUS!

What the hell is going on here?

In tiny black letters at the bottom of the bag is written: SPOKANE, WA.

Is this the direction Rosenstein is guiding me? Am I supposed to go to Spokane, Washington? Is that where my family is?

Sean does not know exactly how far Spokane is from here, but he knows that it is a long haul. If he wants to unravel this mystery, however, Spokane appears to be his destination. For Sean, he simply hopes that it is the place where he will find his family.

FIFTEEN

Port Sheldon, Michigan

Navy First Class Gunner Michael Eisley, retired, always enjoyed the sunset. It occasionally occurred to him how many a human being can possibly witness in one's lifetime, but he had never bothered to do the calculations himself. Nevertheless, he thought it amazing how we oftentimes neglected to say goodbye each day to that wonderful energy source in the sky that keeps Earth from skipping off into the vacuum of space. He could completely understand why ancient people, such as the Babylonians, worshipped the sun, albeit for far different reasons than he does.

I guess we simply figure that the sun will be there tomorrow, just like it is every day, Eisley thinks.

But what if someday it isn't?

This is why Eisley pays homage to the old girl every chance he gets. Besides, he does not know how many more years he has left to watch her as she slowly sneaks over the horizon each day, especially with his diabetes and various other ailments. Every day seems to be a crapshoot, his body sometimes feeling all of its years and then some, but he still manages to continue plugging along. Since his retirement, his schedule has become wide open, and he tends to make it in time for the show. What a damn fine show it is, too.

Eisley's house sits on the shores of Lake Michigan, and when the sun's rays strike the lake at exactly the right spot, it casts an array of light shimmering off the surface, making for quite a beautiful sight. It is even more spectacular when the lake is calm and placid, with few or no boats stirring up the waters, as it is now. It appears almost like there are two suns, cut in half by a glass prism that reflects the light to all corners of the earth.

The lake has been calm for most of the day, with the majority of people staying close to home and not particularly in the mood for fishing or boating. Similar to the aftermath of 9/11, a feeling of shock, sadness, and anxiety consumed the nation once word of the terrorist attack at Tamawaca reached the ears of the American public. No one feels like doing much of anything, except watching the news reports and thinking about how precious life can be in this new era of global terrorism, where every nation and every person has been dealt a hand, even if they have no desire to play. It seems strange to Eisley how it takes traumatic and sudden events like the attack last night to grab the attention of most people, and to remind them that we are all mortal beings whose own lives are not infinite. The sun sets on everyone's life sooner or later, and it simply becomes a question of *when*.

Ah, fuck it, thinking too damn much.

Eisley takes a swig from his beer bottle. He knows he

has reached the border of sobriety when he begins using metaphors to describe the fragility of life.

He sits at the end of his dock, paying no mind to a fishing pole next to him that receives a tug every once in a while from a curious fish. To his right sits his 34-foot deep-sea fishing boat, and to his left is moored his 18-foot sailboat. No name occupies the fishing boat, which he once again reminds himself is bad luck, seemingly daring the seas to punish him for this transgression. A good 'ole Navy boy, no less, failing to name his boat, a lapse that would cause him endless grief from his fellow sailors. He would get around to naming it, sooner or later.

The sailboat is a different story. While the fishing boat is where he installs his latest "toys," the sailboat is his muse, his siren, a possession he prizes above all else. He takes her out only once a week in the summer, on what he dubs "special occasions." The freedom and joy these periodic jaunts produce is something he treasures and does not wish to spoil through overindulgence. The sailboat is special to him because he views it as a Navy man would: a chance to conquer the sea. While these journeys are rarely dangerous, there is something electrifying about being alone in the middle of the sea, utilizing nature to power your vessel while at the same time fighting against the very elements that can capsize you in a heartbeat.

On the rear of the sailboat, in wavy, uneven letters, is written:

DEPTH CHARGE
Port Sheldon, MI

Eisley sailed this morning in an attempt to occupy his mind with a slight diversion, but it was of little help. Tamawaca Beach is close to Port Sheldon, and he even considered taking a trip to the site to determine if he could help, but the television reports warned all civilians to stay away because of a possible contamination alert. Although he had heard nothing else on TV concerning any type of lethal pathogen or biological weapon that had been released at the site. However, the news reports made it abundantly clear that there are no survivors and therefore, no need for blood or plasma donations.

Giving blood, however, is not what Eisley has in mind. He has information. He saw something strange while on his fishing boat a couple nights ago, and the more he thinks about it, the more he believes the chance of it being a random event unrelated to the attack does not seem likely.

What the hell had it been doing out there?

Maybe his eyes or the patchy fog that night were playing tricks on him, or maybe he dozed off and simply imagined it. Or maybe Eisley is trying to manufacture a plausible excuse for what he saw because he still cannot believe it himself. Now, however, it seemed almost like a... premonition.

Eisley unwraps one of the cheap cigars he buys at his local grocer and the lone vice he allows himself in a given day. He takes another swig of beer and thinks, *Well, make it two vices.*

But what the hell, he is retired. Drinking your brains out as you slowly coast into senility is part of the territory, and it is a territory that he intends to fully immerse himself in.

After his active duty ended, Eisley worked in military intelligence for years, and he still keeps in close contact with many of his former colleagues, several of whom remain employed in the same capacity. Curiously, just before the Fourth of July weekend, he spoke to one of his former colleagues, who happened to mention that nothing interesting had been received lately. No alerts, no threats, no juicy intelligence for the upcoming holiday. This was somewhat surprising given that since 9/11, around every major American holiday many of the intelligence agencies are inundated with large amounts of information or data suggesting specific cities or targets. Eisley's friend jokingly suggested that maybe the bad guys are taking the holiday off as well. Needless to say, Eisley is certain his friend's thinking has altered dramatically since the events of last night.

Although Eisley continues to maintain ties with his contacts in the intel business, the calls seem to be coming less and less frequent. Whether this has to do with Eisley getting on in years and they question his value as a prime source of information, or whether his colleagues simply do not want to bother him during his retirement, Eisley does not know and does not care to dwell on what the specific reason might be. Once in a great while though, a former colleague may receive a piece of cryptic intelligence and will ask Eisley his opinion or thoughts on the matter. Eisley, however, no longer holds a top secret (TS) clearance in the government, which previously allowed him access to most types of highly classified documents and files.

The military's security ratings system starts at the bottom of the ladder with "confidential," followed by "secret," and finally, "top secret." The military also uses a clearance for "special intelligence (SI)," which tends to be highly specialized and was a clearance that Eisley also held for some time.

Nevertheless, Eisley still receives questions from former colleagues who may be in a jam. Apparently, they trust him enough to know that what is discussed between them is in no jeopardy of being compromised. And that is something Eisley does not deviate from, ever.

Eisley rises from his chair as the last remaining rays of light begin to fade into twilight and the stars prepare to take center stage. He grabs his beer and with his cigar dangling from his mouth, ambles down the dock, onto the small patch of grass that can loosely be called a backyard, and up a short flight of stairs that lead into the house.

He goes directly to the refrigerator for another cold one.

Retirement sure is grand, he thinks, as Eisley twists off the bottle cap.

And then, he freezes.

Suddenly, his heart starts thumping and his instincts tell him that something is out of place. It takes him no more than a few seconds to pinpoint it, and when he does, he knows his options are severely limited. He remains calm and still, but he is an old man now, and the chances of outrunning or physically matching a younger adversary are slim. At the very least though, he can die with the satisfaction that they did not get the drop on him.

His voice cuts through the silence of the house, "If you're going to kill me, why don't you get it over with? Sun's already set and I ain't got all fucking night."

"How did you know?" a muffled voice behind him responds.

"Are you kidding? I can smell the sweat dripping off you. You got no showers where you come from?" he says sarcastically, still trying to display a semblance of bravado.

"Good one, old man," the muffled man responds. "You can turn around now."

Eisley slowly turns around, expecting a muzzle flash or a blackjack across the head, but nothing comes. No lights are on and the house is bathed in shadows, with only a few dimples of light escaping through the blinds.

A figure stands a few feet in front of him in the kitchen doorway. The figure finally comes into view, snapping a light on to announce his entrance.

Eisley's eyes nearly pop out of his head as he sighs heavily with relief.

"Jay-sus, Jon, you almost gave me a fucking heart attack," Eisley says as he puts a hand over his chest, as if this might slow his heartbeat.

Kaley smiles, the two men look at each other a moment, and then briefly embrace.

Eisley laughs and slaps him gently on the face.

"Well, my boy," Eisley says. "What's wrong with you? Trying to put your uncle in an early grave like that. You should be ashamed of yourself."

"Sorry about that, Mike, I didn't want to sneak up on you out there. You just looked so damn peaceful," Kaley says, motioning towards the lake. "You enjoyed your sunset, I take it?"

"Sure as hell did," Eisley indignantly retorts.

"So is that how you put up a fight in your own home? You tell me I fucking stink?" Kaley needles him.

"You do stink," Eisley replies.

Kaley motions around the kitchen, "I thought at least you'd have that Glock taped to the bottom of a cabinet in here. You going to throw your beer at me instead?"

Eisley grins and reaches past Kaley to the hood over the stove. Kaley hears a slight tearing sound as Eisley removes an object from the bottom of the hood and brings it up to the light to reveal a Glock, cocked and ready to go.

Eisley explains, "I always thought someone would surprise me when I was cooking and not reaching for a beer."

"Why? You drink a lot more than you cook, you should be playing the odds," Kaley says, only half-jokingly.

"I see you still have your mom's sense of humor," Mike says, "she couldn't crack a smile in a room full of clowns either."

"Are you saying you're a clown?" Kaley asks.

"Smartass," Eisley mutters, shaking his head.

He takes a long look at Kaley and says, "Well, as long as we're on the subject, and you've let yourself in, can I get you a beer?" he asks.

"Maybe one over dinner," he replies.

Kaley's tone changes only slightly, but enough to notice. "But unfortunately, this isn't a social visit, Mike. I need your help."

Eisley's voice also takes on a more serious tone, "Shoot, kid."

"I'll tell you all about it over dinner, but first, I got to wash this stench off." He gives his uncle a smirk, "Apparently, it's giving me away."

* * *

Second Lieutenant Julianna Dawson knew right off the bat that Hutchinson had given her a shit assignment. Well, not necessarily a shit assignment, but a shit for an assignment. That shit being one Colonel Malcolm Fizer.

Dawson arrived at Evans barely an hour ago and instantly felt that the welcome mat had not been rolled out for her and her companions, a pair of information technology specialists specifically assigned from General Theodore Parker's command. From what Dawson gathered from the techs, they are responsible for investigating the satellite coverage of last night's attack, which apparently was less than impressive. As for Dawson, she is obviously aware the general did not personally request her to act as a liaison, let alone knows who she is, but she'll focus on the fact General Hutchinson thinks enough of her to give her this assignment. The jury is still out on whether this is a good thing or a bad thing. Either way, if the chain of command here means answering and reporting to General Parker, something very serious and important is afoot.

Dawson enlisted in the Army primarily as a way to defy her parents. A rebellious teenager and constant disappointment to her folks, she practically thrived on making their lives miserable. She had no desire to be like her mom, a housewife content in making dinner for her breadwinning man and the ultimate caretaker of the children and the home. Dawson's father still seems trapped in a 1950s time warp that divides the familial responsibilities on a domestic/non-domestic basis.

Originally, the plan was to complete basic training simply to show her parents that she could, and then find a top job in the civilian world. Well, plans tend to change when you least expect them to.

She loves the Army and everything it has to offer: the structure, the discipline, the honor. Besides having to constantly deal with the underlying prejudices against a woman in a man's army, she believes she can overcome all the obstacles and become the first female five-star general in the United States Army. A lofty goal, she would be the first to admit, but setting one's sights higher than what other people think possible is not only inherent to her personality, but part of her rebellious attitude that still spits in the face of convention.

Of course, five-star generals typically need serious and extensive combat experience, a requisite Dawson invariably is lacking. Here she is instead, working as a "special liaison" to General Parker, an assignment she foresees having little to no chance of producing any action, much less excitement.

Still, it could be worse. General Parker is one of the highest-ranking officers in all branches of the military, and to produce a good showing for him would certainly be beneficial to further her ambitious career plans. Then again, she does not know how much cooperation she will receive from Colonel Fizer, and thus far, the prospects have not been promising.

To say the reception had been icy would be a vast understatement. Fizer seemed downright hostile when they arrived. However, since Dawson and her cohorts are under the direct command of General Parker, Fizer continues to maintain a certain level of professionalism. Dawson noted that Fizer seems to be aware how far he can push the envelope, and he barely remains within the boundaries from openly impeding an investigation led by a superior officer.

Fizer personally escorted the computer techs, Daley and Harrison, to the command center to examine the programming of the satellites that fall under Evans' jurisdiction, an act Dawson initially thought was Fizer simply being helpful. On closer inspection, however, Dawson received the distinct impression Fizer was sizing up the IT specialists, trying to determine exactly what they are after and more importantly, if they would find what they are looking for. Dawson has a feeling that Fizer's concern rests primarily with the chance that something might be found that could potentially embarrass him or show an error in judgment in his command.

Dawson's hunch was confirmed when Fizer then went to nearly extreme lengths to explain that none of the other personnel at the base was able to find anything more regarding the attack, and furthermore, programming of the satellites is personally overseen by him. Therefore, there could obviously be no errors related to that, and he really did not see the purpose of an examination by *outsiders*, a term that had a perceptible tone of maliciousness behind it.

Just following orders, sir, they responded. Harrison explained that they need to reassure General Parker that there were no mistakes due to negligence or other human error.

Fizer nodded impatiently and mumbled something about the absurdity of it all and the waste of important human resources. He reluctantly left the techs to their own devices, and Dawson quickly followed in his wake. Fizer made it a point to walk a few steps ahead of her at all times, nonverbally expressing his displeasure with the sudden addition of a "shadow." He had spoken very little to her thus far, and when he did, it was not at all friendly or even particularly informative. His utter contempt at being assigned a "liaison" to monitor his command seemed to him to be not only undermining his authority, but downright insulting. Dawson wants to explain to him that she is only the messenger, but she is not even certain if this would be an accurate title.

Dawson had not been fully briefed on what her responsibilities are as a liaison, only that she is to periodically inform General Parker any new information Colonel Fizer has unearthed regarding the attacks. At least, that is what she thought she was supposed to be doing. Soon enough, though, it becomes apparent that her job is not at all what she initially believed it to be.

Dawson's purpose appears more covert than General Hutchinson had indicated. She realized that it is rather redundant for her to act as an intermediary between Colonel Fizer and General Parker. In actuality, her assignment is to shadow Fizer, keep an eye on him, report anything unusual, and above all else, ensure that the techs receive full cooperation. What Dawson deduced from this is that someone within the high command, likely General Parker, does not trust Fizer, and for whatever reason she was selected to see if that mistrust indeed seems warranted. Perhaps it does.

Within several minutes of meeting the colonel, Dawson detected a kind of nervous energy on the part of Fizer. At first she chalked this up simply to a character trait he possesses: a get-to-the-point bluntness, bordering on being downright rude. Not unusual for a man in his position, considering the stress level, but this is something entirely different. The colonel seems fidgety, attempting to hurry things along as if he is operating under a rigid schedule that must be followed.

Dawson looked behind the steely gray eyes and cold demeanor, and she saw something that lay hidden, a secret Fizer knows but is not sharing. It is a secret that definitely seems to have him rattled and maybe even...*scared?*

What's your story, Colonel? Dawson thinks.

She sits down at a desk directly outside the colonel's office and begins to review the log of last night's activity. While doing so, she occasionally glances through the doorway into the colonel's office, and what she sees is a man who looks like he could crack into a million pieces at any moment.

*   *   *

A hearty dinner and nearly two gallons of cold water were exactly what the doctor ordered, and what Kaley desperately needed. His uncle still knows his way around the barbecue, and the steak and halibut Kaley devoured were all the proof that one needed. While it was tempting to wash the food down with a couple of beers, it would not do him any favors in rehydrating after the long trip in the sweltering train car. Not to mention that he does not need alcohol impairing his judgment at a time like this, and especially for what he has planned tonight.

With more than a little hesitancy for his uncle's safety, Kaley related everything he had seen at Evans, the assassins sent to his home, Rushmore's disappearance, the fake car accident, and the first-class trip to Michigan on the freight train. Kaley was initially reluctant to involve Uncle Mike, but with a little coaxing and reassurances that he is a big boy who can take care of himself, and the threat of not delivering on dinner, Kaley described everything over their meal. Everything, that is, with the exception of the disc in his possession. Kaley does not want his uncle to have any knowledge of a secret disc in case he is ever asked about it somewhere down the road.

Kaley is not entirely certain what he has on the disc, only that it contradicts everything that has been reported regarding the attack. Still, he is not willing to give voice to outlandish theories and far-fetched conspiracies, at least not yet. After all, he is not Sean O'Connell.

Mike listened attentively as Kaley recounted the story to him, unable to even lift the fork to his mouth the entire time. Unlike his nephew, whose appetite never seems to sour, Mike could not even think about eating after hearing Kaley's story, his mind flashing back a couple nights ago to what he saw on the water.

Kaley puts down his fork with a satisfied sigh and takes a long pull from his water glass. He glances towards his uncle and does a double-take when he notices a strange look on the old man's face.

"Hey, Mike, I know it's unbelievable, but I haven't even got to what I need from you yet," Kaley says.

Mike shakes his head back and forth, as if shaking the cobwebs loose, and leans in towards his nephew, looking at him intently. "I think what you *need* to do is go to the press, get it out in the open, so they can't come after you. And I think what I *need* to do is tell you what I saw the other night cause, after being in my line of work for thirty years, you rarely start believing in coincidences."

This immediately grabs Kaley's attention, and now it is his turn to look closely at his uncle. "What'd you see, Mike?"

"First things first," Mike begins, "what about going to the media, the newspapers? I know you don't have any tangible proof, but you could at least tell your story and get the bloodhounds on the trail. You got anyone you know?"

"Well, yeah, I know a woman who works at the *Tribune*," Kaley acknowledges. "But that's not the point, Mike-"

Eisley slams his fist on the table, "Dammit, Jon, that is the point. You've got to get this shit out for the public to hear, cause right now you've got a huge bull's-eye on your back and-"

"Listen, Mike," Kaley interrupts, "they've already tried to kill me once, and right now I'm sure the back-up team is trying to locate me, if they haven't already."

Eisley suspiciously looks around, as if expecting a group of armed men to burst through the door and haul them both away.

Kaley continues, "I can't go to the press with what I got, Mike. I need something more, something concrete."

Kaley feels bad for lying to his uncle, but he does not need to tell him *everything*. Besides, he truly believes he needs something more, another piece of evidence to hang his hat on in addition to the disc.

"I'll tell you what I need from you, but first tell me what you saw," Kaley insists.

Eisley eyes Kaley for a few moments, considering whether to trust his nephew's judgment, unsure if the kid is making the right decision by not blowing the whistle immediately. Finally, he resigns himself to have faith and trust that Jon knows what he is doing.

Eisley puts down his fork and pushes away the plate, the mere thought of eating incomprehensible. He takes a deep breath and, as if about to tell the most important story of his life, he begins:

"I was tooling around on the lake two nights ago in my fishing boat, just kind of futzing around. Sometimes if I'm bored around here or just get a feeling for my sea legs, I'll spend a night or two out on the lake. Well, anyway, I was anchored a few feet offshore in this little deserted cove, off the main lake, where there are no cottages or houses. Really quiet and isolated, you know. It's a cove that ends in what I thought to be some kind of swamp, and then nothing but forest. Or so I thought.

"I was anchored no more than fifteen feet from shore, in probably twenty feet of water, just dozing out on deck, manning the fishing pole, when I woke up with a start. The water started getting a little choppy, not much, but enough to notice when a minute before it was dead calm. There was no wind and no other boats on the water, so right away I thought it was kind of strange. At first I thought it was some former 'friends' from the business, arriving to collect an old debt."

Kaley tries not to smirk at his uncle's flair for the dramatic. Here is a man who still lives in a world of deadly shadows and old alliances, even though he has been out of the game for several years now. Eisley does not notice his nephew and continues.

"I got my pistol from below deck, came back on top, and then I saw something . . something I still can't believe," he says, disbelief evident in his voice.

Eisley may inject the dramatic into his stories, but there is a reason it is an effective narrative device. Kaley is absolutely hooked now and waits in suspense for his uncle to continue.

"So what do I see?" he asks rhetorically. "The fucking swamp is moving."

Eisley's hands come together and then he separates them. "There's a seam in the middle where two parts seem to be breaking off and separating. It's like a curtain was being pulled back to reveal something."

Eisley pauses a second before continuing, "And it did."

Kaley can restrain himself no longer.

"What the hell was there?" Kaley asks expectantly.

"A boat," his uncle responds, his eyes lighting up.

"A boat? What kind of a boat?" Kaley asks.

"A big boat," Eisley says cryptically.

Jon gives his uncle a quizzical look as Eisley explains.

"It looked like a DD-990," Eisley says.

Kaley racks his brain for a moment, trying to recollect the design of the Navy vessel Eisley is referring to.

"A *Spruance*-class destroyer?" Kaley guesses.

"Almost exactly," Eisley confirms. "It had all the details, same structure and design. But it wasn't flying any flags and there was no name on the boat, nothing to designate that it was actually one of ours."

"Was it stocked like one of ours?" Kaley asks. "What was their armament? Tomahawk missile launchers?"

Eisley shakes his head. "No, nothing like that. It was strange. It was like it was...naked. Like it was the stand-ard issue model built, the base model."

Eisley pauses a moment before continuing, "But I was more interested in what the boat appeared to be carrying. Or transporting."

"What do you mean?" Kaley probes.

"Well, a tarp was covering them, but one of the lines was not secure, 'cuz a breeze came out of nowhere and blew the tarp up for a split second. Granted my eyesight ain't the best, but I know what I saw. There were some bad-ass motherfuckers under there, Jonnie."

"What were they?"

"You read *Guns & Ammo?* The newest issue?" Eisley inquires.

Kaley shakes his head, suppressing a grin. "My subscription just ran out. Fill me in."

"On deck," Eisley says confidently, "there were probably a half-dozen new models of the AH-64 Apache. I mean brand-fucking-spanking-new, you hear me? Like they were just flown out of the showroom, gleaming in the moonlight," Eisley says, always one to paint a picture for his listener.

"You gotta be fucking kidding me, Mike," Kaley says disbelievingly. "The military owns probably no more than a dozen of these Apaches cause they're so ridiculously expensive. And you're telling me this boat that rolls out of a swamp just happens to be carrying a bunch of them on its deck?" Kaley asks, not bothering to hide the incredulity in his voice.

Kaley wonders if the old man is finally starting to lose it. Perhaps his uncle is trying to inject some excitement in a life that has become a bit on the dull side. "You sure your peepers are alright?" Kaley asks.

Eisley will not admit weakness or vulnerability to anyone, a character trait that simply does not mesh with the personality of a tough, macho Navy man. So when someone, especially his nephew, starts prying, attempting to find a weak spot, it irritates him to no end and makes him a wee bit defensive.

"They're fine," Eisley responds through clenched teeth.

Kalcy does not look convinced and he continues to push, "What about the diabetes?"

With barely restrained anger, Eisley says, "Everything's fine, you little shithead, and if you keep at this interrogation, I'll shoot you myself."

Kaley holds up his hands in surrender and laughs. "Okay, okay. Just trying to be sure you're not making things up in your golden years. You know, you're at that age where you old folks like to concoct stories to ease the boredom, make things a little more exciting."

"I'll bury you where you sit, kid," Eisley says, only half-jokingly.

Challenging him, Kaley arrogantly asks, "Oh, yeah, Mike, with what?"

The next second Kaley feels an object shoved into his groin, rather unpleasantly, and the cock of a hammer.

"With this," Eisley says triumphantly.

Kaley looks down to see the working end of a double-barrel shotgun getting comfortable with a couple parts of his body he has always been rather fond of.

The shotgun rests on a hook attached to the bottom of the table, allowing the person holding the shotgun to swivel it in a wide angle to any spot around the table. In this case, the man holding the shotgun is, thankfully, his favorite uncle.

"What? You think I only got the Glock stashed around here?" Mike says incredulously. "I could be sitting here at this table having dinner with one of my very best friends from back in the day, and for all I know, he may have come here to kill me. I have to be prepared to defend myself, Jonathan."

"Point taken," replies Kaley, as he pushes the barrel away from this most sensitive of areas.

"Good, I didn't want you thinking you could get the drop on me twice in my own home. That would be plain unforgivable," Eisley says, with a note of pride in his voice.

Eisley puts the barrel of the gun back into a leather sheath attached to the bottom of the table. He absently picks up some food from his plate before throwing it back after reconsidering. He leans back in his chair and eyes his nephew for a moment.

"Now that it has been re-established that I'm still sharp as a tack and top dog around here, I've got one more thing that could blow your socks off."

"Try me," Kaley responds.

Eisley leans forward and continues his story, "As they cruised by me, I heard a couple voices on the deck, completely garbled from where I was, but it's not what was said that's important, but who was saying it."

"You recognized one of the voices?" Kaley asks excitedly.

"Well, no, not exactly," Eisley concedes. "But one thing I do know: one voice was definitely American and the other voice, and I'm sure of this, was Arabic in origin."

Kaley digests this information and starts trying to put the pieces together: a large, Navy-like vessel carrying the newest model Apache helicopters, stealthily cruising through deserted waters at night, with Arabic-speaking or Arabic persons on-board, and a couple nights later the "attack" was launched.

Something is missing, Kaley thinks. *Still not enough pieces.*

Kaley is certain there is so much more to this story than he can possibly understand at this point. What is contained on the disc is simply one piece of the puzzle. It is eerily coincidental, however, his uncle mentioning the group of Apaches considering what Rushmore and Kaley witnessed at Evans.

"Now, your turn," Eisley indicates, encouraging his nephew to ask his favor.

Kaley snaps out of his reverie and bulls ahead, "Mike, I have the coordinates for the location in Lake Michigan where Rushmore and I first detected that signal. It's kind of a haul from here, but I think I should take a look. It may be a waste of time, I know, but I really don't have a lot of other leads. You still got your diving equipment, sonar, all that stuff?"

A twinkle appears in Eisley's eyes as the thought of adventure suddenly materializes before him. Finally, something to break up the monotony and routine of his daily life.

Eisley pops up from his chair as if someone lit a fire under his ass, and it looks like this is exactly what Kaley has done. "I got it all, with a few toys to boot. Let me make a quick phone call."

"To who?" Kaley asks suspiciously.

Eisley sees anxiety and concern etched across his nephew's face, and God knows, he has seen that look before. "Don't worry, Jonnie boy. I've known this guy for almost twenty years. I trust him with my life," Eisley assures him.

Kaley stares at his uncle for a few moments, stone-faced, "Mike, I cannot stress to you enough the serious-ness of what I've gotten involved in, and now what I've gotten you involved in, too. If anything were to happen to you, I'd never forgive myself."

"Jonnie-" Eisley begins.

"I have an unknown and dangerous enemy chasing me," Kaley interrupts, "and I cannot guarantee your safety, let alone my own. Make the call only if it's necessary, and you feel that this man is trustworthy. Give what info you only need to, nothing more. You got it?"

The last statement sounded more like an order than a question, but Eisley clearly discerns the fear and anxiousness in his nephew's voice.

"Jonnie, you worry too much. I've somehow managed to take care of myself for most of my life. I'll be fine. And my friend might even be able to help us out, see if he's heard anything about this mysterious signal. But you're right, I'll only let him in on what's necessary, okay? I'll use my utmost discretion," Eisley winks, trying to ease his nephew's apprehension.

Kaley studies his uncle for several moments and finally, slowly nods his head, "Okay, but only what he needs to know."

Mike nods, "Absolutely, be back in a minute."

Eisley hurries down the hall to his bedroom door and opens it. He picks up his house phone and dials a number he knows from memory.

"Alex, it's Mike. How are you, pal? Well, I've got something strange . ."

*　*　*

A moment later, Alexander Moriah hangs up the phone and smiles. Mike Eisley has absolutely no idea what he has just done. He cannot possibly know the extent to which he has sealed his and his nephew's fate. For he has managed to seal it tight, in a watery grave no less.

Moriah's first call is to Michael English, the CIA agent, to give him an update on Kaley's whereabouts, in case the assassin Sloan contacts the intelligence officer anytime soon. Moriah's second call is to the commander of the group of men that "stormed" Tamawaca Beach the night before. Their services would be needed again in this unexpected and very delicate situation. Fortunately for Moriah, half the men are still in the area and probably will not mind a little overtime. Better still, all the men are accomplished scuba divers, but more importantly, they are all accomplished killers, and it seems that in this instance, the latter will be as important as the former.

Sorry, Mike, friendship cannot save this one. Godspeed, comrade.

SIXTEEN

Tamawaca Beach – Headquarters

One of the largest cottages in the town of Tamawaca, dubbed the *Easy Does It* by its owners, sits practically in the middle of the dozen cottages that front the beach. In fact, the cottage appears to be the largest in the small town, and it was chosen as a makeshift headquarters for this express purpose. The more room, the better. Plenty of thinking space, one might even say. The choice seemed even more logical given the cottage's central location to the beach and the rest of the town.

As you enter the cottage through a screened-in front porch, a dining room that spans nearly the length of the house is immediately to the left. To the right is a living room, richly furnished, the walls covered with several paintings and tapestries, the perfect amount to avoid looking tacky and cluttered. In the far corner of the house is a large kitchen, with a small laundry room adjacent to it. There are a total of three floors, with the top two floors comprising a whopping fifteen bedrooms and three bathrooms. A small veranda on the second floor rests directly above the front porch, and on the third floor, a tiny balcony is located off one of the bedrooms at the back of the house.

No one would argue there is a lack of space, and in fact more than enough to house a small army. And this is the cottage's sole purpose at the present time, and for that matter, indefinitely.

After arriving at Tamawaca Beach, General Parker, Lieutenant Colonel Hermann, and Private Anderson slowly strolled down the sidewalk that spans the beach. They walked in a state of hushed reverence, reluctant to utter even a word to each other in respect to the recently deceased. Although all the bodies had been cleared from the beach, a melancholy air hangs over the site, like a suffocating fog that has rolled in off the lake. The small town is blanketed in a kind of surreal destruction, as it seems unfathomable that one moment, people were laughing and enjoying themselves during the holiday weekend, and in the next moment, they were gone, annihilated, *vaporized.*

The day has turned out much like the mood in the air: gloomy and cloudy. The humidity has eased slightly and the appearance of storm clouds on the horizon has caused the forensic team to hurry their evidence-gathering in case the storm hits the beach.

All three men watched somberly as members of the forensic team, numbering as many as twenty, conducted their work throughout the beach and around the cottages near ground zero. Samples of everything were taken, spots were marked with miniature flags where blood was found and body parts had settled, inanimate objects such as stones and driftwood were bagged for further analysis, clothes fibers were gathered, and a sealed on-site lab was constructed in front of the *Easy Does It*. All manner of tests are being performed in the lab and every type of analysis one can think to do is in the process of being completed.

Parker does not directly involve himself with the scientific aspect of the situation, but instead prefers to leave it to the experts. He does not need to know every detail of a particular experiment or why certain analysis is conducted, but rather is more interested in knowing how accurate and factual the conclusions are that are being drawn. He simply wants to understand the end results of their findings for the purpose of making an informed decision on how to proceed forward.

As twilight fades into darkness, with only intermittent streetlamps providing illumination, the forensic team has erected standing lights encircling the entire blast radius and beyond. The team anticipates working around the clock, weather permitting, sleeping in brief shifts, and generally working as fast as they can the first day after the attack. Not only are they driven by a profound sense of duty to their country and to the people who perished, but the first several hours of evidence-gathering is crucial in their line of work. It is similar to the oft-compared belief that a homicide detective's best chance of finding a killer or even catching a break are within the first 24-48 hours after the murder, before the trail begins to turn cold. The men and women of the forensic team believe the evidence as it stands, before the elements of wind and weather can interfere and contaminate their findings, provide the most accurate clues to determine exactly what happened here.

Pairs of soldiers stand at intervals along the sidewalk, ensuring that any curious members of the press or civilians do not inadvertently wander too close to the beach and corrupt potential evidence. In fact, the throng of television and newspaper reporters has been relocated about one hundred yards from the beach, where they stand at a makeshift gate guarded by a group of soldiers. The soldiers check everyone who wants to enter, scrutinizing press credentials, denying those who have not been granted proper clearance. The military were forced to make concessions to several of the top network news anchors, but for the most part, the media has been barred from direct access to the beach. They were also warned of federal prosecution if caught inside the gates without proper authorization, which keeps most of them at bay, while others search for different ways to gain access. Unfortunately for them, Tamawaca is bordered on both sides by trees and steep, sandy dunes, not exactly terrain that is easily traversed.

The number of soldiers at the site has dwindled since around mid-afternoon. They were initially summoned to assist in the removal of bodies and to scan for survivors. The latter job had been a lot easier than the former, in more ways than one. Many of the soldiers were recalled once it was apparent that the primary objective now is to gather as much evidence as possible, which falls squarely on the shoulders of the forensic team.

In terrorist situations where there is concern over the detonation of a Weapon of Mass Destruction (WMD), the military employs special response units, known as SRUs. The purpose of these units is to provide technical and analytical support to the civilian response teams. In this case, the Chemical Biological Rapid Response

Team was immediately called in by the Michigan governor. As a result of the governor's paranoia over recent news stories of chemical and biological agents, and the ease with which the media portrayed terrorists' ability to obtain such lethal agents, the governor did not hesitate in requesting military assistance as soon as he heard news of the attack. In fact, the SRU was the first group on the scene, within an extremely short amount of time after the attack occurred, a fact that did not seem to capture anyone's attention.

The SRUs are the military's first-response teams that provide information on the extent of the damage done and pave the way for follow-up military assistance. In this case, the Civil Support Team, or CST, which is a high-priority response unit supporting civil authorities in responding to a Weapon of Mass Destruction situation, was dispatched after the SRU. The group is typically headed by a lieutenant colonel, and jointly staffed with Army and Air National Guard personnel. However, the President nixed this command structure upon hearing word of the attack, opting instead to have one man, a general, in charge of this post. The President is notorious for despising top-heavy, bureaucratic institutions, ironic considering the endless number of federal agencies that comprise the government of the United States. Nevertheless, the President wanted only one man for the job, a person he could trust and who would not obstruct the pipeline of information that needs to flow freely to the White House, albeit confidentially.

General Lyle Cozey arrived within several hours of the attack, along with two of his aides, and the authority to coordinate soldiers around the site in terms of clean-up, stabilization, and assisting the forensic team in whatever may be needed. Cozey's unit is federally trained, equipped, and sustained, with the Michigan State National Guard providing additional troops and command support. While in standard circumstances, the CST supports the state response under the direction of the governor, the President had a brief chat with the latter and they mutually decided who would be in charge. Although no suspected Weapon of Mass Destruction had been released, the President and governor were briefed on an unusual radioactive substance found at the site, and they agreed to keep the CST there under the command of General Cozey. The Chemical Biological Rapid Response Team was dismissed several hours ago.

The CST consists of 22 full-time National Guard service members, divided into six teams: command, operations, communications, administration, medical, and finally, a survey team. Instruction is provided by a number of Department of Defense schools, along with agencies like the Federal Emergency Management Agency (FEMA), the Department of Justice, the Environmental Protection Agency, and the Department of Energy. The CST is equipped with high-end detection, analytical, and protective equipment. The equipment is required to detect a wide range of substances, including toxic industrial chemicals, organic substances, radiological agents, and chemical and biological agents. In this particular instance, an unknown type of radiation had been detected and is currently being analyzed by the forensic team, along with members of the SRU.

Along with the CST, the United States Marine Corps Chemical Biological Incident Response Force, which provides emergency relief to victims of a WMD attack, was deployed. Upon learning there was neither a WMD attack nor any victims to assist, the group was recalled to their home base. In addition, after it was determined there was nothing the American Red Cross workers could do, they were sent to a neighboring town to establish a grief center for the relatives and friends of the victims who came calling on their loved ones.

Finally, the Centers for Disease Control (CDC) was briefly called in and after a rather cursory examination, at least by their standards, they concluded that no disease organism was released at the site of the attack. Many of the CDC officials complained to whomever would listen that they were hastened in and quickly escorted away after an all too-brief examination of the area. The contingent was recalled to their offices in Chicago, where they would pass their information onto their superiors in Atlanta, the location of their headquarters.

Even the Department for Homeland Security, the federal department established in the wake of the 9/11 terrorist attacks, was practically turned away at the gates by Cozey. An organization oftentimes looked upon with suspicion and distrust, Cozey is unfamiliar with any members of the department and therefore, not apt to let them wander around and possibly compromise the site. A few members of the department are still lurking around Cozey's headquarters and the beach area, but their presence is more in an official capacity of ensuring that everything is running smoothly and efficiently. In addition, they are here to assess the risk of another attack in the foreseeable future, and what weapons may be used in the attack.

Behind the scenes, closely monitoring the flow of information to and from General Cozey, and therefore determining what the media and public needs to know, are the general's keepers, Lieutenants Michael Bason and Cheryl Stringer. In several military circles the pair are likened to two hunger-starved pit bulls, prepared to lash out at anyone or anything that could potentially cause harm or embarrassment to the general. They have been with Cozey for a number of years, are notoriously protective of his affairs, and will defend his decision-making to the death. They keep the general well-informed and well-connected, and one or the other can usually be seen covertly whispering into the general's ear at any given moment of the day. They are ever-present around the general, and the long-standing joke about them is that they even accompany the general to the latrine, where they each wipe one of Cozey's cheeks.

Cozey established HQ in the *Easy Does It,* and the long, ornate, wooden table that spans practically the length of the dining room is essentially the conference room. Papers, charts, graphs and the like are scattered on top of the table, and several aerial photos of the beach and the surrounding area had been tacked onto the walls of the dining room. A multitude of circles and arrows were hastily drawn on many of these photos. Several television monitors occupy the corner of the room, various scenes being played out on each one: pictures of Tamawaca Beach from this morning, the President in Air Force One, a shot of the White House, a live feed of the beach as the forensic team continues to comb through it, an overhead shot from a news helicopter hovering as close to the beach as the military would allow. A number of fax machines and computers had been set up in the living room, with several soldiers typing away at the consoles. The whole cottage is bright as a Christmas tree, and the bustling activity inside might, at first glance, give the impression of a holiday party. Inside, however, it is apparent that no one is enjoying themselves with the grave business at hand.

General Cozey's uniform jacket is slung across a chair and his shirtsleeves are rolled-up above the elbow. He sits at the head of the table, his eyes darting over a piece of paper in front of him. His hounds, Bason and Stringer, stand a few feet away, reviewing some notes written in a leather binder. Cozey has been in contact with the President several times throughout the day, providing brief updates on any new information gathered at the site. The calls were unnervingly short for both men's liking because there is so little new information to report, and the information they do have is inconclusive from a scientific perspective. Although the unusual radiation discovered at the site was conveyed to the President, the forensic team has thus far been unable to determine where it originated from or explain how traces of it were found at the site.

Cozey looks exhausted, already frustrated with a lack of clues and the multitude of questions that circle around inside his head like a neverending merry-go-round:

Why? What prompted the attack? Why in this remote town in the middle of the heartland, in the middle of nowhere really? Did the enemy even need a reason anymore? Is it simply another case of anti-Americanism, antiwesternism, anti-imperialism? A blow from the chosen people onto the infidels? An attack to let us know that we are not invincible, that we are fair game as any other country and its citizens? An attack to show that even after 9/11 we are still vulnerable, still susceptible to the whims of terrorists?

Parker sensed a feeling of relief in Cozey's eyes when he and Augie arrived in Tamawaca. Nevertheless, Cozey still wants to appear in control of the situation, properly delegating responsibility, managing the press, and detached from emotions that can possibly cloud one's judgment. Though both men are generals, Parker is clearly the senior of the two men, and as such, Parker's direct authority from the President trumps any other officer's. Cozey is not necessarily ecstatic to see General Parker, whose presence could be viewed as undermining his own authority, but Cozey reasons that in this type of situation, the more higher-ranking officers running the show, the better. Cozey would defer to Parker, and the latter would expect nothing less.

Parker likes General Cozey and believes the man to be a straight shooter. It is Cozey's two hounds Parker does not trust. Bason and Stringer are constantly looking out for the best interests of their general, and while this is usually an admirable quality, it is also exactly what worries Parker. Their unwavering devotion to Cozey and their belief that he can do no wrong, along with their future political aspirations for the general, is a potentially volatile mix that could raise certain conflicting issues and concerns. Parker hopes all of this can be put aside for the moment.

After touring the grim landscape of Tamawaca Beach, Parker, Augie, and Private Anderson met with Cozey and his two aides and received the most current situation report. There is no additional information concerning the radiation bands found at the site, but they believe they have determined a plausible scenario for how the attack was carried out the previous night.

According to a preliminary report prepared by the forensic team, it appears that a number of extremely powerful bombs, perhaps as many as ten or fifteen, were planted at various intervals along the beach. The bombs went unnoticed because they were contained within coolers or other containers that would not look unusual in a beach setting. Melted plastic parts were found at several of the detonation locations, suggesting that the bombs were encased to hide their true identities. The melted parts were initially thought to be merely debris, but upon closer examination, it appeared the pieces were in such close proximity to the blast, their composition had been noticeably altered. Only something that was practically sitting on top of the bomb could have been affected in this particular way.

The bombs themselves appeared to have been made somewhere in the Far East, but what startled investigators is that partial Arabic markings were found on some debris from the bombs.

"Who's in charge of the forensic team?" Parker asks.

"A man named Waterston," Cozey responds, "you know him?"

"Yeah, I think I met him once years ago, seen him at several functions in D.C. You?" Parker inquires.

"Yeah, he's good and his team is one of the best," Cozey responds. "Very professional, and so far no errant leaks to the bloodhounds," he notes, referring to the media.

"Good, let's keep it that way," Parker nods, noticeably pleased. "The press is licking their chops to snag any piece of juicy info. We need to keep whatever we have under our hat for now. And we also need to be sure that if the President is declaring war on those responsible, we got the goddamn right ones, whether it's the Sword or some other group."

Cozey looks confused for a moment and indicates, "But I thought they already confirmed specific details of the attack given to us by the Sword, and they received a couple of witness reports putting their people not far from the scene."

Parker looks at Augie, who shrugs his shoulders in surprise. Now it is Parker's turn to appear confused. "What reports? We never heard of any witnesses turning up," Parker says, a touch of suspicion in his voice.

Bason speaks up, "Sir, witnesses in two separate locations reported seeing a boat carrying Arabic-looking men several hours after the attack, hundreds of miles from the attack site."

"Well, to be accurate," Cozey interjects, "several hundred miles north of the scene. Near the towns of.... "

Stringer quickly hands Cozey a slip of paper, which he gratefully accepts.

"Ah, thank you, Lieutenant. Here we are. Near one town in northern Michigan called East Jordan, and again near a town in the Upper Peninsula called St. Ignace."

"Why am I just hearing this now?" Parker snaps, in a failed attempt at hiding his anger.

"General Parker," Bason explains, "these accounts were reported shortly after the President spoke, after it became known the Sword was responsible."

For the first time, Stringer speaks, "The witnesses

came forward once they realized they had seen the possible perpetrators of the attack. It was only after they arrived home from a long day of . ."

Stringer pauses.

"Yes?" Augie presses.

"Fishing, sir," she finishes.

"Excuse me?" Parker asks, thinking he misheard her.

Cozey shakes his head in amazement as he relates the story. "It was extremely early this morning, around dawn, when the first group of witnesses were motoring out to spend the day on the lake fishing, and they saw a boat carrying several Arabic-looking men. A few hours later, another group of fishermen evidently spotted the same boat. None of the witnesses even heard news of the attack until they returned a few hours ago. They eventually put two and two together and called their local police departments."

Parker looks around the room in disbelief.

"You're telling me that two separate fishing parties a couple hundred miles apart saw the same boat with several 'Arabic-looking' men on them? And neither party of witnesses heard news of the attack until they returned?"

Bason indignantly says, "It makes sense, sir, think about it-"

Cozey holds up his hand to cut off a potentially insulting remark Bason may let slip to a superior officer, and Bason instantly complies with Cozey's stern gesture.

This action, however simple, impresses Parker for its unquestioned authority and the immediate obedience it instills in Bason. Perhaps Cozey is not merely a pawn of the dynamic duo of Bason and Stringer, and maybe

Parker jumped to some rather unsubstantiated conclusions about their relationship.

Cozey casts an annoyed glance in Bason's direction before continuing, "General, it's not so far-fetched when you get down to it. A bunch of fishermen from the boonies not paying much attention to the outside world go to bed early, wake up at the ass crack of dawn, and do not come into contact with any type of civilization save a group of Arabs floating around in an area not really known for its diverse culture. They return home, hear the news, and figure out what, or who, they have actually seen."

Parker considers this for a moment, then says, "Even so, these 'witnesses' need to be thoroughly examined and their stories checked for inconsistencies."

"Agreed," Cozey concedes with a nod of his head.

"Lieutenant Colonel Hermann, get someone on it right away," Parker orders.

"Yes, sir," Augie responds.

"And I'd like to speak to Waterston as soon as possible to see how everything's coming along," Parker states, to no one in particular.

"He should be reporting any new developments immediately, General, but regardless, I'll have him brief you on what his team has found so far," Cozey indicates.

"I'll fetch him, General," Stringer says, and she hurries out the door, apparently leaving no room for debate.

"And what about the Canadian authorities?" Parker questions. "No one strange or unusual turning up at the border today?"

"They were put on alert immediately after the attack," Bason responds, "but so far, we haven't heard anything from them."

Cozey shakes his head, "No, nothing from the Canucks, and they claim they practically frisked or questioned everyone crossing from our side to theirs in the last fifteen, sixteen hours."

"Frisked?" Parker repeats with a wry grin. "We all know what our neighbor's idea of security means, and it usually includes stopping every fifth car. Augie, get somebody to do a check of everyone who was frisked or questioned at the border in the last few hours. See if any passport names match up with ones that have been flagged."

"I'm on it, sir," Augie responds, and quickly takes leave.

"Private Anderson?" Parker asks, finally turning his eyes to the quiet, yet attentive, private.

"Yes, sir?" Anderson inquires, a flash of eagerness lighting up his young face.

"Can you dig me up an aspirin around here?"

SEVENTEEN

Somewhere in the Dakotas

Adding to his worries, as if he needs something new on his plate, Sean's gas tank is extremely low. In fact, this is beyond anything that falls under the definition of "low." His tank, to Sean's dire realization, is parched, bone-dry, utterly vacant, waiting for its all-important liquid tenant to resume its stay as quickly as possible. The needle is practically buried in the red and the "E" is now almost completely obscured.

The Buick *Skylark* is a workhorse when it comes to gas mileage, and it seemed, at one point to Sean, that the full tank of gas would take him clear to Washington. Thus, Sean had pushed the seemingly mundane task of filling up the gas tank to the back of his mind, and told it to take a number behind some of his more pressing concerns.

Sean anticipates the car belching out the last of its fumes in the next few miles before dying a very slow death. While Sean knows he only has himself to blame, this fact does not stop him from cursing the car under his breath.

He has been riding her hard since he "acquired" her, hovering around 90-100 miles per hour the entire duration on the highway. It is a miracle of the highest order that, with it being a holiday weekend, he has not been pulled over by any of the Midwest's finest for speeding and possessing a stolen car. Or as Sean likes to think of it, a gift from the used car lot of *Raymond's Rough Riders,* located just within the westernmost boundaries of Chicago. The lot had been closed for several hours by the time Sean waltzed in, and a stolen car in that particular neighborhood would certainly not be a headline on page one. At a minimum, he figures he has at least eight hours before it is reported stolen, and possibly even longer considering the size of the lot at *Raymond's*. Sean even found an old license plate under several used engine parts that he tacked onto the car after he was safely away from the city. He decided he would rather have a cop run the plate and receive an expired notice than a stolen notice.

As for solving the problem of starting the car without keys, Sean definitely owes an old friend big time. It is truly remarkable the vital things you can recollect so many R&Rs ago. Like, for instance, how to hotwire a car. If he emerges from this alive, Sean will remember to drop a line to Sanchez, formerly a repo man in the greater Los Angeles area and member of his basic training class in the Marine Corps, and thank him profusely.

The *Skylark* has been running low for quite some time now, and Sean is certain he has not passed a gas station for over sixty or seventy miles on this lonely stretch of highway. His car contained a quarter tank the last time he passed a gas station, and he simply figured he would fill up at the next one. Unfortunately for him and his wretchedly thirsty vehicle, and because he is avoiding most major highways, he is still waiting to find the next one. He certainly has to thank the leprechaun on his shoulder for helping him elude the authorities thus far, considering his tendency at the moment to propel his car into light speed. But the gas situation, the more he thinks about it, is something that could have dire consequences.

Besides completely halting the search for his family, he has no idea where he may find the next sign of civilization, let alone a generous soul who would allow him to "borrow" their car in order for him to reach his final destination. If no one passes him tonight and he cannot hitch a ride on foot before sunrise, his chances of dying from exposure suddenly come into play. With the vast flatland of the Dakotas spreading out before him in all directions, it offers little hope of providing any shelter from the brutal rays of a summer sun. In all actuality, a more favorable scenario for him at this point is to be pulled over by a cop, accost the unsuspecting officer, and steal the car in order to keep moving forward. It seems like a better alternative than the car breaking down out here in the middle of what he sees as a barren wasteland, albeit without the apocalyptic red sky and vultures circling overhead.

After finding Rosenstein's clue, Sean thought it best to follow the apple trail to Spokane. When he examined a map to determine Spokane's exact location, Sean also read some general information about the city. Spokane, Washington, originally known as "Spokan Falls," is located approximately 280 miles east of Seattle, situated at the falls of the Spokane River, where the river descends from the Rocky Mountains into the Columbia Plateau. The city contains a population around 200,000 and is considered the commercial center of eastern Washington and northern Idaho, with the state line only several miles from the city center. On the map, Sean also noticed that to the west of Spokane, a few miles from Spokane International Airport, there is an active military base: Fairchild Air Force Base.

The *Skylark* buckles for a moment, but continues its breakneck pace, as if the car itself is pushing onward, knowing full well the urgency of its driver. Sean knows the fumes will only last so long, sensing that the car probably has no more than a mile or two left in it. How he longs for a *Shell* or *Amoco* or *Texaco* sign to come looming out of the darkness, like an oasis shimmering in a vast desert. He wants a large sign in neon lights boldly proclaiming:

WE HAVE GAS! FOOD! RESTROOMS!

Amazingly, Sean's dreams suddenly come true. He blinks his eyes several times to ensure it is not a mirage, and to his utter relief, he realizes it is not. A green exit sign announces the town of Redstone in 1½ miles, and attached to the bottom of the sign is a smaller, white sign, which simply states:

GAS UP

That sign will do, too. Sean nearly cries tears of relief as he realizes the silliness of it all, considering how trivial it seems when compared with the disappearance of his family.

I suppose one obstacle at a time, Sean thinks. Of course, he needs to avoid putting obstacles in his own way next time, as the task before him is difficult enough.

He floors the gas, not caring if he coasts into the station on the hiccup of a few good fumes. Sean only hopes the exit ramp is on a decline.

Then a momentarily terrorizing thought creeps into his mind as he approaches the exit. *What if the station is not directly off the highway?*

Especially in smaller communities with a concentrated population, the stations are typically located in the center of town, which is generally a few miles away from the highway. The Buick hardly has a few more blocks in her, let alone a few miles. *Worse yet, what if the station is closed?* The thought of a fully-functioning station closed for the night would be too much to bear. Sean would be forced to become a gas thief as well.

His heart thunders inside his chest as all the dire possibilities of not reaching the station converge. Sean thinks of what he would do in each scenario and none of them are especially-

Suddenly, he sees a beacon of light emerge out of the darkness. He reaches the exit ramp and spots what appears to be a well-lit, perfectly open, and seemingly functional gas station located two to three blocks off the ramp. He flips on his turn signal for no one in particular and coasts off the highway, glad to be doing something other than sticking his thumb out for a ride in the barren wasteland.

A minute later, Sean rolls the car into the oasis, which is assuredly real, and pulls in at the nearest gas pump. A small convenience store is located directly in the middle of the station, with two sets of pumps on either side of it. As he slides out of the car, Sean notices an old man behind the counter of the store, the first sign of life he has seen in a while and the only sign of life around here.

Sean thrusts the gas nozzle into the tank, as if the swiftness of this action is a sign of his appreciation to the car for struggling to reach this point. He takes a panoramic look across the surrounding area, only to find a whole lot of nothing and a moderate breeze. While his car gets healthy, Sean enters the bathroom on the side of the station to clean up a bit.

He splashes a few handfuls of cold water on his face and runs his hands through his disheveled hair. Once again, Sean has to reassure himself that the image staring back at him in the mirror really is him. Although brief, it is an immediate shock each time he catches a reflection of himself in a window or the rearview mirror. He repeatedly forgets about the hastily arranged disguise he applied this morning.

This morning, he thinks, *seems like a millennia ago, while the previous night has practically faded into an eternity-aged memory at this point.* His world has moved from the surreal after the events at Tamawaca to the stark reality of finding his family and punishing those responsible for their disappearance. He no longer feels like he is aimlessly wandering around in a dreamworld, but rather he has established a concrete destination, a solid lead in this mystery, and hopefully, the location where he will ultimately find his family.

Sean listened to the news reports on the radio, the Sword of Allah's claim of culpability for the attack, the President's speech to the nation from Air Force One, and the talking heads lamenting the fact that this could happen again on American soil after September 11th.

Had we not tightened security on our borders and within them? Had we not re-covered our citizens under a blanket of assurances that nothing like 9/11 could ever happen again, with the nation's newfound focus on protecting its citizens? Had we not displayed to the world our mighty strength and resilience in the face of extremists? Had we not shown the terrorists of the world what might become of them and their organizations if they threaten our way of life? Has our unwavering "War on Terror," which has sacrificed so many lives in Iraq and Afghanistan while seemingly depleting the ranks of these extremists, not provided any currency in protecting our nation from further acts of terrorism?

The questions were fired back and forth until Sean could no longer stomach the chatterboxes speculating who was responsible. He switched the radio off with a curse and instead, attempted to concentrate on the road ahead, both literally and figuratively. The news reports and discussions of a terrorist attack made him uneasy, still unable to come to grips with how the whole world could believe one thing while his eyes saw another. Whatever he witnessed, he does not believe it to be the work of Islamic fundamentalists, radical Muslims, or any kind of religious *jihad* declared by a terrorist organization or cell. Granted, terrorist organizations are evolving into ever-more regimented and disciplined groups with larger budgets and the latest technology, but it was the manner in which those soldiers *moved* on the beach that registered something long dormant in Sean. They reminded him of someone a long time ago, and to even give a second thought to what that suggests provokes a dispiriting feeling within him.

Adding to the assortment of conflicting emotions within him, Sean has tried to determine how Abraham and Rosenstein's research on an extraterrestrial invasion fits into the equation. It's like jamming two mismatched jigsaw pieces together in an effort to make sense of the puzzle. Unfortunately, Sean knows there are more pieces yet to be uncovered. Complicating matters even further, he does not know what the completed puzzle is supposed to look like.

Sean dries his hands on one of those soiled, white cloth towels commonplace in gas station restrooms. They never seem quite sanitary to him, but at the moment he is willing to disregard his own personal hygiene.

He exits the restroom and as he approaches the car, he notices the hose has been reconnected with the pump and the gas cap has been replaced on his car. The windshield and side windows even appear to have been cleaned.

Guess you can still get the royal treatment at some places without paying for it, Sean thinks.

He looks toward the store, but it is empty. Even the old man, who seemed to be a permanent fixture behind the counter, is nowhere to be seen. The place does not give the appearance of a full-service station, let alone any signs to indicate that. He seriously doubts someone looked under the hood and checked the tire pressure.

Sean instinctively looks around, his eyes darting across the lot, the pumps, the surrounding fields, and finally, back to the store. Nothing. Not even a breeze anymore.

Sean checks the price on the pump and walks toward the store, unfolding a couple of bills from his pocket as he continues to look around. The stillness of the night air suddenly has him on edge.

He enters the store and conducts a cursory inventory of the few shelves stocked with chips, candy and the ever-present gas station staple, beef jerky. Several other shelves contain motor oil, portable gas tanks, windshield wipers, and car deodorizers. A single camera sits in one corner of the store, currently trained on the area around the counter and cash register.

"Hello?" Sean calls out.

The sound of his own voice nearly startles him. Maybe it is because he has not used it in such a long time, or perhaps because it sounds so empty and meaningless in this place. The very solitude of his journey and particularly this area produces a strange feeling in Sean that he is the last living soul on Earth, and his voice is like a desperate searchlight, probing the darkness for a human response. Sean waits a few moments, allowing someone, *anyone*, the chance to answer.

But nothing comes.

"Is anybody here?" Sean calls out.

Sean waits another moment, uncertain whether he even wants someone to answer, or if the silence is more comforting and reassuring. Sean reaches for the gun in his waistband to find it missing.

Shit, he thinks. He left his gun on the front seat. He admonishes himself for leaving his sidearm behind, knowing a potential enemy would have little empathy for his plight.

Sean glances outside, his eyes drawn to the bright white lights of the station, which are teeming with thousands of little bugs. The image strikes a chord in him for some reason. A sliver of moon is visible, but it can hardly compete with the fluorescent glow from the lights. He turns back towards the front of the store.

At that moment, Sean fails to notice a car stealthily

pull up across from the station, its headlights off. The car practically blends in with the tall grass of the surrounding fields.

Sean grabs a couple bags of chips and a can of *Pringles* from the shelf. He walks to the side of the store, where several glass doors shield the cool beverages inside from the warm, humid air outside. He selects a few drinks from the cooler, mostly highly caffeinated and chock full of sugar.

As he reaches for a second bottle of *Mountain Dew*, he suddenly makes eye contact with someone directly behind the rack in the cooler.

Sean jumps out of his skin and into a rack of postcards that stand behind him. He nearly falls to the floor, but is able to maintain his balance without ever taking his eyes off the cooler. He notices that the person staring back at him has not moved an inch.

Sean deliberates whether to run back to the car to fetch his piece when a familiar scent suddenly registers in him. He is surprised he did not notice it immediately, as it is a very distinct and sordid smell. When he opened the cooler door, he received a waft of death traveling along the cool air: the coppery smell of recently spilled blood.

Sean looks to the left of the cooler and sees a silver door marked **EMPLOYEES ONLY**. He drops his groceries and stumbles towards the door. As he grasps the handle, he feels the cold from inside pulse across his hand. Without a second thought, he yanks open the door and dives inside, hoping to avoid any gunfire.

There is none, the only sound the humming of the refrigerator system inside the cooler.

Sean rises from a crouched position behind an assortment of cardboard boxes. He glances around the boxes before quickly pulling his head back. When a barrage of bullets fails to come whizzing through the air at him, he peers around the boxes again, this time more slowly. And what he sees takes his breath away.

The old man who was sitting behind the counter of the store when Sean first arrived is now propped on top of a large box in a sitting position, staring straight ahead. A garrote has been wrapped and tied tightly around his throat, almost completely severing his head from his body. It is amazing the head is still attached to the torso given how deep the wound across the man's throat is. A large amount of blood has escaped through the slit in the man's throat and pooled in his lap, giving the man's dirty, gray overalls a new crimson pattern.

Sean instinctively reaches his hand out to check for a pulse and pulls back, realizing there is no purpose in leaving behind fingerprints on a man who is very much dead and gone.

Like the helicopters at Tamawaca Beach, Sean again hears something that sounds like imminent danger, a forewarning, coming from outside. This time, it only takes Sean an instant to identify the sound. It is the drone of a motorcycle, the noise gradually intensifying as it approaches the station.

Sean sprints from the cooler and, as he remains low to the ground, cautiously approaches the door to ensure the threat is not directly outside. He stares out the window, focusing on the single headlight of the motorcycle as it approaches the station, only a quarter mile away now. Sean exits the store and heads immediately for the driver's side door of the Buick. Right now, his sidearm is his only salvation, his only chance, and he needs the weight of the gun in his palm for immediate reassurance.

As he reaches for the handle of the car door, Sean suddenly hears a *whizzing* sound overhead and in the next instant, the front of the *Skylark* is blown to pieces. Sean is knocked backwards from the blast and absorbs a few pieces of shrapnel over various parts of his body. He feels a sharp pain on the side of his head and numerous searing pains throughout his body. But all his extremities are still intact for the moment, including his head, which he takes a small measure of solace in. He is uncertain if he will ever regain his hearing until he hears another *whizzing* sound whistle by, causing Sean to cover his head. A moment later, the rear of the car, near the gas tank, receives a direct hit, causing a second explosion.

Sean stumbles like a drunk backwards toward the store, knowing it is only a matter of time before the gasoline from the pumps becomes ignited. He steals a glance back at the road to see a car suddenly come roaring from the opposite direction towards the motorcycle, a spontaneous game of chicken suddenly materializing on this deserted country road.

A large, bearded man wildly fires a gun from outside the driver's side window at the figure on the bike, the whole time screaming at the top of his lungs as if he is a Japanese *kamikaze* fighter pilot about to go down in flames.

The man fires at least a half-dozen shots in quick succession.

BAM! BAM! BAM!

The figure on the motorcycle apparently is hit as the bike rolls out from underneath him and skids along the pavement towards the car. The motorcycle narrowly misses the car and continues to skid past when Sean notices a small, round object floating through the air, as if in slow motion, heading directly for the car. The figure rolls away from the car as it passes, and a moment later, Sean hears the distinct sound of breaking glass.

The bearded man hurriedly tries to open the driver's side door with the car still in motion, but before he can accomplish this, a large explosion from inside the vehicle propels him out faster than he would have preferred.

Nearly simultaneously, Sean hears a couple more *whizzing* sounds around him. He immediately leaps and hurtles himself through one of the glass doors of the store when a pair of explosions rock the small station. He comes to a stop in a pile of broken glass and other debris, with a strange, calming silence enveloping him as he lies there.

The smell of burning fuel fills his nostrils and the sound of fire wreaking havoc can be faintly heard. Billows of dense, black smoke drift into the store, which has suddenly become an open-air convenience station. He attempts to lift his head, but to no avail. Instead, he reaches for something to drag himself up by, but his fingers grasp only at air.

For a moment, Sean thinks he hears the *thwack, thwack* of a gun being discharged, but he is not certain. He only knows that if it is the sound of a gun, he is not the intended target. Yet.

Again, Sean attempts to haul himself off the floor, but he fails miserably. His eyelids flutter as the smoke rapidly enters his lungs and poisons his circulatory system. He is breathing nothing but noxious carbon dioxide now, and should be dead within a few minutes.

Sean is certain he is entering the pearly gates when he sees a gorgeous woman float, as if on a cloud, into the store and approach him. She calls out to him.

"Professor?"

She shakes him rapidly, "Professor?"

He smiles weakly and nods his head, thinking there definitely could be worse guardian angels out there, or at the very least, less attractive ones.

The last thing Sean remembers before the black surrounds him is being jostled away from the heat and smoke across someone's back, only to hear one last explosion and to taste the earth once more with his new companion.

* * *

The July night has surprisingly become unseasonably chilly after the sun descended beyond the horizon. The constant breeze that gusts across the surface of Lake Michigan is blowing mightily tonight, and appears to be bringing a cold front with it. Kaley and his uncle are currently in the middle of the lake, and they can feel firsthand the cold, buffeting winds. They are lucky, however, in one rather important aspect: the water is unusually calm in the face of the gusting wind. Typically, it only takes a stiff breeze to whip up the tides of the lake, invoking the wrath of one of the strongest undertows on the face of the Earth. But for now, while the current remains strong, it is certainly manageable for the 34-foot fishing trawler, and definitely diveable. Of course, no diving instructor in their right mind would recommend a dive in such precarious circumstances.

First, the dive is at night, which automatically presents a host of problems, first and foremost the possibility of becoming disorientated and lost underwater. Second, Kaley has no diving partner to accompany him and thus, can only rely on a 70-year-old diabetic for assistance if he is to have any problems below the surface. Lastly, he is diving in the middle of nowhere, with no reference points such as a nearby lighthouse or reef, and absolutely no land in sight.

The more Kaley thinks about it, the more he believes he is several sandwiches short of a picnic to be doing this. It has been a number of years since he last conducted a night dive, a fact he is trying not to dwell on. Furthermore, he is diving at a set of coordinates that may or may not contain anything useful in his pursuit to determine exactly what happened in Tamawaca the previous night. He wonders if this is simply a huge waste of time, and whether he even needed to involve his uncle in the first place.

But what the hell, I can't turn back now, he thinks.

He is determined to go ahead with the dive, and he can only hope all his training and experience will come back to him the instant he penetrates the water's surface. He knows that the sliver of moon will offer little to no guidance once he is underwater, but fortunately, his uncle tends to maintain the very best in diving equipment, although the old man probably goes only once or twice a year.

From a visibility aspect at least, Kaley feels confident in the flashlight his uncle will provide for his jaunt under the sea. Kaley will be carrying a pistol-gripped underwater kinetics light cannon flashlight with HID, or high-intensity discharge technology, which makes it seem, as advertised, he would be "taking the sun underwater." Not that Kaley knows what he is looking for. He has no idea what to expect once he is underwater or even if the expedition will provide a clue to what occurred on Tamawaca Beach. His instincts are simply telling him the trail leads to this spot, and he prepares himself to anticipate *anything* that may be located at the coordinates in his pocket.

The depth meter on Eisley's boat displays a reading of 140 feet at their present location, but they remain a short distance away from the exact coordinates. For now, Kaley sits back and marvels at the vast array of monitors and gauges that occupy the cabin below decks. From the exterior, it appears to be an ordinary fishing boat with the exception of several large antennae located on the crown of the boat.

Upon entering the cabin, however, one finds all the bells and whistles are present and accounted for: a sonar radar, a depth meter with the discernible outlines of fish and vegetation below, a global positioning system, and several underwater cameras rigged fore and aft of the boat, installed with special lights to cut through the murkiness of the lake. There is one additional "unique" feature designed by Eisley in the lackadaisical days of his retirement: two .50 caliber machine guns hidden inside secret panels located at either end of the boat, operated either manually or from the chair Kaley occupies. Obviously, Eisley installed them more for posterity's sake and less in preparation for an attack or to assault a beachhead. Eisley continues to envision himself a player in the game, even if his team already retired his number.

Kaley notes they are rapidly approaching the coordinates when suddenly, the depth meter shows a reading of 245 feet, dropping over a hundred feet in a matter of seconds. Perhaps there is a sea ledge or chasm far below.

Damn, Kaley thinks.

He is hoping to keep the dive within a reasonable range, around 175 to 200 feet. Now, however, they are nearing the danger zone of 300 feet, a depth any skilled diver remains extremely wary of. Kaley is not ready to panic or abandon the dive, but he fully realizes the peril his life will be in at such a depth when he enters the dark, cold, and assuredly hostile environment.

He takes a deep breath as the adrenaline begins to stir. *Time to suit up,* he thinks.

Kaley moves to a compartment in the back of the boat that contains the diving gear and begins hauling it out. As he retrieves the gear, he recalls his training in an attempt to unearth any hidden gems he was taught that could mean the difference between life and death in the underwater environment.

Kaley's training in SCUBA started at the Naval Diving & Salvage Training Center (NDSTC) in Panama City, Florida. The NDSTC is considered the premier military deep-sea diving school in the world because it offers a number of controlled training environments. Additionally, because of its location, the school has direct access to open water diving in nearby St. Andrews Bay and the Gulf of Mexico.

The NDSTC maintains a four-pronged approach to instruction: formal class work, lab areas for students to become familiar with all facets of diving equipment, a large pool for physical training and SCUBA skills, and finally, three Pressure Vessel Assemblies (PVA). The PVAs are complex, multi-lock chambers that allow year-round training for deep qualification diving, emergency recompression skills, and pressure training. The last element involves the type of pressure a diver feels from the weight of the water, not the pressure associated with stress. However, in all fairness, when you are a couple hundred feet underwater, the meanings associated with the word quickly become interchangeable.

Since the school's completion in 1980, it has been responsible for selecting the most qualified American and international students from every branch of the military. Students in training are required to display to their instructors a certain level of comfort and ease while performing a multitude of tasks underwater. These tasks, dubbed "projects," are created to test the students' ability to function efficiently in a foreign environment, and to ensure they are able to avoid bouts of panic or nausea that may arise in an underwater situation.

The majority of students who fail to complete the training is not a result of the projects, but because of class work and academics. Students are taught the basic gas laws associated with diving and diving medicine, recompression chamber operations, and aspects related to salvaging. The training is focused and demanding, requiring students to not only be in peak physical condition, but also possess a sound and well-balanced mind. Training at NDSTC is difficult by design in order to eliminate any potentially weak individuals who may harm themselves or others in a dangerous, deep-water environment.

Kaley nearly washed out a couple times because of the demanding academic challenges. But, as always, Kaley persevered, and completed several different programs offered at the school. He initially completed the Second Class Diver (2C) program, an entry-level program for most deep-sea diver applicants. The course lasts over three months, and instruction and training is provided in surface-supplied air and SCUBA diving techniques. In addition, the course covers underwater repair, salvage, and search procedures. The primary focus of the classroom instruction includes diving physics and medicine, SCUBA-supported diving systems, underwater tools and work techniques, and underwater cutting and welding procedures. The course qualifies students to become skilled at diving at depths of up to 190 feet.

Kaley, although in the Army, also completed a Marine Combat Diver course and an Amphibious Reconnaissance Corpsman course. The latter is a requirement for anyone assigned to a Marine Recon platoon and the former's ultimate goal is to designate the status onto someone of a "Marine Reconnaissance Combatant Swimmer." The course is 35 days in length and focuses on physical conditioning, combat diver fundamentals, and various areas of SCUBA training. The course provides underwater infiltration training according to current Marine Corps mission performance standards. Or, as several of the instructors like to inform their pupils at the beginning of training, "It helps make someone who is already a badass motherfucker on land, a badass motherfucker underwater, too."

Kaley slips on an isothermal suit ideal for diving in temperatures between 38-72 degrees, and he figures the deepest depths of the lake will be somewhere in the middle of that range. Of course, the further down he ventures, the colder it becomes, and he must anticipate the temperature plummeting to the low end of that range. Constructed within the suit are waterproof 2-millimeter compressed neoprene socks, which he squeezes his feet into. Next, Kaley pulls on a pair of isothermal boots with ankle seals that almost completely eliminate what is called "water exchange." Water exchange is the primary cause for the greatest amount of heat loss while diving at extreme depths.

Next comes a pair of ankle weights, which are used at the discretion of the diver. Kaley prefers to wear them to act as a counterbalance in stabilizing buoyant fins, which, if too severe, could cause a diver to lose his sense of direction and become disoriented and even worse, lost in the depths below. Kaley then slips on an isothermal hood that seals at the neck like a magnet to the rest of the suit. It is definitely a snug fit, but not to the point of being uncomfortable. Besides, when diving at such extreme depths, the last thing you need is a chink in the armor, and he would much rather prefer a tight-fitting suit than something loose and baggy.

Last but not least, his lifeline, the OMS-C134 tank: a low-pressure steel cylinder considered one of the lightest and most neutrally buoyant cylinders in the world. It is lighter than an aluminum tank and therefore, facilitates easier access from a boat or dive site, resulting in less physical stress. Attached to the tank is the regulator, which is responsible for supplying air to the diver at ambient pressure. Kaley adds an ankle weight around the tank and underneath the valve to ease the weight on his hips.

Kaley attaches to his wrist what looks like an over-sized watch with three gauges on it: a compass, a depth meter, and a percentage bar displaying his air supply. The letters and numbers on the gauges all glow in the dark, which will be essential on this dive. On the outside of either leg, in a sheath attached to the isothermal suit, Kaley places two titanium knives.

Kaley then checks his mask, which contains on either side a *FireflEYE* video camera. The cameras are 37½ millimeters, nearly 1½ inches in diameter, and are for depths of up to 1,000 feet. He switches the cameras on and checks the feed. The picture appears clear as day on a couple of monitors in the cabin, which Eisley will be closely watching.

Eisley will be able to communicate with Kaley through a tiny transmitter in the latter's ear. From his perch at the monitors, Eisley can warn his nephew of any looming obstacles below, such as an unexpected ledge or how far he is from the bottom of the sea floor. Although Kaley will not be able to respond verbally, a keypad with over-sized letters to accommodate his gloves is attached to the inside of his forearm. Obviously, this is not for the purpose of writing a novel, but simply for brief communication describing his condition or specific details of the dive.

Finally, Kaley dons a pair of gripper gloves with wrist seals similar to the ankle seals on the isothermal suit. Kaley pats his hands together and hops up and down several times to loosen up, feeling as bundled as a kid going outside to play in the snow on a blustery, winter day.

Kaley checks the depth meter on the boat and notes it is hovering around 250 feet. Lake Michigan's average depth is approximately 280 feet, with its deepest point a little over 900 feet. Kaley says a silent prayer that his coordinates do not correspond to a suicidal diving depth such as that. Otherwise, he got all dressed up for nothing.

Kaley looks at the coordinates jotted down in front of him and then back at the depth meter. He reaches for the two-way set connected to the wheelhouse where Eisley is at the helm.

"Alright, Mike, ease her back around here," Kaley instructs him.

There is a crackle of static followed by Mike's voice.

"Easing her down now, aye, sir," Eisley wryly responds.

A grin spreads across Kaley's face. *You can take the man out of the Navy, but you can't take the Navy out of the man,* he thinks.

Kaley grabs the flashlight, turns his regulator on and takes a puff, checking to ensure the air is flowing freely and without restriction. He breathes deeply several times and makes his way up several stairs to the deck.

Eisley ambles down the stairs from the wheelhouse, a strained look on his face. Kaley knows that as much as his uncle loves the adventure of the open sea and a chance for action after several years in the slow lane, his concern for his nephew's safety is first and foremost, and readily apparent on his face. Kaley anticipates the impending speech and quickly tries to cut it off.

"Listen, Mike," he starts, before he is hastily waved away.

"Just shut up a minute," he says sternly, but without malice.

Eisley gathers himself and looks Kaley up and down. He emits a long, exasperated sigh.

"Ever since you were a kid," Eisley says, "you were always getting into trouble, always testing your limits. Seeing how far you could go, how far that envelope could be pushed. You never wanted to be told that you couldn't do something, that you couldn't figure something out."

"So nothing's changed, is that what you're saying?" Kaley asks. "You trying to talk me out of this?"

Eisley shakes his head, "No, I just want you to be *sure* you want to do this, Jonnie boy."

"I got to know what's down there, Mike. I got to know if there is something, or nothing or . . "

Kaley searches for the right words, but they are not immediately forthcoming.

"Yeah," Eisley sighs, "you got to know."

Eisley pauses a moment before continuing, "Well, I'll be a mosquito in your ear. Just try and keep your wits about you down there."

With a nod of understanding, Kaley simply says, "Narcosis."

"Yeah," Eisley confirms, as if even uttering the word will bring a curse upon them both.

Unspoken between them, they both know that at these types of depths, nitrogen narcosis is a very real and dangerous factor. Nitrogen narcosis, also known as the "raptures of the deep," is a condition that can afflict divers at depths greater than 130 feet. Since Kaley would be nearly doubling that depth, the threat of it occurring exponentially increases the deeper he dives and the longer he stays underwater. The condition is caused by the narcotic effects of the air's nitrogen at high pressure, and is marked by a loss of judgment that often causes foolish behavior in a diver. One reaction to nitrogen narcosis is discarding equipment that is vital in staying alive. Although not directly related to it, the element of darkness could also factor in the disorientation process that accompanies nitrogen narcosis.

In an attempt to reassure his nephew, Eisley notes, "I've got several powerful halogen lights on the hull of the boat that I'll turn on. Should get you down there about fifty feet or so. After that, the HID flashlight will take you the rest of the way."

"Right," Kaley responds, as he moves over towards the side of the boat.

"Jon, remember," Eisley advises, "if you're having problems down there, any problems at all, don't risk something as important as your life to see what's down there."

Kaley does not respond, trying not to think about any potential "problems" he may encounter below.

With more than a little irritation, Eisley adamantly asks, "You hear me?"

Kaley turns toward his uncle. "Yeah, I know, Mike," he says softly.

Eisley's look of concern does not vanish completely, but for the moment it noticeably diminishes.

"And if I have any problems up here," Eisley says, "I'll let you know with the word, um...how about...'Hemingway'?"

Kaley grins and asks, "*The Old Man and the Sea* still one of your favorites?"

"Always," Eisley confirms proudly.

Kaley makes a few final adjustments and conducts a last-minute check of his gear to be certain everything is secure and nothing will drag in the water, risking entanglements of any kind. He does it as a necessity, but also to avoid looking into his uncle's face for fear he may start second-guessing his decision.

"Alright, Mike, ready to roll," Kaley says confidently.

He takes a couple deep breaths of fresh air, knowing they could be his last for a while. Before putting his breathing regulator in his mouth, he says, "Watch my back down there."

"Always," Eisley says once again. He gives his nephew a brief, encouraging pat on the shoulder, which Kaley accepts as one of the higher forms of affection his uncle is wont to give.

"Trust your instincts, lad," Eisley intones.

With that, Kaley enters the cold, dark water with a small splash, and very quickly, he disappears into the mysteries of the deep below.

EIGHTEEN

Tamawaca Beach – Headquarters

Parker slowly scans a list of families who either own or were renting cottages in Tamawaca at the time of the attack. It is depressing reading the roll call of names, but even more so when Parker realizes the amount of children who perished in the attack. Until proven otherwise, all the people included on the list are missing and presumed dead. It seems that, at least this year, you are one of the lucky ones if you *were not* spending the holiday in this small sliver of paradise.

At this point, however, no definitive method could be used to identify the bodies, or what is left of them. To be able to identify the victims, DNA samples would be needed from relatives and dental records would need to be examined. It was readily apparent to those first on the scene that there is not much left of any of the bodies, and in the majority of cases, hardly anything at all.

The deceased list was culled from people who had called authorities to inform them that his or her brother, sister, best friend, aunt, uncle, cousin, grandparent, coworker, or parents were at the lake house this weekend. And all of them invariably asked the same frantic question:

Are there any survivors?

While no one wanted to confirm the death of a loved one without conclusive proof, they also knew they could not skirt the truth or offer a glimmer of hope in a hopeless situation, and sadly informed them that there are no survivors. If the person on the other end of the line did not start wailing or sobbing uncontrollably, the authorities tried to comfort them as best they could, offering words of condolence.

Parker continues to peruse the list while simultaneously thinking of something else, a fact that nags at him.

The bodies, or lack thereof, Parker thinks over and over again.

He cannot help but believe there is something significant directly in front of him to grasp, to wring a bit of truth from.

What types of bombs were detonated here? What kind of bomb could obliterate everything in its path, leaving the faintest of evidence and a minimal amount of human remains?

To Parker, it seems that only the intense heat and energy concentrated in a nuclear bomb could have wrought the damage inflicted on the people here.

"Sir?" a voice asks, startling him from his reverie.

Parker turns around to see Lieutenant Stringer, a rather bland expression on her face. But it is in the eyes that Parker sees something odd and...*mischievous?*

"Yes, Lieutenant?" Parker asks, annoyed at the interruption.

What bothers him even more is that in the last few

hours, his level of tolerance for others besides his inner circle has plummeted, while his distrust has conversely increased. He seems too preoccupied concocting new conspiracy theories every few minutes since his discussion with Augie about the possibility the attack was carried out by *fellow Americans.*

"Sir, Dr. Waterston says that he is in the middle of some 'delicate procedures,' which is how he described them, and will not be available for several hours," she says matter-of-factly.

"*Several hours*, Lieutenant?" Parker asks incredulously.

"Yes, sir, that's what the doctor claims," Stringer responds.

It strikes Parker as odd that Stringer seemed to have been gone an inordinate amount of time for her to return to inform him of that.

Goddammit, there I go again, he scolds himself.

"It's over my head, sir," Stringer remarks, "and if you ask me, a questionable resourcing of precious time and energy."

To Parker, Stringer's comment sounded rather arrogant and ill sighted. The forensic team, Parker assumes, wants to nail the bastards responsible as much as the next person. Whatever "procedures" that need to be completed to narrow the list of suspects, to determine how the attack was coordinated, or anything that seems relevant to determining the who and the how, then these would be essential items on the "to do" list. And they would certainly not be overlooked.

"Why do you say that, Lieutenant?" Parker asks, challenging her.

"Sir, if I may speak frankly, we all know the sons-of-bitches responsible for this. We also know the retaliation that needs to be brought, as quickly and as mercilessly as possible," she says, the coldness in her voice clearly evident.

Parker is surprised by the sharp tone of her voice and her unwavering belief in the culprits responsible. She sounds almost...bloodthirsty.

"Lieutenant," Parker notes, "sometimes the most obvious answer is not always the correct one."

"And sometimes, sir," she sternly responds, "the simplest explanation is the correct one. Occam's razor, sir."

Parker retorts, "This is not a science experiment, Lieutenant, remember that."

"But who else would launch an attack on a day so loaded with symbolism for this country?" she asks rather insolently. "Seems like someone is trying to send a message."

Parker notes the venom in her voice and the lack of a *sir* in her last comments. Parker is typically not a stickler for such formalities, but Stringer is practically on the verge of talking down to a superior officer.

Before Parker loses his temper, Augie suddenly appears and interrupts. He always seems to know when his assistance is sorely needed.

"General, I think you better take this call," Augie indicates, holding a cell phone towards him.

Parker turns away from Stringer, who exits the room immediately upon hearing Augie's voice. Parker glances at Augie and does a double-take when he notices the look on the lieutenant colonel's face.

Augie is excited about something.

"Who is it?" Parker whispers.

"Daley, sir," Augie responds.

Parker gives him a bewildered look until Augie explains, "Our tech at Evans, sir."

Parker nods and then shakes his head in frustration. "Fucking memory, Augie. That thing's going, too. Don't ever get old, man."

"I won't, sir," Augie confirms.

Parker takes the phone and exits the room. He walks out to the front porch of the cottage with Augie following closely behind.

"Daley?"

"Sir?" a crackling voice responds.

Goddamn cell phones, Parker thinks.

Reading his thoughts, Augie whispers, "We don't get very good reception out here, sir."

Parker responds sarcastically, "Must be the satellites."

"What's that, sir?" Daley asks.

"Nothing, son. What have you got for me?" Parker asks.

As Daley's voice veers in and out of clarity, Parker attempts to discern the more relevant points.

"Sir, Harrison and I found something unusual with the satellites assigned . . Evans. There doesn't appear to be anything missing, as far as time being erased from our recordings or . . along those lines. However, sir, we did find . . unusual as far as the loop these birds are supposed to run on."

"Yeah, go on, Daley," Parker encourages.

"Well, sir," he breathlessly continues, "the satellite they call Plymouth Rock, which by all rights should have been retired . . we found to be re-tasked around two weeks ago. Besides covering an area that she normally does not cover, she also was covering an area too large for her to handle. Specifically, around the area where the attack took place, sir."

Daley sucks in a breath, waiting for the general to absorb this and, at the same time, allowing himself a much-needed intake of oxygen.

"And, General, I believe you were informed of the black patches around the country that our birds typically don't fly over. Remote areas in the desert, in the plains, places like that . ."

"Yes, these patches can last anywhere from a few seconds to what, a couple of hours?" Parker asks.

"Uh, yes, sir," Daley confirms. "The military allows for no longer than twelve hours for a particularly desolate area to go unmonitored, if only for a few seconds. With terrorists and domestic militias, and you know the attorney general has been on the war path-"

"Yes, Daley, please go on," Parker impatiently interrupts. The last thing he needs is a political roundtable discussion concerning the current administration's policies.

"Sorry, sir. Well, as far as we can tell, there are no records for the area of Tamawaca having even been glanced at in the last two weeks, since the satellite was re-tasked."

"Say that again," Parker demands.

"It's true, sir," Daley asserts. "They maintain computer records of clips from the most recent flyover of certain areas, and the last retrieved record for the area around Tamawaca was June 21, at 2:15 AM."

"How can that be?" Parker inquires.

"I don't know the answer to that, General, but it gets worse," Daley says uncomfortably, unsure how to deliver the remainder of his rather sobering news.

"The re-tasking was authorized by one Major Thomas Halliwell, who was stationed at Evans until about two weeks ago," Daley reports.

"And where is the major now?" Parker presses.

Daley pauses, reluctant now to continue.

"Daley, you there?" Parker asks. A small knot has suddenly begun to form in the general's stomach.

"Yes, sir," Daley responds. "The major was killed in a training accident on June 19, sir. His card access should have been voided and his authorization numbers deleted from the mainframe."

Parker knows what to expect now and angrily states, "Say what you're going to say, son."

"Sir," Daley explains, "Colonel Fizer is the only one at Evans, besides the major, who could have even had access to the satellite re-tasking."

"Son-of-a-bitch," Parker screams, capturing the attention of everyone within shouting distance, which includes nearly the entire beach.

"Uh, sir, one more thing," Parker hears from the other end of the line.

Parker pauses, holding his breath for the next bombshell.

Daley continues, "Fizer must have seen us creeping around inside the mainframe, cause he got spooked and-"

There is a garble of static, followed by another, and then Daley's voice can be heard again.

"Sir, did you hear me?" Daley asks.

"Say again, Daley, what about Colonel Fizer?"

"He-"

There is another outburst of static as Daley's words become lost into the abyss of the cellular world.

"Dammit," Parker says, and moves towards another part of the porch.

"Can you hear me, Daley?" Parker shouts.

"Did you hear me, sir?"

"Daley?"

Finally, the general finds a magic spot where he hears everything clear as a bell. Although he is not going to like what he hears.

"I said, the colonel's gone, sir, and Dawson went after him!"

*　　*　　*

Julianna Dawson did not think much of her assignment initially, but it finally seems to be coming around. After a couple of dull, uneventful hours at Evans perusing the logs and getting up to speed on the base's latest training manuals, Dawson's patience was rewarded, all thanks to the colonel.

Fizer's level of anxiety had gradually increased as the minutes ticked by, and the restless manner in which he conducted himself did not go unnoticed by Dawson. She maintained a constant, if inconspicuous, watch on him through his office door, trying to avoid Fizer catching her watchful eye. On several occasions, Dawson held her gaze on the colonel for an instant too long, and they would exchange a momentary, and rather awkward, bit of eye contact. She tried to discern something in those mercurial eyes, while at the same time he appeared to be sizing her up. Dawson also noticed him intermittently talking in hushed tones on the telephone, his back turned towards the doorway. She was surprised he had not attempted to close the office door, but she suspected the colonel did not want to appear like he was hiding anything.

Fat chance of that, she thinks.

Dawson is growing impatient and frustrated with the lack of information she is receiving from him. She would gladly endure a couple of snide comments from him if that would grant her entry into the information loop. But thus far, zilch. Dawson is uncertain, however, whether the lack of information is a result of Fizer intentionally keeping things from her, or the fact that there does not appear to be anything new to share. No leads, no breaks, no mind-blowing discoveries, nothing new to report. This scenario seems highly suspect to her considering the vast number of people working to piece together the events of last night. For the time being, however, she maintains her professionalism and her tongue.

Finally though, something shakes the colonel to the core. Dawson initially thought it was a computer problem when the colonel started impatiently tapping at the keyboard. Then Fizer began pounding the keyboard, as if he were trying to crush it into tiny pieces. He did not seem to be paying attention to her at all, or maybe he simply did not care any longer that she was watching him. Either way, it gave Dawson the opportunity to stare at him uninterrupted. It was then that Dawson noticed a look of absolute disbelief on the face of the colonel. A moment later, as if the water was slowly being drained from a cooler, the blood in Fizer's face disappeared, leaving behind a milky, lifeless, almost hollow look to the man's head. She thought his head was going to crumple like a deflated basketball.

After a few minutes, Fizer composes himself, rises from his chair, straightens out his uniform, attempting to iron out the creases that seem permanent, and heads for the door. The colonel attempts to regain a look of equanimity on his face after his brief loss of composure, but he nevertheless appears rattled.

As for Dawson, she has had enough of being ignored and disregarded. She has a job to do and a duty to fulfill for General Parker, and if it means being a hard-nosed bitch, she could play the role to critical acclaim, especially with Colonel Fizer.

As the colonel reaches the doorway, Dawson springs up from her perch and addresses the colonel with a speech she has prepared in her mind for the last hour or so:

"Sir, I'm going to need a brief update on the situation here, however trivial any new information may be. As special liaison, I was ordered to report directly to General Parker every several hours with the actions being taken by this base, particularly by yourself. I need you to help me do my job properly, sir, and without problems," she concludes, praying she sounded assured and self-confident, polite yet stern.

Dawson knows she has more to say, but suddenly she cannot remember it. She only hopes she did not sound too desperate.

Surprisingly, Fizer acquiesces, nodding his head, acknowledging her brief, rehearsed speech.

"You're exactly right, Lieutenant," Fizer concedes. "We all have our duties to carry out, however small, and to shirk those responsibilities at a time like this would be bordering on disrespectful.

"Hell, even unpatriotic," he adds, with a little mustard on it. "I'll have a briefing for you in just a moment. First, I need to use the latrine. I feel an upset stomach coming on," he says, placing a hand over his midsection.

I wonder why, Dawson thinks.

She does the only thing she feels she can do, and that is to say, "Certainly, sir, I'll wait for you right here."

What could she do anyway? Follow him into the head and hand him the toilet paper? She feels like an idiot caving so easily, but the colonel does not leave her much choice.

Barely a minute passes after the colonel leaves that her phone rings, with one of the tech guys, Harrison, on the other end. After establishing the fact that Fizer is not within earshot, Harrison informs her what they had discovered. One of Evans' satellites was re-tasked by a dead man, a dead man whose access should have been eliminated upon his demise. Instead, the major's access numbers were utilized nearly 36 hours after his death, and he had, from beyond the grave, been very adept at re-programming the satellite. For a dead man, that is.

Upon the elimination of Major Halliwell's access numbers after the re-tasking was complete, every action the man had undertaken in the mainframe had been erased. Only when Harrison and Daley rummaged through each person's access on the base did they notice the discrepancy between the last action taken by Major Halliwell and the date of his demise. They discovered this information only after reviewing the last documented footage of Tamawaca prior to the night in question.

Pray tell, Mr. Harrison, who at Evans has the authority to view every soldier's access number?

A minute later, Dawson bursts through the men's room door on a mission, unclasping the button on her holster. She withdraws her sidearm, only to discover the place empty and one of the three large windows at the back yawning open, a stiff breeze blowing through it. She hurries over and peers down, half-expecting to find a string of sheets tied together leading to the ground.

Instead, Dawson notices a large, steel drainage pipe running down the side of the building, with an abundance of handholds and footholds. The pipe runs four stories from the roof to the ground, where a small patch of grass circles the building. It is only about fifty feet, not a bad little shimmy.

That nimble motherfucker, she thinks.

Dawson cannot believe the colonel had it in him. Fizer does not appear to be in peak physical condition, with one of his more obvious features a slight but noticeable paunch. Of course, that does not imply he cannot negotiate a simple drainage pipe. She underestimated Fizer and it had cost her.

She holsters her gun and also decides to take what appears to be the fastest exit, courtesy of the original trailblazer, the good colonel. Dawson steps up onto the windowsill and grabs a hold of the pipe on the far side with one hand, and with the other hand, she latches on to the near side. She steps off the windowsill and for a moment, she is only anchored to the building by the muscles in her arms, which strain against her uniform jacket. Her legs dangle for several seconds, searching for a foothold.

Stupid, stupid, stupid, Dawson thinks, as she quickly

realizes she should have removed her jacket before she ventured into the merciless Midwestern humidity.

Sweat droplets have already blanketed her forehead and around her hair. She maintains her hair cut short, not because she is attempting to be "like one of the guys," but because she likes the way it feels. Besides, it only seems sensible to keep it cropped short in the summer.

Dawson cannot find a foothold, so instead she wraps her legs tightly around the pipe. She quickly slides down, careful not to go too fast and tear the skin clear off her hands. If her parents could only see her now, what a sight she must be. She reaches the ground within seconds and immediately sprints towards the one place Fizer would likely go if he is trying to flee: the motor pool.

The motor pool is located on the other side of the base, in a large hangar the size of a small museum. Dawson sprints towards it, knowing that precious seconds are ticking away. She notices a large cluster of activity at the pool, with vehicles coming and going. In fact, the whole base is a blur of activity as a designation of a high terrorist alert has been issued. The base is being reinforced for any kind of attack, for who knew if, or *when*, the next strike would come, and where.

About fifty yards away from the hangar, Dawson notices a young soldier holding a clipboard saluting none other than Colonel Fizer. The colonel quickly returns the salute and hops into a military-style Hummer, guns the engine, and takes off towards the gates of the base.

A pained expression crosses Dawson's face as she arrives at the hangar, her legs a little rubbery from the sudden exertion of energy in the heat and humidity. She grabs the young soldier's arm as he makes a note on his clipboard. He looks at her in surprise and disbelief, wondering how anyone could manhandle him like this, especially a woman.

Between large intakes of air, Dawson tries to talk, but it comes out somewhat ragged.

The soldier raises an eyebrow. "Can I help you," he says, peering at the rank on her jacket, "Second Lieutenant Dawson?"

His tone sounds skeptical, as if he does not believe she is actually a lieutenant in this man's army.

Although she looks disheveled, with sweat pouring down her face and an intensity blazing in her eyes, she puffs herself up a bit, and with an air of superiority, she says, "Yes, actually," looking him up and down, "you can, *Private.*"

As if embarrassed by his lower rank, the private suddenly seems deflated.

"You can tell me what Colonel Fizer said to you," Dawson demands, "and where he might be going."

The private, sensing her desperation, figures he has suddenly regained the upper hand.

"Well, sorry, Lieutenant, that's classified information," he smirks. "Can't help you, ma'am."

The private gives Dawson a smarmy smile that instantly gets Dawson's blood boiling.

Dawson looks back towards the gates of the base to see the colonel passing through them, quickly turning left and accelerating, but more importantly, getting away. She turns back to the private, rapidly running out of patience.

"Alright, well at least give me a car I can use for a little while," she says. Then she lamely adds, "I need to run an errand."

The private looks shocked, dramatizing the look for pure theatrical value. "Yeah, right, take anything you like," he sarcastically says.

The private chuckles, "If you hadn't noticed, it's a little busy around here at the moment, Lieutenant, and we can't just issue vehicles out to anyone. I haven't even seen you around here before, are you stationed-"

"I'm not just anyone, Private," she begins, and reaches into her pocket. "I'm a special liaison to General Theodore Parker-"

As the private looks down to see what she pulls out of her pocket, with the other hand Dawson uses the butt of her pistol and smashes it across the top of the private's head, driving him instantly to the ground.

Desperate times, Dawson thinks.

She bends down and retrieves a key from a huge chain attached to the private's waist. No one has noticed anything unusual yet, but that would soon change. She notes the number on the key and runs to the corresponding spot in the motor pool. She hops into an older model military jeep that looks like it has been around since World War II. She turns the key and gives it some gas, not sure if the old girl is going to turn over. But like all things in the military, and like every great general, it may be old, but it always seems to work. She reverses the jeep and speeds off towards the gates of the base.

Dawson does not ease up on the gas pedal once, not even when the MPs begin shouting and shooting warning shots into the air. The MPs dive for cover as she plows through the gates of the base, the same ones that hours before, Jonathan Kaley had sped away from before nearly being seized by these same MPs.

This similar point of reference, although arrived at nearly 24 hours apart, is a precursor of a future and inevitable collision on fate's timeline where their lives will intersect. It seems, at the time, to be one of life's little coincidences and consequently, one of its mysteries.

Dawson turns left and jams her foot down to the metal. She intends to receive the briefing she was promised only minutes ago.

NINETEEN

The Depths of Lake Michigan

There is blackness, nothing now but blackness. The powerful beam from his flashlight tries to pierce through the darkness to reveal...anything, but the blackness is all-encompassing. It is as if the light is being reflected back at him, as if something down here has no desire to unmask itself. Kaley feels like he has wandered into a dreamland, that mystical place where you become an apparition, floating, looking down upon the land. Except in Kaley's case, there is nothing but the cold, black vastness of the lake around him, where not even a fish seems to be lurking. At times, Kaley does not even feel that he is underwater, but rather floating aimlessly through the vacuum of space. He has, of course, never been there, but he imagines an astronaut may experience a similar kind of disconcerting feeling during a space walk.

Kaley has reached about a hundred feet on his depth meter as he gradually continues descending. He does not even glance upwards, as the halogen lights on the hull of his uncle's boat long ago disappeared from view. A slight pressure begins to grip his head, like a hand has been placed on the top and is gently squeezing.

This is perfectly normal and no cause for alarm, he reminds himself.

Any severe change in the atmospheric pressure a human body is accustomed to will cause physiological alterations within. Kaley has dived often enough to know and anticipate this, but it has been so long since his previous dive that he wants to reassure his nerves, for safety's sake. The last thing you want to do down here is panic and become disoriented in any way. The depth of the water can do that all by itself without the aid of the human mind to accelerate the process.

As if sensing his uneasiness, Eisley speaks for the first time, "Jonnie, we doing okay, buddy?" he asks.

Kaley has nearly forgotten that he is connected to his uncle on the surface. It is corny, but he feels like his uncle is an angel on his shoulder, his reassuring voice in his ear. Suddenly, he does not feel so utterly alone down here.

Kaley touches the oversize keys and sends back a response:

G-O-O-D.

Eisley's confirmation of the reply is almost instantaneous. "I'm glad you're good. Just remember everything you were taught, kid."

There is a pause as Eisley checks something. Everything that Kaley sees and knows, Eisley is also monitoring from upstairs.

"Jon, I got you at about a depth of one hundred twenty-five. Is that the same reading you got?" he asks.

Kaley checks his meter and briefly confirms it with his uncle: Y-E-S.

"And the total depth reading of where you are at is around...two hundred seventy feet," Eisley says, as if he is calling out bingo numbers at the community center.

Approaching the danger zone, soon to be fully immersed in it, Kaley knows his uncle wants to tell him to get his ass back to the surface, to quit dicking around and come back up, but Mike would never say that to him. Besides the fact that Kaley would not listen anyway, his uncle rarely discourages him from doing something he has resolved to accomplish. Especially with the determination and purposefulness readily apparent on his nephew's face, Eisley refuses to place negative thoughts in his head. In any case, Kaley could do that all by himself.

At a time like this, 150 feet below the water's surface, somewhere in the depths of a rough and tumble Lake Michigan, with nothing but a few gauges and an aging uncle as backup, you can begin to second-guess your rational thought process fairly quickly. Kaley is not sure what he is supposed to find down here, or what may await him far below. He has a set of coordinates, this is true, but what exactly do they mean? All the coordinates represent is the source where a barely perceptible signal was traced and identified. For all Kaley knows, it could have been an electronic malfunction on their end. Some type of errant transmission burst that was . . .

But who am I kidding?

Kaley's gut and his instincts are telling him he is on the right track. There was something here last night, something that might still be lingering. What it is Kaley cannot even begin to guess, let alone speculate. He does not know what to expect in the murky waters below because he has no idea what he is looking for. He believes that he will obviously know it if he sees it, but will there be anything to see? Kaley's worst fear at this point is that his instincts are unreliable and he has entangled himself in the proverbial wild goose chase, with nothing but a whole lot of water to find.

The murkiness of the lake becomes cloudier with each foot he descends, giving Kaley a feeling that he is in freefall, with no sense of direction or beacon to guide his way. Once again, sensing his nephew's mounting anxiety, his angel from above speaks, "Jon, it looks like you got a ledge of some kind coming up. It's about fifteen feet down, a little east of your position. Then the depth of the lake drops dramatically."

Kaley recalls the ledge they passed over only minutes before as they approached the coordinates. It appears he is swimming back towards it. He kicks his legs, rather cautiously, not wanting to barrel straight into the ledge, but also trying to obtain any type of marker as he descends into the unknown. Maybe he simply wants to see something besides the all-encompassing blackness of the water.

A moment later, the beam of his flashlight reaches the end of the ledge, which Kaley slowly pans over, as well as the surrounding area. He pulls up for several seconds and observes the ledge before swimming past it into the dark chasm below. The ledge is large widthwise, stretching in both directions as far as Kaley can see, which, in this case, translates into how far the beam of his flashlight can penetrate. So that does not tell him much.

There is something about the ledge that catches his attention, however, a quality that seems unusual. The end of the ledge appears rather jagged, not smooth like you would expect from the dulling effect the constant flow of water would have on it. It looks as if the floor of the lake was abruptly severed at this point, like it was...broken off. A strange image pops into Kaley's head, one of the giant from *Jack and the Beanstalk*. He pictures the massive giant stomping across the lake in his size-250 shoes and putting holes in the floor of the sea with his thunderous footsteps.

"What the hell?" Kaley hears, muffled in his ears. "Strange, ain't it?"

Eisley expresses Kaley's sentiments exactly.

Kaley plays the beam over the ledge once more before he continues his descent into the chasm below. He glances at his depth meter to find he is around 160 feet deep. The pressure on his body and his head has steadily increased throughout the descent, but it has not reached the point of being uncomfortable or painful. Kaley can feel, however, that this stage may not be too distant. The pressure in his eardrums is where he has noticed the most dramatic change, and he can feel them starting to disagree with what he is doing. They feel as if they have begun to curl up, to shrivel the way a flower would from a lack of water and sunshine. He knows, of course, that he is being ridiculous, that his ears are still perfectly normal – for now.

Kaley can feel his body trying to readjust, attempting to acclimate itself to the foreign environment so that its normal processes will not be interrupted. The blood needs to keep pumping, the organs need to keep running, and most importantly, the brain needs to receive a steady flow of oxygen.

Kaley does not necessarily worry about the physical

aspect of the dive. He is in excellent health, with less than 4% body fat, the stamina of a Kenyan marathoner, and the strength of a bodybuilder. The constant kicking of his legs does not tire him in the least, and he has surprisingly felt stronger as the dive progressed. He is like a running back whose legs have become sturdier by the fourth quarter, while the defense has all but lost theirs. Unfortunately, Kaley is uncertain who the defense is, let alone where they are.

"Jonnie, everything kosher?" Eisley asks. "I need to take a quick spin," Eisley says casually.

Kaley is momentarily surprised, a sudden feeling of abandonment washing over him. He cannot think of a worse place to be stranded than out here in the middle of Lake Michigan, with not a speck of land in sight.

He quickly realizes he is being foolish. His uncle would sooner die than desert him out here.

Kaley writes in response, W-H-E-R-E-?

Seconds later, Eisley replies, "Just around, be back in a jiffy."

That's weird, Kaley thinks. Even though Kaley cannot physically see Mike at the monitors, watching his every move, speaking reassuringly into his ear, he simply imagines his uncle not sitting in that chair and the panic starts to set in. Not knowing who invited it to the party, Kaley tries to clear his head.

Jesus, I need to work on my abandoncy issues, Kaley thinks flippantly. He promises it will be something he addresses after this is all over.

Kaley glances at his depth meter to see he has edged over the 200-foot barrier. His eardrums feel like someone is slowly screwing them into his brain. The pressure in his head is more intense, as the previous gentle hand has suddenly become angry. The isothermal suit has begun to feel several sizes too small. Kaley focuses on the deep below and tries to maintain his wits about him. Any experienced diver would tell you that at a depth of this magnitude, your wits are all you can rely on. They feed off of and sharpen your instincts, which Kaley must have the utmost confidence in if he is to survive a dive as dangerous as this one.

The suit has managed to keep him insulated from the cold temperatures for the majority of the descent, but now he can feel a certain chill to the water at this depth. Maybe it is the mind's perception of the water, which creates a certain understated reality for him, but nevertheless, it still *looks* like the water is unimaginably cold.

Kaley remembers when he was a kid, swimming with his old man and his Uncle Mike, in waters not too far from here. Every summer his family would visit for a couple weeks with his mother's brother, and every summer when he first stepped into the lake, it was as cold as a witch's tit. He remembered wondering if the lake ever got warm, even in the heart of summer. He could still recall that first time, reluctant to venture any further than the three-foot deep water he had waded into. The lake seemed so cold and mysterious that first time. His uncle, his old man, and his older cousins were splashing around what seemed like a mile offshore, although it was probably no more than twenty or thirty feet. He was reluctant, maybe even scared, by the prospect of diving into the cold unknown.

What if there is a giant sea lizard waiting for me, ready to snatch me down into the deep, never to surface again?

He recalled fantastic thoughts like this running through his head that first time.

His uncle and his old man – big, tough Navy guys, the picture of masculinity and machismo – swam over to him and reassured him with the following phrase, as they pointed towards their nether regions:

"Don't worry, boy, all of our battleships become dinghies in this freezer."

The raucous laughter that followed made him feel part of the guys, and forever after, his mother would have to physically haul him out of the water to come eat his dinner.

Of course, it would always remain a mystery to the family why he joined the Army and not the Navy. *That's just Jonnie, trying to be different, carving his own path,* they all thought.

Or maybe, in the back of his mind, the sea lizard still exists, waiting . . .

His brief reverie catches him off-guard as he returns to the present. He looks at his depth meter and, if he could, he would gasp. *260 feet!*

He is fast approaching the danger zone, if he is not already immersed in it, and the sea floor is nowhere to be found, nor is his wingman.

Are my coordinates incorrect? Is this simply all there is? Had my gut been wrong?

He really did expect to find something down here, despite his nagging doubts. What, of course, is anyone's guess. Still, he thought-

"JON!" his uncle shouts in his ear.

Kaley nearly jumps out of his skin when he hears his uncle's voice. The man sounds out of breath, wheezing.

"Jonnie, you still with us?" he asks. "You're at two hundred and seventy-five feet, you wouldn't believe-"

Eisley is interrupted by Kaley's rather urgent question: W-H-E-R-E/F-U-C-K/W-E-R-E/U

The words cannot come out fast enough as Eisley says excitedly, "Yeah, I know, I'm sorry Jonnie. I just took a little tour of the fairgrounds, and there is definitely something strange going on."

Eisley takes a breath before continuing, "Now don't freak out or anything, but you're essentially swimming in a big fucking hole."

Kaley stops kicking and pulls up for a moment. He looks up and points the flashlight beam, as if this might reveal what his uncle is talking about.

Kaley then types, ?-?-?, and sends the inquiry.

"Yeah," Eisley stammers. "I know, sorry, kid, um...I took a spin around your dive area after I saw that ledge. And...uh...it's weird, it's almost a perfect circle. The depth reading outside the circle is around one hundred thirty feet, and then you come inside the circle, it drops to almost three hundred feet where you're diving.

"It's like something crashed through the bottom of the sea floor there."

Kaley once again thinks of the giant trudging across the lake as he looks at his depth meter: *280 feet!*

Suddenly, Kaley does not feel the cold of the water anymore. In sharp contrast, the water feels lukewarm, like a bath that has been sitting for several minutes. Immediately, Kaley thinks this sensation could be a result of nitrogen narcosis and his mind is trying to fool him into believing that he may not even need his isothermal suit. That somehow he has found a small area of the lake where warm water circulates, or maybe he is directly above a fissure in the bottom of the sea floor that releases steam from the Earth's core.

Whatever the case may be, Kaley does not think he is imagining the feeling of warmth that has suddenly engulfed him. He tries to orientate himself to his surroundings and take an inventory of his body and his mind, hoping that neither is beginning to fail him. He remains stationary, for the first time a bit of hesitancy, a dash of reluctance, and a sprinkle of fear have entered his psyche. He slowly points the flashlight beam below him, afraid he has found the lair of his mysterious sea lizard, who has been slumbering but will surely awake from this unexpected intrusion. What a fine meal Kaley will make.

"Jonnie? You okay?" Eisley shouts in his ear. "Are you still with me, kid? You're too deep, Jonnie, you can't stay down there very long, do you hear me?"

Eisley's voice has become like a beacon in the darkness. And almost instantly, a different sort of beacon materializes, followed by another, and another.

For the second time since he has been underwater, his uncle expresses the exact same sentiments Kaley is thinking. Far above on the surface, Eisley peers at the screens before him, unable to comprehend what the cameras on Kaley's mask reveal.

"What in God's holy name-"

*　　*　　*

The four boats blaze along the water in a V-like formation, each boat carrying six men armed to the teeth for an enemy that only numbers two: one who is currently underwater and the other older than is commonly thought of as "fighting age."

Some of the men are equipped with the standard Colt M-16, the American military's workhorse since its inception in the 1960s. The M-16 holds twenty to thirty rounds of .22 caliber bullets and has a range of four hundred meters. Of course, at that distance, the soldiers' confidence in the weapon's accuracy begins to dissipate. Nevertheless, because of an in-line recoil that maintains the barrel from wandering off target during firing, it is considered one of the most accurate rifles in the world.

The other men prefer the M4, the immediate descendant of the M-16, as the former borrows about eighty percent of its parts from the latter. The M4 is currently the weapon of choice for Special Forces throughout the world, primarily because it is for close-range combat, situations Special Forces are intimately familiar with and indeed, specialize in.

Two of the "lucky" ones in the squad are equipped with the newest in military technology, a weapon believed by most of the gun-educated and many a card-carrying NRA member only to be in development. The four-barreled firearm is a handheld gun and, with the help of a group of microelectromechanical thrusters, capable of firing 15-millimeter heat-seeking mini-rockets. In addition to the mini-rockets, the gun also holds a clip of 4.6-millimeter bullets for what the top brass sees as essential in the next frontier of warfare coming soon to a news channel near you: urban warfare. Despite what most people believe, the head honchos in the military did garner a few lessons from their troops' excursions into urban jungles like Mogadishu and Haiti. Not many, but a few.

Certainly, the word *overkill* comes to mind when looking at this newest technology in weaponry, and in fact, could also be applied when comparing the amount of men and weapons against the enemy they face. It is like a couple dozen tanks squaring off with an Amish village.

This, however, is the way they have been trained and drilled: to always be prepared. To be overly prepared in fact, for any extenuating circumstances. They will certainly not lose a fight because they are outgunned or their enemy is better prepared. It is not a matter of confidence for these men, as they all hold the highest amount of regard for their abilities, bordering on sheer arrogance. One can see it in their commander's face, a look he has somehow etched onto his men's faces, like a gene he has managed to pass on to every soldier who serves under him. It is a look of impassivity, with no mercy or warmth radiating behind the eyes, knowing that they cannot be defeated by anything or anyone.

It is a look that can be summarized in two words: *stone cold.*

The men all look forward as they approach the target. They do not make last minute adjustments or check their weapons, for they have already done this several times over. Their target is in sight and their focus and concentration is completely on the objective before them. Many of them are simply jacked to have a mission on consecutive nights. Of course, tonight's mission is unexpected and they have not specifically trained for it, but how difficult can two men be?

The boats begin to fan out and approach the target from several directions, knowing full well the "capabilities" the retired Navy man has installed on the ship. They were briefed on the Navy man's expertise and what to expect from his unique vessel. Regardless, every man on these four boats believes these "capabilities" will be no match for them.

The stretch run begins as the boats are only a few hundred yards away from their target. The men remain calm and collected, but added to the mix is a look of raw determination on their faces. It is a look of motivation to do whatever is necessary to achieve their objective. They have never failed before, so why start now?

A burst of gunfire signals the start of what looks to be a very brief battle.

*   *   *

Kaley peers below him, but is unable or possibly incapable of processing, quantifying, or registering it properly. As the flashlight beam moves over the bottom of the sea floor, a strange phosphorescent light spreads like wildfire. The sudden warmth Kaley felt before becomes more intense and he is slowly enveloped in the light from below. He feels as if someone has parted the clouds to reveal the shimmering stars in the night sky. Only he is floating along with them rather than gazing up into the heavens to observe them.

The wildfire continues across the sea floor, spreading madly and without disruption. There is no obstacle or impediment that seems capable of halting or even slowing this raging lightshow. There seems to be no "off" switch.

Kaley's astonishment is tempered by the fact that he does not know what is happening or what harm it might do to him, if any. He does know that it is...well, *beautiful*, which would be the apt word to describe it. The feeling of warmth he felt before has now fully transformed into a more powerful sensation, something deeper and all consuming. He feels as if he has just swallowed a kettle of hot chocolate, but instead of occupying only his stomach, it occupies his entire insides. His body, followed by his mind, begins to tingle. He catches himself trembling, like an earthquake is shaking his entire being right down to the core.

Suddenly, he wonders if he has been captured by the "raptures of the deep." Maybe this is all an illusion that has invaded his mind and taken over his cerebral cortex, his hypothalamus, his . . .

Only moments before, he was afraid of a sea serpent emerging from its lair and swallowing him whole. And now, the world to him has become a rock concert, a roller coaster ride, an explosion of light and sensations. He does not think the sight before him is an aberration, a trick of the mind, or an illusion he has conjured. *Besides, Mike sees the same thing I am seeing, right?*

Perhaps his oxygen supply has quickly diminished at this depth and he is simply floating away from this world and into another. Moving towards the white light, as so many across the globe have reported seeing when approaching the gateway of death.

Kaley attempts to shake the strange sensations from his head, but to no avail. He is fully absorbed in its grip, and he feels powerless, helpless even. Succumbing to the warmth and then-

He explodes back into the world.

"Jonnie!" his uncle exclaims. "Hemingway is here! We got company."

Kaley hears a short burst of gunfire before his uncle keys off the transmitter.

*   *   *

Eisley saw them coming. Two blips on a screen, and then four blips. Fanning out to surround all sides of the boat. He definitely saw them before he heard them, which seemed unusual. On a deserted stretch of water in the middle of nowhere, sound tends to carry over the lake like a bolt of electricity. Eisley can only surmise his enemies have some type of silencer or stealth mechanism on the engines of their boats. They obviously do not want anyone to know they are coming, which, to Eisley, suggests he and his nephew are about to have a potentially lethal encounter. But Eisley intends to test that theory with a little surprise.

In addition to the .50 caliber machine guns fore and aft of the ship, Eisley, on the crown of the ship, installed a grenade launcher with a nearly flawless targeting system. Of course, anyone who knows Eisley would suspect these are no ordinary grenades.

Besides the inherent problems one may face installing a missile system on a deep-sea fishing boat, missiles tend to be bulky and unwieldy for intimate, close encounters with enemies. Obviously, finding conducive places on this type of boat to store the missiles, let alone building a system capable of launching them, proved extremely difficult. Eisley pondered this small dilemma for a long time before resolving it with a more practical, albeit insane solution.

The grenades look in appearance like any other grenade fired from a weapon: compact, sleek, flat on one side and cone-shaped on the other. When it comes to weaponry, however, everything concerning Eisley must contain an asterisk. In this case, each grenade contains a small microchip that makes this particular brand of projectile very, very smart. At least, quite intelligent as far as weapons go.

The grenades are called *"sound-seeking"* projectiles. Radically different from the heat-seeking variety, the grenade can be programmed to recognize the sounds of enemy tanks, all terrain and amphibious vehicles, and even the click of an enemy reloading his rifle. Conversely, the grenade is programmed according to its owner's arsenal using one of two methods: serial numbers from the weapons themselves, or lacking those, burning a compact disc from a vast online database that contains the audio discharge of nearly every known weapon and downloading the owner's specific "tracks" onto the chips contained in the grenades. In other words, the grenade becomes familiar with the sounds of its master's weaponry and when launched, becomes like a bulldog and sics those foes whose weaponry it fails to recognize.

It is called the XJ-4, and why it was bestowed with this name, Eisley has no idea. He only knows that he had to have them after seeing a demonstration. He obtained a stash of them from a friend formerly employed by the Mossad, the Israeli intelligence arm. Eisley has remained friends with quite a few people from his days in intelligence, at least those still alive, and it always amazes him the kinds of goods he is able to procure simply by asking. That, and a few thousand American dollars always help.

The grenades are intended solely for short-range combat and, just like a bulldog, cannot effectively fight with a blindfold on. The grenades are not simply launched into the air and magically know where and whom to attack.

The programmer must enter some type of directive: a set of coordinates, a certain direction, and/or an approximate distance to the target.

Eisley decides to enter a general direction and the grenades can lock onto the steady *whirrrr* of the enemies' propeller blades. The microchip also allows its owner to download sounds associated with their respective "mode of transportation." In this case, Eisley programmed all the sounds related to his boat. From the firing of the .50 caliber guns to the emptying of the bilge compartment, the grenades know Eisley as much as any weapon can without taking him out to dinner and a movie.

In addition to his two choice weapons of design, he also installed a three-inch thick steel door in his command center to ensure all the privacy he needs when operating his defense system. It would take a hell of a blast for the door to be compromised. The only drawback is in the event of a fire breaking out in his command center, in which case Eisley is as good as cooked anyway. Eisley deploys the door and hopes such a scenario does not present itself in this battle.

Last, but certainly not least, Eisley has his trusty Browning .22 if the steel door does happen to be penetrated.

Despite all of his outer-defense weapons, Eisley wishes he maintained a couple of automatic weapons on board. Of course, not many people plan for an attack on their deep-sea fishing boat, so Eisley would have to be content with what he has.

According to the scope, Eisley sees that the boats are still approaching from only one side, with the two inner boats a little closer than the two outer ones. It appears likely the outer ones will move around to flank him, which any good commander would order as long as the cross fire does not pick off the men on the opposite flank.

Eisley hits a switch on his console and instantly, the compartment doors covering the machine guns release and the guns move forward several feet. Eisley constructed the pod they maneuver on to allow the guns as much space as possible in order to cover a wider firing zone. But he also does not want them jutting out conspicuously from the boat, inviting a would-be enemy to target the entire gun. Reinforced around the area, as with the majority of the hull of the boat, Eisley installed a durable, lightweight metal similar to steel, but not quite as heavy, which would create unnecessary and uneven ballast to the entire structure.

Eisley fires several shots across the bow of the nearest two ships to let them know he is here, waiting and ready. Almost instantly, however, he hears a loud blast from the front of his ship, which rocks the boat backwards.

Eisley looks at his monitors to find the forward .50 caliber gun has been either destroyed or at least incapacitated. Whatever the case, based on how quickly one of his guns has been removed from the equation, it is obvious to Eisley that his foes have done their homework.

Eisley has only twelve of his "special" grenades, which he had not planned on expending this early in the game. When your enemy makes a statement like that, however, you have to craft an equally effective and damaging response.

He punches in several numbers for the grenade launcher and prepares to unleash a small slice of hell on the approaching boats.

Eisley looks at the screen in front of him, waits a moment, and then fires the first grenade.

*   *   *

Within seconds of the first round of bullets sprayed by the Navy man's .50 caliber, one of the two soldiers carrying the four-barreled gun launches two of the 15-millimeter heat-seeking mini-rockets from a standing position on the boat. His legs are spread wide, his stance perfectly balanced despite the choppiness of the boat churning over the water. The boats began to rapidly accelerate once it became apparent they had been made by the Navy man.

No one else in the squad has fired yet on orders to wait until the mini-rockets have taken out the boat's forward perimeter defense. The soldier who was issued one of the two four-barrels in the company is one of the most accurate men his commander has ever seen, the primary reason he was chosen to launch the attack. With the four-barrel gun, however, the commander could have selected the worst marksman in the group, although it would be a difficult task to select among his men a single candidate for that rather indistinct title. Because, despite the precise accuracy of each of the soldiers in his squad, it is not a necessity the shooter is dead-on target. He simply needs to be close and the minis would do the rest.

The rockets lock onto the heat generated from the barrel of the .50 caliber and within seconds, completely incapacitate the gun, leaving the barrel and other pieces of it scattered on the surface of the lake. The reasons why they employed the mini-rockets instead of a rocket launcher are two-fold: first, they do not want to destroy the boat and anything potentially valuable that might be in the possession of its occupants; and second, their orders are not to kill – just yet.

The two closest boats now have an open avenue to the front of the boat and nothing, it seems, to stand in their way. Unbeknownst to the squad, however, not all of their intelligence is complete. Every soldier who has been in battle on the side with superior numbers and firepower will tell you that inaccurate intelligence and underestimating an opponent are two cardinal sins when fighting an unknown enemy.

Although the motorboats' engines are nearly at peak speed, the engines have been equipped with a special silencing mechanism, stifling the amount of sound that would typically be reverberating across the lake. This allows the men in the boats to hear a sound not unlike a bottle rocket being launched. A brief flash of light appears from the crown of the Navy man's boat, followed by a *puff* of smoke.

The commander sees this from his vantage point and immediately orders the man steering his boat, *"Veer port!"*

The man reacts instantly and splits away from the other boat it is traveling beside. The commander's boat is now about forty yards away from the Navy man's boat, on the starboard side.

The commanding officer turns and looks at the boat it was traveling parallel to just in time to see a projectile strike the stern of the craft.

KA-BOOM!

A deafening explosion echoes across the lake, scattering men from the boat into the cold, dark water. Several lifeless bodies float on the surface. The front of the boat, which has not been completely obliterated, travels several more yards before coming to a stop, trailing in its wake debris and human bodies. The middle of the boat, which is actually now the back of the boat, is engulfed in flames. Within a couple minutes the boat will disappear beneath the surface, carrying with it the only occupant left onboard, the driver, whose head pierced the glass windshield upon impact.

To the utter shock of the commander, he realizes the Navy man has outfitted some type of grenade launcher on his *fishing boat.* The commander returns his gaze forward to determine the status of his other two boats. They are practically equidistant from either side of the back of the Navy man's boat, approaching fast, trying to obtain an adequate firing angle on the aft .50 caliber.

Radio communications are strictly prohibited on a mission such as this one, just as they were during their mission the previous night. The risk of being overheard over any communication lines, be it a military frequency or simply by an ordinary citizen who monitors the air-waves, is far too great to justify using them. Besides, the essence of an effective unit is their ability to communicate with each other through non-verbal gestures and signals, not relying on the spoken word to transmit vital information that could possibly be captured by an industrious enemy. In this regard, the men are practically telepathic in their ability to communicate with one another.

Of course, an obvious drawback when separated into small groups is that each team is on its own, and the commander must rely on the team leaders to act appropriately and decisively. While the commander has total faith in his team leaders, he is not one to relinquish responsibility and control, to delegate his duties to others. He trusts his team leaders will act in the exact same manner in which he would if he were present.

And now, the commander only hopes that his men in the other two boats have taken heed of their enemy's hidden and thoroughly deadly weapon. This thought is nearly simultaneous with the launch of another projectile from the crown of the ship.

*   *   *

The second grenade Eisley launches does more harm than good in the long run. The grenade barely clips the propeller of one of the speedboats, which is cruising towards him at a tremendous speed on his port side. The grenade is certainly not a direct hit, but the aftermath of the explosion more than compensates for the seemingly errant shot.

When the grenade grazes the propeller and strikes the water, the force of the impact lifts the stern of the speedboat into the air like a champagne cork being popped off a bottle. The rear of the speedboat completely capitulates, dumping the men into the water. One man lands at an extremely awkward angle and his neck snaps like a twig.

However, Lady Luck is not on Eisley's side tonight, preferring instead to favor the side with greater numbers, perhaps simply playing the odds. As the speedboat sails through the air, it skips over the water several times before slamming into the back of Eisley's boat in a jarring collision.

Eisley tumbles from his chair as if he has been physically pushed from it and he lands on the floor with a *thud!* His head slams against the side of the steel door, and a sudden surge of blackness surrounds his eyes.

The fishing boat heaves to its starboard side before

bounding back to an upright position, but it continues to rock unevenly back and forth.

A small trickle of blood rolls down Eisley's hairline and hangs over his eyelid, frozen there.

Eisley staggers, grabs the side of his chair and pulls himself up. He blinks and suddenly, his right eye sees only red. He paws at his eyes and attempts to clear them.

A blind enemy is a vulnerable enemy, he thinks. Eisley cannot recall where or when he first heard the phrase, but he can certainly relate to it at the moment.

He looks at his console and sees with a sinking feeling that the aft .50 caliber has been incapacitated as well, whether from enemy fire or from the collision is not clear.

At this point, is the reason really important?

More importantly, however, are the large, urgent letters flashing on one of his screens.

The hull of the ship has been breached!

The speedboat must have struck a weak spot in the hull where the armor was not securely reinforced. Water is quickly filling the interior of the hull and within several minutes, the boat will be submerged.

Shit!

The remaining two enemy boats are now stationed alongside his own vessel.

Seconds later, Eisley hears several pairs of heavy boots on the deck outside the steel door. It soon sounds like a small army has boarded. What seems odd is that he does not hear any muffled voices, talking or directives outside, only the echoing footfalls. He knows they are coming for him.

Eisley picks up his Browning .22, realizing the short amount of time he may be able to hold them off with the small pistol.

Eisley quickly considers his other options and they appear limited. One thought, however, does pop into his head, and its rather absolute outcome pleases Eisley in a strange way.

Eisley hits the TALK button on his console.

*   *   *

"Jonnie, you there?"

After what seems like an eternity, Kaley hears his uncle come back to him. Initially ecstatic to hear his voice, Kaley instantly notices the weariness in it, and a feeling of dread sweeps through him. His uncle typically does not sound like a cheerleader at a pep rally, but he certainly has an ever-present feistiness to his tone that now seems to have vanished in the span of a few minutes.

After Eisley informed him that "Hemingway is here," Kaley immediately knew that their unwelcome visitors are surely associated with the same people who paid a visit to his home in the middle of the night. It is only a hunch, but Kaley senses that he and Rushmore inadvertently involved themselves in something greater than they could have possibly imagined.

There is a sensation Kaley feels down to his bones that a plan was set in motion last night. There is some kind of predetermined course at work here and Kaley and Rushmore disrupted it. The word courses through his mind and Kaley instantly thinks of his friend, Sean O'Connell: *conspiracy.*

This is the only word Kaley feels can adequately describe it. Now Kaley wonders if there is anything or anyone that can possibly stop it.

Kaley began swimming towards the surface upon hearing his uncle's warning, keeping his eyes trained on the sea floor below, still dazzled by the light surrounding him. Kaley fully anticipated that the chaotic explosion of light on the sea floor might cease once it reached the walls of the chasm he was in, but the light continued snaking up the walls. The tiny beacons of light finally stopped around eighty feet above the sea floor, encircling the entire circumference of the hole. Kaley looked around the chasm and noticed that indeed, the light stopped at virtually the same level on the walls throughout.

What amazed Kaley even more, however, was when he looked around the chasm, he received the distinct impression he was swimming in the midst of a giant crater. As Eisley pointed out, it was as if an object had crashed here with such force that it penetrated the first stratum of land in the lake and settled on another level over a hundred feet deeper. It might explain the jagged edges he noticed on the ledge where the chasm began.

Kaley's initial instinct was to hastily kick towards the surface at the sound of his uncle's warning. With the beacons of light racing up the walls of the chasm, he absentmindedly attempted to follow, as they seemed to guide the way for him. Much as it pained him mentally and emotionally, Kaley could not rapidly ascend to the surface to come to his uncle's aid because it could pain him even more *physically.*

Kaley's ascent to the surface must be extremely gradual on account of a condition that can develop called "the bends," which occurs in deep-sea divers who ascend too quickly to the surface. The bends are caused by a rapid decrease in atmospheric pressure, resulting in the release of nitrogen bubbles into the body tissues. When the body is subjected to high atmospheric pressure, such as that found underwater, the respiratory gases of the body are compressed and larger amounts are dissolved in the body tissues. During an ascent from depths greater than thirty feet, these gases flee as the external pressure decreases. The decrease in air pressure releases nitrogen in the body in the form of small gas bubbles that block small veins and arteries and collect in the tissues, cutting off the oxygen supply and causing various unpleasant symptoms, such as nausea, vomiting, and pain in the joints and abdomen. In severe cases, the effects include shock, total collapse, and death. The ascent to normal atmospheric pressure must be conducted gradually in order for the nitrogen to be released slowly from the blood and expelled from the lungs.

While Kaley would be foolish to attempt to violate this established law of science, because after all, there would be nothing he could do for Eisley if he is dead, he is also fully aware his uncle desperately needs him. The ascent has been agonizingly slow, even though Kaley is probably pushing the envelope as far as he can. He does feel dizzy, another symptom of the bends, and his joints are on fire. He continues to look above him, as if expecting to see something more significant than water from this vantage point. Kaley thinks he hears faint rumblings on several occasions, but they might be a figment of his imagination.

Kaley swims at an uneven pace towards the surface,

ignoring the fact that he needs to stop at certain intervals for a set period of time before continuing his ascent in order to avoid the bends. He simply continues when he feels he has spent enough time at a certain depth or when his patience runs thin, whichever comes first. It is hardly scientific and without a doubt stupid, but he cannot bear the thought of Eisley on his own against God knows who on the surface.

Kaley passes the ledge he initially inspected on his descent, noting he is still well over a hundred feet away from breaking the surface.

And that is when he definitely hears a loud impact above.

*   *   *

"Jonnie, you hear me?" Eisley asks.

Eisley looks at a small monitor connected to a camera directly outside the steel door. He sees several men, about ten yards away from the door, all holding automatic weapons and looking rather determined and exceptionally pissed off. They are dressed in black from head to toe, with some wearing black camouflage on their faces while others wear hoods with only slits for their eyes. It would be only a matter of moments before they barrel through the steel door, taking out their rage on him.

The screen beeps with a reply: Y-E-S.

Eisley grins approvingly and nods, "Atta boy. I knew you were okay. I got you around a hundred feet here, Jon, you should be well outside the blast radius."

Kaley does not like the sound of those words. He punches in a couple of question marks on his keypad and sends it.

Eisley sighs and sadly says, "Now listen, Jonnie, don't worry about me...I'll be okay."

Eisley again glances at the monitor and sees that, with the exception of one man who positions himself directly in line with the center of the steel door, pointing an odd-looking, four-barreled weapon, the rest of the men turn away and cover their heads.

The man takes aim . . .

"Retirement was too boring for me, anyway, Jonnie," Eisley says with a chuckle.

He places his hand over the button for the grenade launcher, knowing that the timing needs to be perfect.

Eisley lets out a deep breath, watches the monitor, and whispers into Kaley's earpiece . . .

*   *   *

"I'll take these guys, Jon boy, you get the rest of 'em."

Kaley would scream if he could, but with the breathing regulator in his mouth, it is impossible. He looks towards the surface, feeling disoriented and nauseous, unsure if it is because of the decompression sickness or because he is in absolute anguish over his own helplessness.

Suddenly, he hears a couple of nearly simultaneous whistles like fireworks, and then, for a brief instant, what sounds like an explosion is transmitted to his ears before the communication link abruptly ends.

This time, he is certain he hears a rumble above him, and a few seconds later, he feels a force against him like an undertow. The water, as if it has suddenly conjured up a few hundred hands, pushes him deeper underwater. He initially tries to swim against it, but it is hopeless.

Instead, he allows the water to take him where it wants to. His disorientation is starting to become acute and he tries to focus on...something, anything.

He looks to the gauges on his wrist and has the good sense to note his air supply is becoming dangerously low. With the panic of the moment and his rush to reach the surface, he may have inadvertently consumed more air than was absolutely necessary.

The shockwaves that swept over him only moments before appear to have dissipated. He begins to regain his bearings and slowly restarts his ascent, feeling like he is running in quicksand, making little to no progress. He decides he can take his time now, seemingly since no one would likely be there to greet him when he reaches the surface. At least, not anyone he would want to be there.

The anger and guilt begin to well up in Kaley. He knows his uncle is dead, and he knows it is his fault. All Kaley believed he was doing was asking for some much-needed help, and perhaps giving the man a little adventure in a rather routine life, certainly nothing fatal. Instead, he is responsible for bringing his uncle to a watery grave, entombed now in the sea that he so dearly loved. Kaley does not see the poetry, beauty, or irony in that which another person might see. All he wants now, all he thirsts for, is revenge.

Several minutes later, Kaley bursts through the surface of the water and looks around. Debris is scattered everywhere, much of it aflame. Numerous bodies lie strewn about, one of them possibly Eisley's, but perhaps not.

My uncle is dead, and it is all my fault, Kaley thinks

again. If he never came to him for help, Eisley would still be alive, retired, waking up early to go fishing or just puttering around the lake, beer in hand. Or adding armaments to his deep-sea fishing boat. Or . . .

Kaley suddenly realizes tonight's sunset had been his uncle's last, and this thought fills him with an unrelenting sadness that he cannot begin to confront, not now.

Suddenly, Kaley hears a sound in the distance. Maybe he is wrong about that welcoming party.

On cue, Kaley hears the distinct sound of helicopter blades cutting through the night air, followed shortly thereafter by a spotlight combing the lake. The chopper is no more than 300 yards away, but how it was able to arrive here so quickly or where it came from, Kaley has no idea.

Within thirty seconds, the helicopter is practically on top of him as he continues to bob in the water, trying to discern markings on the side of the craft before attempting to flag it down. The spotlight scans the lake, illuminates the burning wreckage, and finally, comes to rest on Kaley. Suddenly, a light clicks on in Kaley's head: it is the newest model Apache helicopter, exactly what his uncle described only hours before.

Kaley places his hand over his eyes to shield them as he simultaneously squints into the glaring spotlight. The helicopter suddenly banks left, hovering only about twenty feet above him. The rotors churn up the water and extinguish the burning debris surrounding him.

Now, it is only the blinding spotlight Kaley sees. Instinctively, he reaches for one of his knives and pulls it out. His eyes momentarily clear for an instant through the roiling water and glaring light as he spots a crouching figure in the hull of the chopper. The figure is dressed all in black and appears to be holding an object in his hands. The only thing Kaley sees are the whites of the man's eyes because a mask covers the rest of his face.

Suddenly, the man raises his arms, pointing what appears to be a gun at Kaley. Kaley raises the knife in his hand, attempting to gain some leverage in order to throw it more accurately. As he prepares to release the knife, he suddenly feels a sharp pain in the side of his neck. Nearly instantly, Kaley's whole body becomes numb as his head slowly lolls backward in the water, his arms and legs feeling disconnected from his torso. His mind begins to cloud and as he loses consciousness, his last thought is that he really hates the fucking water.

TWENTY

Somewhere over the Continental U.S.

Moriah, Bellini, and several other members of the Foundation sit quietly in a 10-seat jet cruiser, the only sounds the low whine of the engines and the occasional cough or clearing of the throat. The men are quiet for a reason: they are all lost in thoughts of the night ahead of them, the unfolding of the plan, and any obstacles that may arise and need to be overcome in the meantime.

Their well-laid plans are not foolproof, this they all know. Every man and woman in the Foundation knows even the most well-conceived plan that explores every possibility and accounts for every detail can still come crumbling down in the blink of an eye. Nevertheless, the group places all of their trust in the plan because they possess a unique expertise and a vast amount of experience in this particular area. Indeed, the group has been in the planning business since they were formed.

Plans to improve the country and make it stronger, plans to ensure the integrity of its borders and protect the people within them, plans to guarantee this lone superpower remains at the pinnacle for as long as they have a breath in their collective body. Their plans have extended externally as well, to foreign governments and institutions, influencing political movements and regime changes, completely altering ideologies to better suit and benefit the American way of life, and above all else, doing whatever is necessary in faraway lands to advance an agenda that has been undertaken for nearly a century.

To an outsider looking in, the members might acknowledge what they have done throughout the years has not always been right, or humanitarian, or even just. People of all nationalities, including Americans, have sometimes suffered at the hands of the group because of the actions they have carried out. The damage now is irreversible and irrevocable, a fact not only long forgotten by these men and women, but seen as absolutely necessary. They are able to justify it to their consciences and able to sleep soundly at night because they know everything they do is always in the interest of the greater good. They follow the doctrine that you cannot advance the interests of the whole without small sacrifices from its parts. These small sacrifices might include people's lives, but to them, this "collateral" damage is justifiable and completely warranted if it benefits the greater good.

The Foundation's agenda has always been fairly simple and straightforward. For most of its existence, the group's best interests are those of the United States', or more specifically, those they believe the U.S. should possess. Tonight, however, it is not only their own nation that concerns them. It is humanity whose existence they strive to preserve and indeed, save from possible extermination. It is humanity the Foundation has decided to cradle in their protective arms and rock back to sleep, safe and warm in their beds.

And at last, the members, the *actual* members of the Foundation, save a few of them, are ready and willing to put their money where their usually silent mouths are. Tonight decides whether there will be a tomorrow.

The shrill ring of Moriah's cell phone causes everyone's head to turn. A phone call at any point during the night does not signify good news or bad news, but nonetheless, each man tenses and anxiously awaits the latter, simply to be prepared.

Moriah reaches in the inner pocket of his suit coat and pulls out the phone. He hits the talk button and greets the caller with a brief:

"Yes?"

He listens for several moments, the other members not daring to look away from him. They study his face, looking for clues to the news on the other end of the line, checking for any indication something has gone horribly wrong.

Moriah is typically a picture of calm and cool. He does not allow his emotions to get the better of him, and he never lets them control his life or dictate his decision-making. It is a trait he inherited from his father, a characteristic found in most good leaders and one necessary to manage effectively and rationally. But now, suddenly, the façade does not appear so unruffled.

"Shit," he whispers as he disconnects the call.

The other men wait, bracing themselves for the next blow, the next coronary, the next stroke. It is a seemingly neverending parade of challenges, obstacles, and health risks.

Moriah clutches the seat back in front of him and stands up, looking slightly ill. He walks a few paces into the aisle and turns around. He takes a deep breath and looks at the others.

Speaking softly, he explains, "That was one of ours in Tamawaca. He just finished conducting a sweep of Abraham's house. He found a pool of blood in the basement, with a class ring a few feet away. He just confirmed the ring belonged to Abraham's nurse."

"*What?*" Bellini asks, aghast.

"That means," one man says, "the man with Abraham on the beach was . . ."

"*Jericho,*" Moriah whispers. "He found out."

"But how?" Bellini asks.

"Who cares?" Moriah snaps. "Jericho knows, he knows a lot more than he is supposed to at this point."

There are murmured whispers among the men, anxiety-ridden declarations and wide-eyed speculation.

"That means he knows-" another man begins.

"Enough!" Moriah shouts, irritated at the sudden panic in the men, the furor it has caused.

"We continue as planned," Moriah states. "We simply won't have as many surprises for Jericho as we initially thought.

"It does not change anything at this point," Moriah emphasizes.

The men look around at one another nervously, but remain silent despite their belief that *everything* can change in a moment's notice, especially knowing the cunning nature of Jericho.

They slowly sit down in their seats one-by-one, looking expectantly at Moriah, hoping, *praying* that their supreme confidence in his reassurances is not foolhardy or unfounded. Their faith may be shaken, but it remains fully invested in Moriah and his judgment. One can only speculate as to how the rest of the human race would feel about this unwavering devotion.

Location Unknown

Isabella O'Connell's eyes flutter open for the first time in what seems like years. She blinks a few times, attempting to clear away the haziness at the corners of her eyes, but to no avail. The haziness remains, in parallel to the feeling that seems to envelop her brain. She feels like she has been heavily drugged: a strange, almost euphoric sensation, a similar feeling she had a few years ago when waking up after an emergency appendectomy. She had felt groggy then, too. Now, however, the sensation is even more intense, and the level of sedation seems amplified a thousand-fold. She recalls gripping the cold, steel rods running alongside her hospital bed when she awoke, and within a second, her husband's hand gripping one of her's.

Isabella's eyes momentarily roll back in her head, but she manages to stave off unconsciousness for the time being. She reaches her hands out instinctively, hoping her husband is waiting at her bedside once again, but her hands cannot move. Or will not move. She feels a strange sensation on the top of her head, but she cannot reach out her hand to explore it further.

"Sean?" she inquires, barely reaching a whisper level. It hurts to speak, even a whisper. Her vocal chords feel like they have been stretched taut and dried out in the desert for several days. They are irritated and sore and the only thing she wants more than anything at this moment is a sip of water.

She tries to call out, but it does not even make it past her lips.

Oh my dear God, where is my family? she thinks. *Where am I and what has happened to them? And to me for that matter?*

Isabella recalls Sean going to the cottage to grab a few drinks for them, and then the fireworks began...*didn't they?*

Conor started – *Where the hell is Conor?* – clapping, as if in approval. Then...for some inexplicable reason, she keeps hearing over and over again in her mind an extremely sharp noise, like a thunderclap but a hundred times louder.

Next she remembers...as she held Conor in her lap, both of them being pushed back . . or was it pulled?

Isabella does not know what to believe is reality. She feels she has been asleep for so long that she cannot distinguish between the tangible world and what is simply part of her dreams.

But am I dreaming now? Or is this real? Am I lying in a hospital bed somewhere, or am I dreaming that I am in a hospital bed? Was the scene on the beach real or imagined? Is my mind playing a cruel joke on me?

Her eyes flutter open again as she concentrates on clearing away the cloudiness infiltrating her vision. She is determined to find her bearings, become aware of her surroundings, and then act rationally and pragmatically from there.

Isabella realizes she is not immersed in darkness, that there is a dim light present, as if the light bulbs themselves have not been replaced in a while and are dirty and blackened, releasing only a fraction of their potential light. A low humming noise radiates around her, but she is unable to pinpoint the exact location, finally conceding that the noise is surrounding her from all sides. Isabella hears no voices or sounds of movement around her. She thinks that in the periphery of her left eye, a much brighter light is evident, but her neck feels like it is bolted in place.

In fact, all of her extremities feel like they have been completely immobilized. She cranes her neck as far as she can in order to look down at her hands and feet, and suddenly, she realizes she is in fact not horizontal, but rather vertical to the ground. Her legs arc clasped together at the ankles, and both her wrists are also locked in place at her sides. She is not in a hospital bed, she is certain of that now.

Isabella's vision clears enough for her to focus in front of her, and what she sees amazes and confounds her. She gasps, unable to comprehend the scene before her.

Row upon row of the vertical tables similar to her own stretch out in front of her. Unfortunately, she can only see the back of each one. However, for the first time since her eyes fluttered open, and though she cannot see any other people, she *senses* she is not alone, that others are imprisoned in the same type of mechanism she is in. Above the rows, all she can discern is darkness as the faint glow from the dim lights does not seem capable of penetrating the blackness that permeates this . . place.

Where the hell am I? she thinks.

A rising wave of panic begins to well in her stomach and quickly swells throughout her entire body, as if a virus has been unleashed capable of spreading based on her level of fear. Isabella's breathing becomes labored as she frantically looks around for someone to help her. She wants to cry out, to scream at the top of her lungs, but she feels utterly powerless to accomplish such a monumental feat. Her eyes begin to roll back as she tries to maintain her focus, anticipating another loss of consciousness at any moment. Suddenly, her eyes catch something to her left, where she spotted a brighter light.

She cranes her neck as far as it will go, ignoring for the moment the intense pain that washes down her spine. She wills her eyes to focus on a table practically diagonal from her own, in her peripheral vision. She immediately recognizes the familiar little hand.

All the more familiar because she sees the scar on the side of his wrist as a result of a particularly nasty chicken pock.

It is her son's hand.

Tears well up in the corners of her eyes, making the haziness seem like she had 20/20 vision a moment ago.

"Conor?" she softly cries out.

The hand does not move.

Suddenly, all of the tables begin shifting to a horizontal position, Isabella's included.

Alarmed, she looks around and then back at her son, crying out again, "Conor, can you hear me, baby?"

Isabella is looking directly up now, even though she is trying to keep her eyes on Conor for as long as she can. The bright light in her periphery moves closer to him, and with a shock like a bolt of lightning, she sees the top of his head, *literally.*

It has been opened up like a can of peaches, with the

top of his brain clearly visible. The light moves closer and from out of nowhere, several mechanical arms jut out from around her son's head and start to . . .

With a strength she does not think she possesses at the moment, Isabella screams as loud as her lungs will allow, simultaneously feeling a painful prick in her arm.

*   *   *

Dawson tailed the fleeing colonel for several miles outside of Evans before concluding she would have a difficult time persuading him to pull over even if she does catch up to him. They are driving on a long county road where they nearly double the posted speed limit of 45 miles per hour. She ruled out trying to force him off the road, as his Hummer appears slightly more rugged than her borderline-antique jeep. Instead, she decreased her speed and fell back to maintain a distance of around 50 yards behind the colonel, deciding to see where he leads her.

After nearly 25 miles of driving on the county road, she curses under her breath when, after coming around a particularly long bend in the road, she no longer spies Fizer's taillights ahead of her. After several more miles without seeing the colonel's Hummer, Dawson decides to double-back down the county road to determine if Fizer possibly spotted her and pulled off the road somewhere, waiting for her to pass.

Driving slower now with a watchful eye for Fizer's Hummer on the side of the road, Dawson arrives at the point where she came out of the bend to find Fizer had vanished. She happens to notice an inconspicuous dirt path that leads through the trees to her right. The path appears just large enough to accommodate a car, or jeep for that matter. Dawson reasons that it is certainly worth a try because if she is wrong, either way Fizer is twenty miles away from her by now.

Dawson pulls the jeep over and glides it gently into a small clearing of trees next to where the dirt road begins. The trees should provide plenty of cover in case the MPs from Evans decided to pursue her. In fact, a person must be no more than a few yards away to even spot the vehicle, so good is the camouflage of the surrounding brush.

Dawson hops out of the jeep and checks her cell phone once again to find it still has no signal out here in the boondocks. While tailing Fizer, she had tried unsuccessfully several times to call Lieutenant Colonel Hermann, General Parker's assistant.

Lieutenant Hermann and General Parker probably think she has gone AWOL at this point, leaving her post and abandoning her mission. After Harrison informed her about the access numbers, she abruptly hung up on him. Not out of rudeness, of course, but for the express purpose of saving face in front of the colonel. Dawson cringes at the thought that Fizer believes he can brush her off so easily and get away with it. She knew as soon as she received the information from Harrison that Fizer's excuse for visiting the head was a cover for an impromptu fleeing of his command post. Her only goal at that point was to nab the colonel before he pulled an AWOL of his own, and before General Parker learned she allowed Fizer out of her sight. Thus far, she has been unsuccessful in the former and has not yet answered for the latter.

Dawson checks her sidearm again, noting it is fully loaded and the safety is off. She only wishes she has a pair of handcuffs for when she finds Fizer, or at least a pair of the plastic flex cuffs the military uses when detaining prisoners. How she would love to slap a pair on the colonel when, *not if,* she finds him. Cutting off the circulation to his hands is only one of the various ways she can think of to gleefully torture the colonel.

Dawson unbuttons another button on the top of her shirt, which has been completely soaked through with sweat now. Who says that ladies do not perspire? A person with no sweat glands could perspire in this Midwestern humidity.

Dawson scans the back of the jeep for a flashlight, but her lack of luck holds for the moment and she finds nothing. She has a pen in her pocket that has one of those tiny push-button lights at the top, and decides this will have to do. Besides, her eyes should quickly become accustomed to the gathering darkness around her.

She starts down the dirt road, sticking close to the edge in case an unexpected vehicle happens to drive by, forcing her to scurry into the underbrush. Dawson clicks her miniature flashlight intermittently to see where she is stepping. The only sounds she hears are the chirping of crickets and the constant buzz of mosquitoes around her ears, which are currently enjoying a bloodbath courtesy of her body. She swats them away every few seconds, only for a hundred more to resume their comrades' place. What can she do though? It is the middle of summer and she is strolling through a thicket of woods – this is where the mosquitoes come to party and apparently she is the guest of honor.

Or maybe not.

Dawson hears, or thinks she hears, the faintest of voices

through the trees ahead. She cautiously edges her way forward as she strains to listen, not risking using her flashlight and trying not to make any noise of her own. Unfortunately, every step she takes sounds like a jet engine to her, with twigs snapping left and right underfoot. She decides to stop completely, waiting to ascertain whether there are voices ahead or she is simply imagining them.

Dawson hears nothing for a few moments, but then she hears the faint murmur of a voice again.

YES!

She definitely hears voices and then, the revving of an engine. Nothing loud or abrasive, more like the *purring* of an engine in a luxury car. She continues moving towards the sound when suddenly, there is a flash of bright light, which is quickly extinguished. The bright light leaves a cluster of dots in its wake as Dawson squeezes her eyes shut and shakes her head back and forth, trying to clear the dots from her vision.

She hears a man's voice snap, "I told you, complete blackout. I don't want anyone to see from the ground."

Dawson hears another person start to protest, and the first man quickly cuts him off.

"No! No lights, goddammit!" the first man shouts.

Dawson is positive the first man is Fizer. She could recognize the familiar whiny voice anywhere. She crouches low and continues along the path. After another ten yards, she arrives at the edge of a clearing.

A twin-engine Cessna sits idling on a long, narrow airstrip that has been carved out of the forest. The runway appears no more than 15 yards wide and possibly the length of a football field, but Dawson thinks she may even be overestimating it. How someone could land and take off in such a compact space is beyond her. The pilot must be experienced enough to do so, although she would not want to personally find out for herself.

Unfortunately, she may have no other choice. Through the darkness, she can discern the colonel, now dressed in civilian attire, standing outside the right side of the plane, apparently checking a few items on the exterior. The pilot is sitting behind the controls, saying something to the colonel, but she is too far away to hear. If Fizer is taking off on that plane, which is readily apparent, that means she is, too.

But how? They look ready to take off at any moment and it is not as if she can stroll up to them and ask for a lift.

Think, dammit.

One of her father's friends owned a twin-engine prop plane similar to a Cessna, and he had taken her family for a ride one evening at sunset years ago. Altogether ignoring the spectacular view, Dawson grilled her father's friend on all the intricacies of the plane: how much fuel it needed, what each instrument signified, what you do in the event of a crash, what is the top speed, and of course, the landing gear.

What if it does not deploy? What if one of the wheels is damaged? Has your landing gear ever malfunctioned? What do you do then?

All the questions were partly a result of Dawson's inherently curious nature, but mostly because she was nervous as hell. The Air Force was definitely not in the cards for her, as she has never been a "comfortable" flier or one to enjoy the experience of being thousands of feet up in the air. It is not necessarily because she is afraid of a crash, but more the unnerving thought of placing her fate in the hands of a stranger, of a person who does not know her. Ultimately, she hates the idea of being unable to control what could happen to her in the skies above. Trusting another person to ensure her safety is not something that comes easily to Dawson.

Fortunately, her curiosity and anxiety reaped a substantial dividend from her barrage of questions: she knows that the landing gear, when retracted, is stored in a compartment large enough to accommodate a fully-grown adult. At least that was the case in the plane of her father's friend. She recalled the compartment was located directly underneath the floor of the cabin. As long as they do not happen to check under there during the flight, which is typically only necessary in the event of an emergency, she should be safe.

Now, how to snake her way up to the plane . . .

Dawson hurries back to the jeep, taking off her shirt as she goes. She is wearing a tank top underneath, so she does not feel like she is completely baring all. Except maybe to the mosquitoes, but fortunately, she does not embarrass easily.

She arrives at the jeep and drapes her shirt over the back of the driver's seat. She quickly scours the ground around the jeep, searching for the perfect weight. A few feet away, she finds a chunk of wood that is perfect, no longer than a person's thigh and possibly just as wide. More importantly though, it is hefty.

Dawson snatches the piece of wood off the ground and throws it into the front seat. She inserts the key and pulls the gearshift into neutral. With half her body in the jeep and one hand on the wheel, and the other half of her body kicking at the ground, pushing the stubborn jeep along, the vehicle gradually starts down the path. As she nears the clearing, she slows the jeep and shifts it into park. She hops out and steals a look at the runway to see Fizer pull himself into the Cessna.

Shit! Hurry!

Dawson takes out a small pocketknife she always carries with her and scurries to the rear left side of the jeep. Despite appearances, the blade is extremely sharp for such an ordinary-looking pocketknife. She crouches down and plunges the knife with all her might into the gas tank on the undercarriage of the vehicle.

Bingo!

The pocketknife penetrates the tank, creating a hole large enough for gas to start trickling out, but not large enough for the whole damn tank to empty in a few seconds. She wipes the blade on the grass, puts the knife away, hurries back to the front of the jeep, and looks out at the runway.

Do or die time.

Dawson pulls the gearshift back two notches into the drive position, hits the headlights, and dumps the block of wood on the gas pedal. She dives into some nearby bushes as the jeep roars out from the path and into the clearing. The jeep has the desired effect as both Fizer and the pilot look alarmingly towards this unwelcome intrusion. Hopefully, the glare from the headlights will prevent either of them from clearly seeing who is behind the wheel.

Fizer unholsters a gun from the front seat of the Cessna, leans out the plane and fires several shots. The jeep is about 35 yards in front of him, but evidently, Fizer has not been polishing his marksmanship. His aim is severely off, but the trail of gasoline may be able to help.

He fires several more shots and finally, the jeep explodes with a cacophony that echoes throughout the clearing. The jeep is not completely destroyed as it continues across the runway, a manic fireball heading for the woods on the other side of the clearing. The jeep explodes once again as it reaches the other side of the clearing, the wheels still turning as the vehicle finally comes to rest in a crop of trees.

Suddenly, the fire from the jeep spreads to its botanical neighbors and within seconds, several of the trees are aflame. The dryness of this Midwestern summer becomes evident very quickly, a fact Fizer seems to realize, too.

"Take off, now," he exclaims to the pilot.

"You got it," the pilot responds.

Fizer takes a last look at the jeep and mutters, "Stupid bitch," before closing the door.

The Cessna starts taxiing down the runway, quickly picks up speed, passes the forest fire on the left, and lifts gracefully off the ground.

If Dawson did not like flying before, she is certainly confronting her fears head-on now. She ducks inside the compartment of one of the wheels before nearly being pulled out by the velocity of the plane.

So Fizer thinks I'm a bitch. Well, he hasn't seen anything yet.

The plane disappears into the twilight of the night sky, blending in as if it has always been a part of it.

TWENTY-ONE

Tamawaca Beach

News of an explosion in the middle of Lake Michigan spread like a cold through the now media-dominated town of Tamawaca. The media horde initially believed it to be another terrorist attack, but this rumor was quickly dispelled once it became clear the explosion involved a fishing trawler. Nevertheless, an explosion in such close proximity to the site of a *confirmed* terrorist attack only 24 hours before certainly piqued the media's curiosity. Especially when they do not have much to report in the first place.

General Cozey had initiated a gag order for all pertinent information related to the attack, and his directive has surprisingly been maintained throughout the day. Cozey, of course, fed the hounds bits and pieces here and there, but nothing that contained great detail or further explained what occurred the previous night. Bason and Stringer scheduled all press conferences for the general as he briefed the media every few hours throughout the day. The information was purposefully vague, highly censored, and lacked specifics, courtesy of Cozey's two handlers. The primary reason for this is that the more details that are excluded, the easier it would be to ascertain who is actually responsible, allowing the group who committed the attack to furnish the specific details that match with the evidence found. Apparently, the Sword of Allah provided enough particulars to warrant serious consideration as the perpetrators of the attack.

Parker agreed with this logic up to a point, but sooner or later, Cozey and his people would have to realize you cannot hold the lid over a jar of swarming bees forever. Although the media has been acquiescent to the gag order imposed by the military, which is backed by the government's threat of potential jail time if anyone is found in violation, they could only be expected to report on nothing for so long. Words like "freedom of the press" and the "people have a right to know" are starting to be uttered throughout the town with regularity. Soon, these mild complaints are likely to transform into cries of suppression and even worse, *censorship,* and they will only continue to increase in volume and intensity as the lack of information continues.

When Parker realized the press was starting to get whipped into a frenzy with the dearth of information, he advised Cozey they needed to issue something with greater detail and significance, something...*important.* Cozey could not have agreed more, but the fact of the matter is, he pointed out, there is essentially nothing new to report. Besides details regarding the type of bombs used in the attack, which they agreed not to disclose for the moment, no new and for that matter, inherently interesting, discoveries have been found at the site. The head of the forensic team, Waterston, is still involved in his "procedures" and has yet to meet with Parker, an apparent snub that continues to irritate the general. Parker was on the verge of storming over to the makeshift lab and demanding an update from Waterston when news of the explosion reached him.

Parker was directly informed by a member of his staff at the Pentagon, who learned the information from another source that an explosion had been detected from one of their birds overhead.

That is all I need, Parker thought when relayed the information. *More fucking satellites.*

Apparently the lack of information is contagious, as details from his staff member were sparse, but the man was "fairly certain" the "hot spot" was identified quickly and the bird recorded the relevant activity around the area. Parker wanted the footage as soon as humanly possible, and the man promised to get right on it.

In the meantime, Parker determined that the head of the search-and-rescue mission at the site of the explosion is an old friend who used to be in the U.S. Coast Guard. He was able to contact her and requested that if anything interesting or unusual from the site is found, to relay it to him directly, not to General Cozey or his two watchdogs. His friend clearly understood and ensured Parker if something interesting is discovered, she would transmit it directly to him. Cozey would not like it, but that is only if he finds out about it, and even if he does, tough nuts.

Unfortunately, word leaked out about the explosion on Lake Michigan, a piece of information Parker was hoping to keep under wraps for the time being. Parker feared the incident would be the perfect catalyst to cause the media to start shouting from the tallest buildings that the United States of America is under attack, that our internal security and infrastructure is in serious jeopardy, that no one is safe, and above all else, the government is doing *nothing* to protect us. Parker's fears were not unfounded.

He had underestimated the media's penchant for creating panic and sensationalizing stories, and he had overestimated their heretofore noble use of discretion and ability to display patience in the event of a national emergency. Finally, their wait for the next sanitized news conference was over. They needed *something* to report and this was the linchpin. The media's reasoning is that the gag order only applies to the events surrounding the attack at Tamawaca, and their justification for reporting the explosion, as well as any wild theories connected to it, is that it is a completely separate incident. Of course, that does not prevent them from concocting their own conspiracy theories and connections between the two events.

Within minutes of learning of the explosion and obtaining a general estimate of the coordinates where it occurred, a half-dozen news choppers headed out to sea to investigate the "mysterious" and "unexplained" blast. The press typically does not believe in coincidences, especially occurring less than 24 hours apart and only a couple hundred miles away. So now the cat is out of the bag. It seems like the gag order never existed and probably never should have in the first place. Parker foresaw this happening and should have acted more decisively. However, in all honesty, neither he nor Cozey received any updates or new leads on the situation to disseminate to the media. Nevertheless, damage control would be the order of the day now, and the first item on the "to do" list is obtain a status update from Waterston, even if Parker has to beat it out of him.

But first, Augie has something to show him.

"What is it, Augie?" Parker asks testily.

Augie gently grabs the general's elbow and leads him up the stairs to the second floor of the *Easy Does It*.

"It's good, General, believe me," Augie slyly responds.

"It better be. I've got some serious ass-wringing to do, Lieutenant Colonel, and no time to waste."

Augie guides him down the hallway of the second floor to the last door on the right, which he pushes open, quickly ushering Parker in. Augie shuts the door immediately behind them.

The room appears to be primarily used as an office, albeit one that is extremely small and cluttered. There are two sagging bookshelves against the wall, loaded to capacity with books, tomes, and encyclopedias. In the far corner of the room, Private Anderson sits at a cramped desk with papers strewn across it. A notebook computer sits open in front of Anderson and, upon seeing the general, he quickly hops to his feet and salutes. Parker waves him back down.

"Yes, yes, Private, at ease," Parker says. "So, what's this all about?"

Augie motions to Private Anderson, who sits back down at the desk. "Why don't you show him, Private?"

"Yes, sir," Anderson complies.

He clicks on the mouse several times and the computer pauses, digesting the instructions, and the screen goes blank. A moment or two passes and then, a picture fills the screen.

Parker puts on his glasses and looks closer at what appears to be a jumble of images. Suddenly, the picture comes into focus. At first glance, Parker would guess that it is a-

"A bar, sir," Anderson states, finishing the general's thought.

Indeed, a smoke-filled, fluorescent-lighted bar appears on the screen. There are people dancing in front of a stage where a band is performing, and in the foreground, several tables can be seen with patrons seated around them. There is no sound on the video, but the images alone can tell you the band is belting one out for the audience.

"I'm not really a music connoisseur, Augie, you're going to have to help me out," Parker sarcastically notes.

Augie responds, "Sir, a couple of my intel guys commandeered this surveillance tape of a blues bar in Chicago called *Kingston Mines*, where they found one of our friends, or to be more accurate, a trace of one of our friends."

Parker looks at Augie, confusion written on his face.

"Private Rushmore, sir," Augie explains.

The name instantly registers with Parker. "The private on duty last night at Evans?"

"The same," Augie confirms.

"Well, okay, where is he now?" Parker asks excitedly.

"Private," Augie instructs Anderson, "bring up the disc drop first."

"Yes, sir," Anderson responds.

Anderson highlights an area towards the side of the stage and clicks the mouse. Immediately, this area now occupies the majority of the screen. The picture zooms in and Anderson clears up the haziness of the image with a few clicks. Several seconds elapse and finally, a person enters the picture.

"That's Rushmore, sir," Augie indicates.

Parker intently watches as Rushmore approaches the side of the stage. He pauses a moment, briefly glances around, casually tosses something into an open guitar case, and nonchalantly walks away.

"Did you see it, General?" Augie asks.

Parker sighs, "Yeah, it looked like Rushmore throwing a tip into the guy's guitar case."

"Seemingly," Augie says.

Augie addresses Anderson again, "Slow it down for the general, Private."

Anderson taps a few buttons and the tape rewinds to the point immediately before Rushmore arrives in front of the guitar case. Anderson zooms in even further and plays the tape in slow-motion speed.

Rushmore clearly drops a bill into the case with one hand while simultaneously slipping an object into a sleeve of the case with his other hand.

"Wait!" Parker exclaims. "Go back. What the hell was that?"

"See for yourself," Augie slyly smiles, holding up a small disc.

Parker looks at it for a moment and a smile slowly creeps across his face. "You son-of-a-bitch," Parker says. "Did you have to put on the dog and pony show first?"

"Well, actually," Augie hesitates as he glances towards Anderson, "Private Anderson insisted you witness firsthand Private Rushmore's rather courageous act."

The smile instantly disappears from Parker's face as he realizes Privates Anderson and Rushmore likely worked together for a substantial period of time at Evans, and are probably good friends. It initially failed to dawn on Parker how terribly agonizing this must be for Anderson.

With several additional taps on the keyboard, another image emerges from a different camera angle. This time, it shows a mass of people gathered around the bar, staring up towards a television. The camera's eye is pointed away from them, more to the side of the group and centered around a cash register behind the bar. Then, coming into view is Rushmore, but now he is slightly slumped over and being half-dragged/half-carried by two men on either side of him. A curious woman appears to address the men, who barely break stride as they continue to haul Rushmore out of the bar as inconspicuously as possible.

Anderson rewinds the scene and plays it again, as if by viewing it a second time they might gain further insight as to where Rushmore was taken. Then, the screen goes black, and Parker realizes that even if they knew where they took Rushmore, any chance of helping him has long since passed.

Parker looks down at Anderson, whose head is slightly bowed, already starting to mourn his friend. Parker places his hand on the young private's shoulder and gives it a reassuring squeeze. They all hold a moment of silence for Rushmore, admiring him for his incredibly brave act. He realized the heat was on and he had the wherewithal to dump the evidence in case something happened to him.

Parker glances at Augie, who motions towards the door, and Parker nods in agreement. Time to give Private Anderson a moment to himself.

Parker and Augie walk outside the room and close the

door behind them. In hushed tones, Augie says, "General, I might also have a lead on our missing sergeant."

"Kaley, right?" Parker recalls.

"Yes, sir. A couple of my people found out Kaley's got an uncle who was a former intelligence officer in the Navy."

"Yeah, go on," Parker urges.

"Sir, his uncle lives practically around the corner from here. If Kaley's on the run, he might have gone there," Augie concludes.

Parker considers this for a moment before nodding his head.

"I suppose it's possible. How long by chopper?"

"Ten minutes, fifteen max, sir," Augie responds.

"Alright, we'll view this when we get back," Parker says. He motions towards the room, "What about the kid?"

"I don't know, sir," Augie says. "He might be a little out of it right now."

"Yeah," Parker agrees. "Alright, we'll come back for him after."

"Yes, sir."

"And Augie," Parker continues, "see if you can grab a couple of soldiers around here who are not wet behind the ears. I don't feel like taking any chances. Who knows what might be waiting for us."

"Understood, sir. I'll have us ready to roll in ten minutes."

"Make it five, Augie," Parker replies.

TWENTY-TWO

Ecuador – 25 Miles Northeast of the Equator
17 Years Ago

The air was so muggy and humid that each step felt like you were walking underwater, which is always the first thing Sean remembers about that day. He often wishes it is the only thing he recalls about that day, but unfortunately, some memories never completely fade away. His nightmares from that day will always remain with him, buried deep after so many years, but still lurking in the subconscious, ready to invoke their gruesome and terrifying images at a moment's notice and with a cobra's lightning-strike. They arrive without warning, without provocation, and are as welcome as a knock on the door by the Devil himself.

Who said we need to remember our mistakes from the past in order to avoid repeating them in the future? Who espoused that we learn invaluable lessons from our errors in judgment? Who claimed our faults and poor decisions enable us to become a better person, and indeed, is simply a sign of being human, of being fallible?

THE FALLEN RACE TRILOGY

Sean does not know who spouted these pieces of philosophical wisdom or, depending on how you view them, philosophical mumbo-jumbo, but he does believe that sometimes, life simply is what it is.

Sometimes people get cancer; and sometimes people are used like lab rats in an experiment; and sometimes people are not who they appear to be and governments are not run *by the people or for the people*; and sometimes secrecy is effectively used as a weapon; and sometimes deals are struck that do not put forth the interests of the common good; and sometimes technology is not beneficial to humanity; and sometimes the wrong decisions are made and people die as a result; and sometimes, you were simply following orders.

It is not cause and effect Sean is arguing with, but rather sometimes in life, things simply happen, and whether they do so for a particular reason or not, they must be accepted. Humanity has not discovered a way to reverse time and change the course of the past in order to alter the present and the future. The ability to acknowledge that life is imperfect, that there is no blank slate on which to record a "perfect" life, is a fact Sean has accepted. Of course, that does not necessarily mean he has to like it, and very rarely does a day pass without him remembering the heat and the horror of the jungle that day.

Sergeant Sean O'Connell led a force of eight men that day, including himself. Their mission: infiltrate and detain the occupants of a small village, which intelligence reports had indicated was harboring several well-known and very dangerous Columbian guerillas. The guerillas were also to be detained if possible, but if not, lethal force had been authorized. The village was several miles from the Ecuador-Columbia border and was believed to be a vital arms cache for the guerillas. American intelligence determined that various smuggling operations, which included not just arms, but explosives, drugs, and even kidnapped foreigners, had passed through this tiny community at one point or another. Sean's team was sent in because American intelligence concluded it necessary to capture the Columbian guerillas and terminate the village's compliance with what were deemed unlawful and terrorist insurgents.

Part of the plan formulated by the government of the United States to help the Columbians regain a measure of control throughout the countryside and over its people, as well as decrease the amount of *coca* shipped to the United States by the guerillas to fund their war, was to eliminate or incarcerate these combatants. While the long-term effects of eradicating the offending plants and attempting to destroy the purveyors of this dangerous drug would show little to no impact on the drug trade, with America continuing to receive a steady stream of more than 80% of its cocaine from Columbia alone, this did not mean the American government did not try. Covert operations and deep excursions into the jungles of South America had become the norm for American Special Forces in the 1980s and 1990s. While the Columbian government knew to cooperate with the United States in their "War on Drugs," they tended to leave a sizable portion of the dirty work for Uncle Sam. Furthermore, the Columbians never officially authorized American troops to operate on their soil. At the same time, this was not Columbia, a fact sure to interest the government of Ecuador, had they ever been made aware of it.

Sean had an uneasy feeling about the mission from the start. In addition to the fact the villagers outnumbered his men nearly four to one, a new wrinkle was added to the mission. More specifically, a new technology. While Sean's team would obviously be armed to the teeth when entering the village, the brass had issued Sean and his men a new weapon that had recently been authorized for use in the field.

The device was no longer than a drumstick, but probably three times as thick. It was a highly polished silver color with a clear tube running through the middle nearly the entire length of the device. At one end of the tube sat a bright blue circular object, approximately the size of a ping-pong ball. On the top of one side of the device was a small switch that jettisoned the blue object out the opposite end of the device.

Sean's team was informed the object contained within the device could only be used once. The device was to be placed in the vicinity of the person's neck or upper torso area and the skin would absorb the circular object almost immediately. They were also informed the object was not lethal, but rather it would incapacitate the victim within a second or two of contact. These devices were to be used instead of their automatic weapons for several reasons.

First, the brass wanted as many prisoners as possible in order to conduct a full and thorough interrogation regarding the village's current activities and any other pertinent information related to the guerillas. Second, although each of the men's automatics was equipped with a silencer, they wanted to avoid inadvertent explosions that could draw other would-be guerillas or other curious types in the area into the conflict. Lastly, and probably most importantly to the brass, they were licking their chops to determine the full extent and capabilities of their new "toy."

This last reason comprised the brunt of what bothered Sean most about the mission. While the brass ensured them the device had already been tested extensively in non-combat situations, neither Sean nor his men were able to use the device themselves before it was issued to them several hours before deployment. Infiltrating a hostile zone was one thing, but entering a hot area outnumbered four to one and being ordered to use a device the combat team was not familiar with was quite another. Of course, Sean's team had been presented with the latest weaponry or newest surveillance gadgets on previous occasions, but this was a whole new beast.

This was a weapon his team had never used and had never *seen* used by anyone. Neither he nor his team knew the specific logistics of the weapon – whether the incapacitation worked instantaneously, what effect it had on the victim, and whether the enemy would have a chance during those precious few seconds to squeeze off a couple rounds at a member of the team. Combat units in the field always like to deal in certainties, weapons they can depend on and know can handle a particular job, like guns, grenades, and knives. The result of these used on another human being is obvious and as predictable as knowing that two plus two equals four.

The new toys, however, were something else indeed. Added to Sean's uneasiness, they were informed the blue objects inside the device were not entirely stable and therefore, were instructed to avoid undue or unnecessary jostling of the devices. Obviously, this was easier said than done and not entirely comforting when humping their way through the jungle. Sean's team was accustomed to moving stealthily, but they did not want to be forced to walk on eggshells because of an object they were carrying in their sacks. Nevertheless, orders were orders, and Sean always seemed to follow them, like any good soldier should. He quickly stifled the moans and groans of his men after they received their instructions and focused their attention on the mission. The men dutifully obliged.

The men were dressed in their jungle fatigues, and their faces were smeared with green and black camouflage. They were all perspiring profusely in the stifling heat, with Sean reminding his men to drink from their canteens every few minutes to avoid dehydration. Despite the intense humidity, the men quickly adapted to the elements because of their excellent conditioning and training.

As they approached the village, Sean gave the signal that there was to be no more verbal communication, strictly hand signals between the team members. Sean's team was fifty yards from the village when he held up his right fist, which halted the rest of his team in its tracks. He then held up two fingers and made a walking motion to the right and pointed, followed by a quick cutting motion with his hand. The two members on the far right of the squad quickly moved off in the direction Sean indicated, aware they were flanking the village on the right side.

Sean then held up two fingers on his left hand and made a walking motion to the left and pointed, also followed by a quick cutting motion. The two members on the far left of the squad followed suit and were the other side of the flanking maneuver, becoming another side of the wall. Sean and the three remaining members of his team would push directly up the middle, creating a funnel whereby the villagers could only go in one direction if they decided to flee. The squad knew that on the far side of the village was a nearly impassable river and essentially, they were creating a situation that left no possibility of escape for the villagers and any guerillas that might be present.

Sean waited for the men on the right and left flanks to move about twenty yards ahead and into position before he led the remaining men straight ahead. They walked gingerly, cautious of their footsteps, aware the villagers could have constructed a multitude of booby traps or warning systems that would alert them to unwelcome intruders. Sean and his men arrived on the outskirts of the village, crouching low to the ground, still hidden behind a dense patch of jungle.

Sean did not like what he saw.

The village was empty, devoid of any signs of life except for a few stray mules milling about. There were eight or nine mud-baked huts that dotted the village, but no sounds emanated from them. A large ceramic pot was suspended over the dying embers of a fire, unattended and appearing forgotten. The air was still, humid, as if holding its breath, waiting for something to happen.

And then something did.

A young woman emerged from one of the huts and moved towards what appeared to be the village's lone water well. She lowered the bucket attached to a rope. Her movements were slow, deliberate even, not the type of movements you would expect from someone who had probably done this same task thousands of times. She, too, appeared to be waiting for something.

Sean glanced back at his men, uncertain of their next move. His men on the flanks were waiting for him to signal for the assault to begin, but something did not feel right. Getting the jump on one woman seemed like overkill, but he also hated playing the waiting game. The more time that elapsed, the greater the chance his team would be discovered. He was hoping a majority of the villagers would be out in the open, and his men could move in simultaneously and surprise them. Pen them in like hogs in a sty.

As Sean's uncertainty mounted and he debated whether to move in or wait, it turned out his next move would be decided for him. When Sean looked back at the woman, she was standing as still as a statue, her eyes fixated on something to her right, near his men on the flank. Her head slowly turned in Sean's direction, and though he was behind a thicket of jungle, he would swear to his dying day that the slightest of smiles crossed her face as he stared at her.

Then, all hell broke loose.

As he continued staring at the woman, in his periphery near his men on the right flank, he caught a flash of light. It was a faint light, occurring ever so briefly, with a greenish hue to it. An instant later, there was a high-pitched screech, similar to a hyena's, followed by an explosion near his men on the right flank. Sean had never heard anything quite like it before, and he doubted he would hear anything like it again. As soon as this thought passed through his head, however, he heard another high-pitched screech, this time near his men on the left flank, followed by another deafening explosion.

They know our positions!

Sean whipped his head around to find a half-dozen dark-skinned men seemingly emerging from below the jungle floor. There was a large hole dug in the ground that had been camouflaged flawlessly, and his men passed over it without so much as a notion they were only several feet away from an enemy trench.

He screamed a warning to the other three members of his team, who seemed stunned by the situation and alarmed that the element of surprise was compromised. How and by whom were questions that would need to be addressed at a later time. For now, however, they needed to gather their bearings, focus on the mission, and keep each other alive. This was not the first time a wrench had been thrown into their plans, and as trained professionals, they were taught not to panic, to clearly evaluate the situation, and to quickly take action.

Sean's men, Johnston, Grant, and Martin, followed their commander's gaze and saw the short, grave men crawling out from the trench that apparently they walked over only moments before. Three of the dark-skinned men held what appeared to be guns in their hands, but on closer inspection, they were unlike any weapon the American soldiers had ever seen. A faint, green glow radiated from what Sean perceived to be the "barrel." At any rate, neither Sean nor his men wanted to determine exactly how the weapon functioned or what type of harm it could inflict.

Disregarding the directive to avoid use of their automatic weapons, and with their lives threatened, Sean instinctively opened fire at the advancing men with his automatic. Johnston, Grant, and Martin followed suit, spraying the men with automatic gunfire that drove their attackers back into the trench.

One of the men teetered on the edge of the trench, miraculously being struck by only one or two bullets, when he started to approach them again, seemingly oblivious to the hail of bullets he was about to encounter. The man raised his weapon and Grant emptied what seemed like an entire clip into him, sending him sprawling into the trench.

After this last round of gunfire, Sean realized the strange sound he had heard when they first opened fire on the approaching men was not an aberration. As the bullets met flesh, a dull thud could be heard with each impact. It sounded more like a bullet striking a stack of dictionaries, a kind of muted noise unlike the sound of a bullet tearing flesh and bone. Sean started to turn back around towards the village when something caught his eye.

It must have caught Johnston's eye, too, as he gasped in disbelief.

"Sarge . . ?"

Grant and Martin had both turned back towards the village, ready to pounce on the next foe, when they glanced over their shoulders to see Johnston and Sean staring disbelievingly at the trench. A hand, followed by several hands, suddenly appeared at the edge. Sean and his men gaped in awe as they quickly did the math in their heads – they figured that the firepower each of them unleashed would be enough to kill six men *apiece*. No man could have survived that kind of onslaught of bullets, but there they were, coming right back at them.

Martin reached for a grenade attached to his hip. He pulled the pin and, just as he was about to toss it into the trench, they heard the high-pitched whine again, but this time the sound was abbreviated. In an instant, Martin's body disintegrated with a strange *whoosh* right before their eyes. Blood sprayed across Sean, Johnston, and Grant as the surrealness of the situation deepened.

They stood there shocked, having trouble comprehending what happened to their comrade, and even more trouble understanding how Martin could have been completely obliterated like that in a heartbeat. These were men who did not become rattled or shaken, but now there was little doubt they had walked into a hornet's nest and they were back on their heels.

Sean tried to collect his wits about him as he turned in the direction he thought Martin was struck from, and he saw three men with those same devices in their-

Suddenly, what everyone had forgotten about, Grant called to their attention.

"Live grenade!" he exclaimed.

All three of them dove for cover, realizing that whatever had obliterated Martin, it had failed to dispose of the grenade in his hand.

A moment later, a blast shook the ground and the three men who had been approaching from the flank were tossed like rag dolls through the air. After the debris from the blast scattered over his head, Sean was instantly back on his feet, assessing the situation.

From his vantage point, he could not see any of his men on the right or left flanks, the woman at the village well had vanished, and there was seemingly nothing moving around him, noting that the hands at the edge of the trench were no longer visible.

Then, simultaneously, the three men within the blast radius of the grenade began to stir. As Sean stared at the men on the ground, something strange registered in him.

There were no marks on the men from the grenade blast: no wounds and no blood.

It was then that Sean realized he had noticed no wounds on the bullet-riddled men who had emerged from the trench.

Sean was about to empty the rest of the clip from his automatic into the men when Johnston beat him to it. He spotted them first and wildly fired at the men on the ground, screaming all the way.

"Die you motherfuckers! Die!" he yelled over the roar of his weapon.

Johnston stumbled towards the men on the ground, attempting to fire from point blank range, when suddenly, several sets of hands grabbed his legs and started pulling him into the enemy trench.

Sean reacted instantly, diving across the ground and managing to grab one of Johnston's arms before he disappeared into the trench below.

"Hang on, bro, I got ya," Sean promised, even though it was evident the men in the trench had the distinct advantage and were about to win this tug of war.

"Don't let me go!" Johnston pleaded, desperation and fear in his voice.

Johnston's eyes bulged in his head, the muscles in his neck strained taut as he held onto Sean's hand with all his might, knowing that if he let go, his fate was sealed.

"Grant," Sean exclaimed, "help us!"

Sean looked towards Grant, only to find two more enemy combatants were approaching from the left flank and Grant was busy holding them off.

Sean's team was on the brink now, in danger of being overrun and worse yet, annihilated. Sean held onto Johnston with two hands and was therefore unable to free a hand to grab a weapon. But Johnston had one arm free, and he grabbed his .38 from a side holster and fired at the men below. Their grip loosened slightly, but hardly enough to spring him from their clutches.

Sean stole a glance at Grant, who turned back the other way to ward off the three men who were momentarily stunned by the grenade, if stunned was even the appropriate term. The men shrugged off the grenade blast as if it was no more than a mosquito buzzing in their ear. Grant continued firing several shots practically point blank at the men, once again the dull thud of the bullets striking something other than...*what?!*

Normal human flesh?

Did they have some type of body armor?

It was obvious the bullets were connecting with their intended targets because the men were knocked backwards, but this only seemed to slow them momentarily, and they gave no indication they were even injured. They reacted as if the bullets were mere pebbles, continuing their relentless assault on Sean and his men. They seemed almost...*inhuman.*

If they did not bleed, how could they be killed . . ?

Johnston emptied the clip of his .38 into the men occupying the trench, but they still firmly held onto him. Johnston's head looked like it was ready to explode, the veins throbbing in his face, the muscles in his arm growing tired.

He dropped the gun and reached for a sheath located on the side of his waist, removing a double-edged dagger. As he raised the dagger to plunge it into the men below, Sean heard the high-pitched sound again followed by a strange *whoosh.* Johnston practically disintegrated in Sean's arms. Johnston's arm directly below the elbow was still clutching Sean's hand, the only physical evidence remaining of the man.

Sean dropped the arm and rolled over towards Grant, springing up and crouching so they were back-to-back now, attempting to fend off the approaching enemy on both sides. The clips were starting to run low because Sean's team had not packed much ammunition for the mission. Partly because they did not think they would need a large supply to subdue the village, and partly because they had received-

"Oh, shit!" Sean exclaimed, a light bulb springing up over his head.

As the enemy closed in, Sean suddenly remembered their newest "weapons."

Reaching into the sack slung over his back, he shouted to Grant over his shoulder, "Use the sticks, Grant, the sticks!"

"What?!" Grant shouted back.

"The sticks," Sean screamed, as he pulled out a handful of the new toys and held them up.

His team was issued thirty of the new weapons, with Sean carrying nearly half of them and the rest scattered amongst the men.

"Let them get in close for us to use 'em," Sean ordered.

"Too late, sir," Grant replied, as he motioned towards the men climbing up from the trench.

Grant looked at his commander desperately, hoping to see a sign that they would survive this mission, that their new weapons would stave off this seemingly invulnerable enemy.

Sean simply nodded his head and said, "Upper part of the body, remember that U," referring to Grant's nickname bestowed by the other men of the team.

It was in reference to Ulysses S. Grant, the renowned Civil War general and president, because the men had noticed Grant reading a biography of the prominent war hero when the team was first formed.

"Yes, sir," Grant responded, as he pulled out one of the new weapons from a sack slung around his shoulders.

"Here," Sean said, handing Grant several more of the devices.

"And stay away from those things," Sean warned, referring to the enemy's weapon that obliterated Martin, Johnston, and most likely, the rest of his team.

As the enemy closed in on both sides of the two men, Sean noticed that not all of the men were holding that strange weapon. Sean casually shuffled a few steps to his left to obtain a better angle on a man who was not holding one.

At the same time, Grant lunged toward one of the men climbing up from the trench and placed the weapon on the man's neck, releasing the mysterious blue orb. As Grant pulled back, he could see the orb grotesquely lodged in the man's neck, which he began desperately clawing at.

When the man Sean targeted was only a few feet away, Sean seized the initiative and shot the man in the kneecap, buckling his legs. Sean once again noticed no blood or wound on the man's knee from the gunshot.

The man began to fall to the ground when Sean grabbed him and applied the weapon to his head and flicked the switch on the device. The man seemed instantly paralyzed for a moment, but Sean's satisfaction that the device actually worked was tempered by what happened next.

The men Sean and Grant "shot" started violently seizing and coughing up what appeared to be blood, but it was an odd, phosphorescent color. Their eyes bulged out of their sockets and they began hemorrhaging the same odd color from their ears and nose. Their skin became practically transparent and they began struggling for breath.

The remaining men stopped in their tracks, staring helplessly at their stricken comrades, seemingly in shock at the damage done to them. They looked uncertain of what to do, whether to attack or retreat, and Sean and Grant took advantage of their hesitancy by using the device on several more of the men.

Each time and for every man they used the weapon on, what followed was the same, bizarre reaction to it: violent seizing and hemorrhaging of a strange liquid, their skin becoming nearly translucent, and a shortness of breath. It ended the same, too: the man clawing at his neck and face, falling to his knees, and finally, plunging face first to the ground.

One of the many things embedded in Sean's mind from that day was one of the stricken men lurching towards him. Sean remembers the man stumbling towards him, not with the intention to harm him, but in a different way.

Sean saw it in the man's eyes. A look that questioned, *What have you done to me?*

Sean did not know the answer to that question because in all honesty, he did not know himself. The new weapon was a wild card, an unknown, whose power and capabilities were known only to its creator. The brass told them the device incapacitated, but what Sean and Grant saw was a weapon that did damage well beyond that. It completely destroyed its victim, and judging from their enemies' reaction, it inflicted gruesome and horrible suffering before doing so.

Sean thought he should have felt a small amount of pity for the enemy, and perhaps in some way he did empathize, but he also reminded himself of Johnston and Martin and the rest of his team. They did not deserve to die like that, with no body to bring back to their families, a pool of blood the only thing left of them.

How do you explain that to their loved ones?

Eight men went out, only two men returned, and barely anything remained of the six killed-in-action (KIA).

Upon seeing several more of their comrades perish the same way the first two had, the rest of the villagers became frightened and fled into the surrounding foothills.

The brass would certainly be proud of their handiwork, and Sean would quickly realize they wanted to admire it sooner rather than later. As Sean and Grant stared at the carnage around them, their breathing heavy and labored, they looked at one another and silently asked each other what the hell had happened here.

That question would not be answered now, and in fact, it would not be answered for a very long time.

No answers would be forthcoming from the brass, and the mayhem and confusion of this day would lead one man to a dishonorable discharge and the other man to suicide.

As Sean and Grant continued staring at one another, a look of recognition passed over their faces as they heard a familiar sound.

Suddenly, the helicopters came screeching from out of nowhere-

*   *   *

Sean wakes with a start, sweat blanketing his face and his shirt damp with perspiration. It is a cold sweat though, as he immediately feels cold blasts of air hitting him from several sides. He hopes he does not have to become accustomed to waking up in strange places on a regular basis, which he seems to be doing more often than he would prefer.

His eyes begin to focus and when they do, he sees the back of a car seat. In fact, he quickly realizes he is in a moving car. The steady drone of the road underneath and the low hum of an air conditioner are the two noises he instantly recognizes. He also realizes he is lying horizontally in the back seat of the car, his head enduring a small pounding as he regains full consciousness.

Sean suddenly recalls the scene at the gas station: the dead attendant, the bearded man firing wildly at the motorcycle, cars exploding, and then his whole world exploding. And then...the beautiful woman.

The guardian angel? My guardian angel?

He gingerly sits up and looks toward the front seat. And there she sits, behind the driver's wheel.

Where are her wings? Sean wonders.

She must have heard him stirring because without looking back, she says, "Glad you're awake, Professor."

A sly grin crosses her face as she looks in the rear-view mirror at him. "Sounded like you were having a bad dream," she indicates.

He must have been tossing or groaning in his state of unconsciousness, something he had done before when dreaming about that day. He knows that because it had scared the hell out of his wife on more than-

My wife! Where the hell is she?!

"Where are we?" Sean asks hoarsely.

"On the road," she replies.

"That's helpful," he retorts.

The woman demurely smiles again, as if she is enjoying herself, like a cat playing with a mouse.

"We're heading the same direction you were going prior to your," she searches for the right word, ". . . rest stop."

"You mean west?" Sean inquires, placing a hand to his head, where a dull, incessant ache has taken root.

She nods.

"You know where I'm headed?" he asks suspiciously.

She nods again.

Before he can say anything, she explains, "I know you have a lot of questions, Mr. O'Connell, and I'm going to do my best to answer all of them. But first, I'm going to ask for your patience."

My patience? For what?

"Who are you?" he asks warily.

She replies, "My name is Sloan, and I have a story to tell you."

She looks back at him for the first time with her piercing eyes and asks, "Do you mind if I start at the beginning?"